Manimekhalaï
(The Dancer with the Magic Bowl)

Manimekhalaï

(The Dancer with the Magic Bowl)

by Merchant-Prince Shattan

Translated by
Alain Daniélou
with the collaboration of T. V. Gopala Iyer

A NEW DIRECTIONS BOOK

Translator's Note: This English edition was prepared with the help of Kenneth Hurry.

Manufactured in the United States of America.
New Directions Books are printed on acid-free paper.
First published clothbound and as New Directions Paperback 674 in 1989.
Published simultaneously in Canada by Penguin Books Canada Limited.

Library of Congress Cataloging-in-Publication Data

Cāttanār.
    [Manimēkalaï. English]
    Manimekhalaï : the dancer with the magic bowl / by Shattan : translated by Alain Daniélou.
        p.   cm.
ISBN 978-0-8112-1098-0
    I. Daniélou, Alain.   II. Title.
PL4758.9.C3M313   1989
894'.81111—dc 19   88–39885
                                                                         CIP

New Directions Books are published for James Laughlin
by New Directions Publishing Corporation,
80 Eighth Avenue, New York 10011

SECOND PRINTING

✦ Contents ✦

❧ Preface ❧

Almost nothing is known of India, its daily life and institutions, in the troubled years of the first centuries of the Christian era. The *Manimekhalaï*, one of the masterpieces of Tamil literature, gives us, in the form of a didactic novel full of freshness and poetry, a delightful insight into the ways of life, the pleasures, beliefs, and philosophical concepts of a refined civilization. The story relates the adventures of a dancing girl who becomes a convert to Buddhism, a rather new creed at the time in South India. Tamil is the main pre-Aryan language still surviving today.

The *Manimekhalaï* calls into question many of our received ideas concerning ancient India as well as our interpretation of the sources of its present-day religion and philosophy. In its clear accounts of the philosophical concepts of the time, the *Manimekhalaï* presents the various currents of pre-Aryan thought (mainly preserved by the Ajivika ascetics and Jain monks) which gradually influenced the Vedic Aryan world and became an essential part of it and, through Buddhism, spread over the whole of the Far East and Central Asia.

Society

The society in which the action of the *Manimekhalaï* takes place has little to do with the Aryanized civilization of the north which we know from Sanskrit texts. Although important cultural exchanges between the Aryan and Dravidian worlds had already taken place by this time, the latter was still able to maintain its independence, some of its features continuing even to our own times.

The center of religious and political power is the king. As in ancient China, the gods' favor and the country's prosperity depend on the king's virtue.

Spiritual and religious life is guided by sages, seers (*rishis*), who lead an ascetic life, living in the mountains or in secluded places. It appears that Dravidian society did not originally possess a priestly caste. However, during the *Manimekhalaï* period, groups of Brahmans from the north had already established themselves in villages or parts of the towns, forming separate communities which were treated sometimes with respect and sometimes with hostility. Anti-Brahman movements still exist today.

The very important middle class is represented by the merchants who could be ennobled by the king, receiving titles such as *Chetty* or *Etthy*.

The caste of courtesans, female dancers, musicians, and prostitutes plays a very important role as the city's adornment and pleasure. Dynasties of dancers, born of celestial nymphs exiled from the paradise of Indra, the king of the gods, have taken up their abode in Tamil country, to the great joy of mankind. They have no apparent ties with the temples; their dance is a profane art which has nothing sacred about it. (Troupes of female dancers attached to the temples as the gods' slaves— *Deva-dâsi*—have not yet made their appearance.)

Male transvestite prostitutes also exist, whose dances are greatly appreciated by the public. They wear a short skirt, probably of Greek origin.

The *Manimekhalaï* describes a wide variety of funeral rites and ways of disposing of the dead. Such customs still survive in various parts of India. Cremation appears to be an Aryan contribution. The practice requiring widows to follow their husbands in death appears to be already widespread in ancient Dravidian society. It is the continuation of a prehistoric custom: the spirits of the dead should be accompanied in the afterlife by all the comforts of their earthly existence. This practice occurs occasionally even today.

The India of this period was a great maritime nation, which had colonized Southeast Asia and Indonesia, introducing Shivaism—which still survives in Bali—and shortly afterwards, Buddhism. In the west, large numbers of Indian ships crossed the sea, exporting their produce to Egypt and Rome. The Greek geographer Ptolemy in the second century mentions the main ports of southern India and, in particular, Kaveris Emporium, the Kaveripumpattinam (or Puhâr) of the *Manimekhalaï*.

Religion

Religion is basically ancient Shivaism, the cult of Murugan (Skanda), Shiva's son, being the most widespread. There are numerous divinities and spirits who are very close to man, playing a constant role in everyday life. Indra, the king of heaven, who rules the elements and upon whose benevolence the rains (source of all prosperity) depend, is the subject of an important cult. Among the goddesses, the goddess of the sea, Manimekhalâ, is especially worshiped by these great seafaring peoples. The rivers also have their goddesses, spirits, and fairies, who continually take part in human adventures. A terrible genie, who dwells at the town's main crossroads, seizes and devours miscreants.

Ancient Jainism, a moralistic and atheistic religion, also appears to be fairly widespread. From Jainism come the theories of non-violence and transmigration taken over by Buddhism.

The religious scene is divided among a great number of sects—religious, philosophic, mystic, theistic, atheistic, ascetic, or of free morals. Theological and philosophical debates are held under the auspices of the various princes.

In such a context Buddhism, in its reformed *Mahâyana* form, irrupted into southern India at the time of the *Manimekhalaï*, spreading its theories on transmigration and *karma*, but without otherwise affecting the structure of society. There were many other sects practicing the monastic life and recommending ascesis as a means of spiritual progress. The main religious and philosophical sects, and especially the Ajivika, Nirgrantha, and Lokâyata, are identical to those which, five centuries later,

fought the famous Shankarâchârya, who codified and uni-
fied these divergent currents, giving birth to what we now
know as Hinduism.

Vedism

In the *Manimekhalaï*, Vedism, the religion of the Aryans,
is merely one religion among many. In a civilization of
oral tradition, the *Veda* (from the root *vid*, to know) represents the seers' (*rishis'*) perception of the universal
laws governing the world. This notion is very close to
the "natural law" (*dharma*) to be developed by Buddhism.
The Vedic hymns were transcribed when the Aryans
finally adopted writing of Semitic origin, under Persian
influence, towards the sixth century before the Christian
era. At this point there appeared a phenomenon which
was to have considerable consequences, and which can
be termed "the idolatry of the book." The sacred texts
would henceforth no longer be considered as the ancient
sages' limited perception of the universal laws, but as a
manifestation of the divine word—the "Word"—revealing those laws. The written *Veda* thus became the sole
source to which all must refer, as in the case of other
"religions of the book" with regard to the Old Testament,
the Gospel, or the Koran.
Even today, one can join Hindu Brahmanism without believing in any god whatever, but not without believing in the supremacy of the *Vedas*. In the *Manimekhalaï*,
we find for the first time a clear statement of the principle
of the "religions of the book."

The Ajivika

The monastic tradition of ascetics practicing incredible
austerities and able to develop magic powers is part of the
pre-Aryan civilization. These indigenous ascetic magicians, living naked and begging for food, are mentioned
with astonishment in the *Vedas*. The basic knowledge of
the wonderful civilization that preceded the Aryan inva-
sions of the second millenium before our era was kept

alive and handed down among these ascetics living on the margins of society. It is through them that the techniques of Yoga, Sâmkhya cosmology, Nyâya logic, and the ritual techniques of Tantra and Mîmâmsâ[1] gradually reappeared in the Aryan world.

The mendicant ascetics were divided into various sects, occasionally associated with strange practices, like the Kâpâlika ("wearers of skulls"), the Kâlâmukha ("black heads" who feigned madness), but the Ajivika were the main repositories of ancestral knowledge. These various traditions have survived on the margins of official Brahmanism right down to our own days.

Makkhâli Gosâla, the teacher of both the Buddha and the Jainist reformer Mahâvîra, was an Ajivika as was Lakulisha, who reestablished Shivaism shortly before the beginning of the Christian era. The *Manimekalaï* gives us important information regarding the Ajivika tradition. Greatly indebted to the Ajivika, Buddhist philosophy additionally borrowed the notions of *karma* and transmigration from Jainism.

The *Rishis*

The formulation of the concepts of the various philosophical schools is attributed to sages (*munis*) or seers (*rishis*). Chiefly known to us from other sources, the most important of these are Agastya, Vasishtha, Makkhâli Gosâla, and Jaimini.

Agastya and Vasishtha are mentioned in the *Rig Veda* as issuing from the sperm of the gods Mitra and Varuna, which was ejaculated at the sight of the nymph Urvasî. Mitra's sperm fell into an earthenware jar, which is why Agastya is called "the son of a jar" (Khumbhayoni).

Agastya was responsible for spreading the Aryan message in the south of India. This is symbolized by the legend that the Vindhya mountains, which separate north and south, prostrated themselves before him. Agastya, who retired into the forest, became the counselor of the exiled Râma.

The sages Vrinchi and Shringi are companions of

Shiva. Achala is a personage deified by Jainism. Kesha-Kambala, "he who has only his hair to cover him," is not known to us from other sources. Jaimini, an authority on logic, must have lived four centuries before the *Manimekhalaï*.

The other heads of schools mentioned are Veda-Vyâsa, author of the *Pûrva Mîmânsâ*, and Kritakoti, alias Bodhayana, author of a commentary on the two *Mîmânsâ*.

Aravana Adigal and Nâgarjuna

One of the main characters in the *Manimekhalaï* is Aravana Adigal, the preacher of Buddhism in the south of India. His name, whose Sanskrit equivalent would be *Dharma-pûrna-svâmî* (the teacher accomplished in the *dharma*) is not known to us from other sources. The Buddhism he teaches is that of the Great Vehicle, the *Mahâyana*. Original Buddhism, the *Hinayana* or Little Vehicle, was essentially a monastic doctrine whose severe rules concerned only limited communities, mainly consisting of Brahmans and converted Kshatriyas living outside society. This form of Buddhism was in its decline when during the first century of our era, under the impulse of Ashvaghosha (a great scholar of Shivaite origin), four persons known as the four suns of Buddhism, at the court of the Emperor Kanishka, developed the universal aspect of the Buddha's teaching. They transformed it into a popular religion open to all without distinction of sex or caste, incorporating into it the Shivaite and Vedic divinities, and placing the accent on the practice of charity and benevolence toward all living creatures rather than on an egocentric search for individual release. This renewed Buddhism introduced the concept of Bodhisattvas, human beings who by their virtue themselves became Buddhas (i.e., heavenly beings). This concept is very far from that of the *Hinayana* which sought solely release or return to non-being. Buddhist sources relate that the *Mahâyana* doctrine was developed and preached by Nâgarjuna, a famous logician from the south of India. According to legend, he received the original teachings of the Buddha which had been preserved by the king of the Någäs, the people of the serpents who lived in an underground world. His name, or surname, means "Light of the serpent." Several works are attributed to Någarjuna, but his teaching is known especially through Chinese translations of Sanskrit texts relating his life and doctrine.

There is an evident correspondence between the teachings of Någarjuna and Aravana Adigal, as well as a concordance of places and dates, which gives great credibility to the identification of the two characters. Like Adigal, Någarjuna had traveled all over India to study the philosophical and religious systems of his time before returning to preach Buddhism in his native land.

In the *Manimekhalaï* we find a contemporary account of the teaching of Någarjuna/Adigal, making it a very important document for the history of Buddhism. The *Mahâyana* must have known a relatively brief diffusion in the kingdoms of southern India before the arrival of the Pallava dynasty in the third century, but it spread throughout the whole of the Far East, where the teaching of Någarjuna/Adigal is considered authoritative.

Philosophy

Apart from its popularized and occasionally humorous concept of transmigration, the *Manimekhalaï* is a document of immense value with regard to the philosophical speculations of ancient India, presented in an easily accessible form.

Sâmkhya cosmology, Vaisheshika scientism, Nyâya logic, and Lokâyata materialism, originally tied to the Ajivika tradition, had forcibly reappeared in the Dravidian world as a result of the Shivaite revival just prior to the beginning of the Christian era. The concepts which had over the centuries gradually influenced the Vedic tradition, henceforth appeared independently in force, later giving rise to the philosophy of medieval India.

It was indeed within the families of missionary Brahmans established in the south of India, such as Någarjuna, Dignâga, and Shankarâchârya, and in the northern marches of Bengal and Kashmir, with Ashvaghosha and Vasubandhu, that the philosophical ideas of Hinduism and *Mahâyana* Buddhism developed, a phenomenon similar to the rediscovery of Greek thought (and its eventually pre-Hellenic sources) by the Christian world.

The Celestial and Infernal Worlds

The *Mahâyana* revived in the ancient religions the notion and description of a series of celestial spheres, paradises where the elect dwell, and nether and infernal worlds inhabited by dark genies or demons. The paradises mentioned are the "world of light" (*Dutita loka*) and the "paradise of perfect bliss" (*Tushita loka*). The good or evil deeds committed in the terrestrial world allow souls to be reincarnate for a time in one of these worlds, in which their stay is strictly accounted for according to their acquired merits. The theory of *karma* is thus strictly connected with transmigration.

The main gods are Shiva and his son Murugan. Brahmâ and Vishnu are often mentioned. Indra, the king of heaven and dispenser of rain, has an important place in Buddhist theology.

The Brahmâs are the forefathers and regents of the various species of living beings.

Champu (Champâpati) is the goddess of the earth, divine protectress of the continent of the jambu-rose-apple (the rose-wood continent), of which India is the center.

Manimekhalâ is the goddess of the ocean.

Chintâ is Sarasvati, the goddess of knowledge.

Durgâ, the terrible aspect of Kâlî, dwelling in the Vindhya mountains, captures all who fly over her territory by seizing their shadow, and devours them.

Of the fairies and genies, the most important in this tale are the Vidyâdhara, inhabitants of Tibet.

The Author

Shattan, the author of the *Manimekhalaï*, was a noble merchant well known as a poet and poetry critic, and was one of the last members of the *Sangam*, the famous Academy of Tamil poets, whose beginnings are lost in history. Shattan was the protégé of King Chera Senguttuvan who, according to *Shilappadikâram, The Ankle Bracelet,* reigned for more than fifty years and made numerous conquests.

He was also a friend of Prince Ilangô Adigal, the author of *The Ankle Bracelet,* whose approval he received for this work, a continuation of that same story. He must also have had the approval of Aravana Adigal, the great preacher of Buddhism in South India.

The action takes place in the three southern kingdoms, whose dynasties fade into prehistory: in the west, the kingdom of Chera (nowadays Kerala); to the east, Chola or Cholamandala (Coromandel, in the Madras region); and in the south, Pandya, whose capital is Madura.

Philosophical Vocabulary

The Dravidian civilization is the heir of the remarkable pre-Aryan civilization which produced cosmology, yoga, logic, and scientific materialism, all gradually absorbed by Sanskrit culture.

Sanskrit (or the "refined language") is derived from primitive Vedic and is a beautifully constructed artificial language with roots which can be used to coin new words to express the most subtle notions. It became the universal cultural language upon the gradual decline of the Dravidian heritage.

The great Sanskrit treatise on logic, the *Nyâyapravesha* written by Dignâna and translated into both Chinese and Tibetan, dates from the fifth century and reproduces almost word for word certain passages of the *Manimekhalaï,* thus clearly of an earlier date.

The *Manimekhalaï* gives highly interesting data on the ancient philosophical vocabulary of the pre-Aryan languages, sometimes mixed with terms from Sanskrit, and rather more often from Pali, the language of Buddhism. In his study on the *Manimekhalaï*[2] the great modern scholar S. Krishnaswami Aiyangar considers that the remarkable figure of Aravana Adigal who preached Buddhism in southern India was probably the master who inspired Dignâna, responsible for spreading the ancient Dravidian logic (henceforth integrated with Buddhism) in the north of India. This appears evident if we accept the thesis that Nâgarjuna and Aravana Adigal are one and the same person.

In the present translation, Sanskrit equivalents of Tamil terms have often been included to facilitate understanding. A glossary at the end of the book indicates which terms are Sanskrit and which are Tamil.

The Date of the *Manimekhalaï*

All the data agree in placing the *Manimekhalaï* in the second century of our era.

Starting from the end of the third century (A.D. 295), the dominant power in the south of India belonged to the Pallavas, of Parthian origin, who came from Maratha country and spoke the Mahrastri dialect. They established themselves at Kanchi[3] and subdued the three kingdoms of Chola, Pandya, and Chera.

The *Manimekhalaï* was certainly written before their intrusion. "There is absolutely no possibility of a Chola viceroy at Kanchi after the year 300 of our era."[4]

Among previous authors, the text mentions Jaimini, whose *Mîmâmsâ Sûtras* date from about 200 B.C., and quotes a verse of the *Kural* of Tiruvallur who is generally considered as belonging to the first century A.D. Gajabahu, king of Ceylon, who is also mentioned, came to the throne in A.D. 171.

Some scholars, however, feel obliged to deny the evidence of the historical context for the sole reason that they refuse to admit that the Tamil text is older than Dignâna's Sanskrit text, forgetting that Dignâna lived in Kanchi and was therefore a southern Indian (like Shankarâchârya later on) with access to traditional Dravidian sources unknown to the Indians of the north.

The *Manimekhalaï*'s antecedence is evident, furthermore, if we accept the identification of Nâgarjuna and Aravana Adigal.

The date of 171 A.D. proposed by Ramachandra

Dikshitar for the *Shilappadikaram* cannot be very far from the true date for the *Manimekhalaï*.

The Text

Traditionally known as one of the masterpieces of Tamil literature, the text of the *Manimekhalaï* was only edited as recently as 1898 by the Tamil scholar Svaminâthârya on the basis of about a dozen manuscripts. Since then it has been the subject of a number of critical studies as well as an incomplete English translation by Krishnaswami Aiyangar and Julien Vinson's attempt at a very abridged French version (Paris, 1928). The present translation, which is the first full and unabridged edition, has been made with the precious help of T.V. Gopala Iyer, on the basis of the 1898 text, taking into account both the ancient commentaries and the recent critical studies.

[1] Alain Daniélou, *While the Gods Play*, 1987.
[2] S. Krishnaswami Aiyangar, *Manimekhalaï in its Original Setting*, 1928.
[3] Kanchi is also known as Kanchipuram or Conjeevaram in the Madras region.
[4] Aiyangar, *op. cit.*

PROLOGUE

With her wild hair shining like the sun, the goddess Champu, divine protectress of the rose-apple continent, Nâvalan Têvu,* abides in the shade of a thousand-branched rose-apple tree, on the peak of Meru, the golden mount.

When she heard that the powerful and cruel Rakshasas were threatening the goddess of the earth, she descended into the south, to the city of Puhâr, and practiced rigorous penance to counteract their evil work.

The Chola king Kantan (Skanda), glorious descendant of a sun-sprung dynasty, betook himself to the divine sage Agastya, entreating him to provide his kingdom with abundant water. Agastya overturned his pitcher. The water flowing from it ran towards the east, forming a wide river which reached the sea not far from the charming spot where Champu stood.

Joyfully, the venerable lady greeted the young river Kaveri, which presented itself before her in the gracious guise of a nymph.

"Be welcome, resplendent child, come down from heaven like the sacred Ganges, bringing with you prosperity and joy!"

Astounded at the great lady's simplicity, the sage Agastya, who had deigned to accompany the young Kaveri, spoke thus to her: "Mother! This most venerable ascetic merits your respect. Pay her your homage!"

The daughter of the Tamil land piously prostrated

---

* According to ancient geography, the continent of the rose-apple tree includes India, the Middle East, and central and southeast Asia.

herself at Champu's feet and stood respectfully before her.

Charmed by her grace and behavior, the old lady took the beautiful young Kaveri onto her lap and said, "This ancient city, whose divine protectress I have been since the day when our great forefather Mahâ-Brahmâ, seated on his lotus, fashioned the genes of the ten species of gods dwelling in the six celestial worlds, as well as those of the twenty sorts of Brahmâ (the generating spirits of the species), which dwell in the twenty subtle worlds, will henceforth bear your name. May you be blessed!"

Since that day ancient Puhâr, whose renown is such that no enemy king dare attack its walls, is known by two other names—Champâpati and Kaveripumpattinam—and the beautiful Kaveri's abundant stream never runs dry even when, due to the movements of the stars, the rains fail to come in the proper season and even when the Chola kings, although known for their virtue throughout the continent of Bhârata (India), fail in their duty.

SUMMARY OF THE CHAPTERS

I   To the sound of the drum, the order is given to the city's inhabitants to initiate the celebration of the annual festival in honor of the god Indra, who, in his former existences, accomplished one hundred sacrifices.

II   Chitrâpati, Mâdhavi's mother, learns that her granddaughter has chosen the monastic life. With a broken heart, she informs her, through Vasantamâlâ, of the entire city's indignation on learning that she had left her profession as a dancer and prostitute to dedicate herself to the religious life.

III   Manimekhalaï betakes herself to a garden on the outskirts of the city to gather flowers.

IV   Perceiving that the Chola prince has followed her, Manimekhalaï closes herself in a crystal pavilion.

V   The Chola prince discerns Manimekhalaï through the glass. Mad with passion, he departs, determined to possess her. The goddess Manimekhalâ arrives in the garden.

VI   The goddess removes Manimekhalaï through the air and conveys her to the isle of Manipallavam.

VII   The goddess awakens Sutâmati, Manimekhalaï's companion, who had accompanied her to the garden and had fallen asleep.

hospice, the prince approaches her, wearing honey-scented garlands of flowers.

throws herself at Aravana Adigal's feet and from him learns the Buddhist *dharma*.

XXX Manimekhalaï practices severe self-denial so as to escape the chains of life and attain release.

All these events have been carefully related in thirty long poems, according to the best rules of Tamil prosody, by Shattan, the well-known merchant, owner of many businesses.

The poems were presented to Prince Ilangô Adigal, the author of *The Ankle Bracelet,* of which this narrative is the continuation. He listened to them all with benevolence.

Manimekhalaï
(The Dancer with the Magic Bowl)

CANTO ONE

The Festival of Indra Is Proclaimed
to the Sound of the Drum

The magnificent city of Puhâr is renowned throughout the world for the virtues of its inhabitants, who jealously preserve the heritage of a most ancient culture.

Still further to increase the city's fame, the great sage Agastya, who dwells on Potikaï, the snowy mountain, counseled one of the Chola kings (bearer of the hero's bracelet for destroying the three flying fortresses of the treacherous demons) to establish a festival in honor of Indra, the king of the gods.

Making obeisance, the king requested Indra to come and dwell each year in the ancient city of Puhâr for the twenty-eight days of a festival celebrating his glory and in honor of all the gods. Learned men, versed in all the sacred lore, assure us that the god benevolently gave his consent, and this is why the festival of Indra was celebrated each year for twenty-eight days.

On this occasion, the followers of the various creeds gathered in the town, explaining the doctrines expounded in their holy books and discussing the value of profane knowledge and of moral concepts as well as the various ways of attaining release. There were also skilled astrologers, who could calculate the periods of the stars and the duration of time.

Many heavenly beings, gods and spirits, not wanting to be recognized, stripped themselves of their glory in order to resemble men, and wandered freely about the city. A great number of strangers, coming from far countries and speaking peculiar tongues, were also to be seen.

1

In the presence of the kings of all the neighboring countries, the state officials were summoned to the palace for the proclamation of the opening of the festival of thousand-eyed Indra. Around the sovereign stood, according to custom, the five groups of high dignitaries who formed the royal council: the high priest, the captains of the army, the spies, and the ambassadors, followed, according to rank, by the eight corps of officials—the tax collectors, the provincial governors, the treasury accountants, the palace servants, the representatives of the people and the officers of the various regiments. Some paraded on elephants, others on horse.

It was asserted that if the festival were not celebrated, the town's guardian genie would be consumed with wrath and molest all the inhabitants. This terrible spirit watched over the bazaars day and night, uttering terrifying cries. He bared his lips the better to show his fangs when he was angered. He stood at the crossing of the four main roads, holding in his hands a rope which he used to capture evil-doers, whom he beat to death and then devoured. It was this same spirit who in ancient times had gone to Amaravati, the everlasting city, and freed Indra, imprisoned there by giants.

The great drum used solely for this occasion was jealously guarded in the temple dedicated to the thunderbolt, Indra's weapon. It was pulled out and fixed by cords to the neck of the royal elephant. The sound of this drum covered with buffalo hide was like thunder and so terrifying that the god of death himself dared not leave his lair. The roar of this drum inspired heroic acts and it was venerated with offerings of blood.

The drummer belonged by right to the most ancient tribe. He beat out the rhythm while proclaiming the edict, "May prosperity long reign over the ancient city protected by the goddess of fortune. May the earth be thrice blessed each month with rain. May the stars follow in their proper courses, thanks to the virtues of our kings."

To thwart the influence of ill-omened planets and the intrigues of perfidious demons, there arrived in the train of Indra their sovereign the four cohorts of thirty-three gods, called Vasu, Rudra, Aditya, and Ashvini, as well as the eighteen Ganas (Shiva's whimsical companions), who had attained the rank of heavenly beings as a result of meritorious acts performed during previous lives in the world of men. These divine beings had all come down to earth to taste the pleasures of the city. So numerous were they that the heavenly city remained deserted, as the city of Puhâr once was when the Chola king Karikâl Valavan departed to conquer the northern kingdoms, as recounted by the learned historians who keep alive the memory of past events.

The herald proclaimed, "Decorate the wide avenues with garlands. Clean the assembly halls. Place at every corner jars full of drinking water, flowering plants in clay pots, and statues holding lamps in their hands.

"Decorate the houses with *areca* branches, palms of *vanji*, stems of bananas laden with fruit, and with sugar cane. Adorn the plinths with flowering lianas. Hang garlands of pearls between the columns.

"Remove the soiled sand and spread fresh in the streets of the old city where the festival will take place, and under the great trees which serve as shelter. Unfurl great banners hanging from cornices and raise the flags attached to their poles.

"Let the priests versed in the rites, one for each of the gods, perform the prescribed ceremonies in their temples, beginning with the god who bears an eye in his forehead (Shiva) and ending with the genie who watches over public order and stands at the center crossroads of the city.

"Let the teachers of civic virtues take their place for their ethics lessons on the fine sand spread under the dais or in the public halls. Let the representatives of the various religions, all of whom claim to hold the truth, gather for debate, seated on the chairs reserved for them in the Hall of Learning. Avoid brawling and violence, even towards enemies.

"Such are the rules to be observed during the twenty-eight days in which gods and men walk in friendship together, enjoying the beauty of nature on the sand dunes, in the flowering gardens, on the river islands, and at the bathing places on the banks of the streams."

3

Thus the herald, to the sound of the drum, surrounded by warriors with flaming swords, chariots, horsemen and elephants, proclaimed the opening of the splendid festival, adding this prayer:

"May hunger, sickness, and violence depart for ever, and may the rain, with increasing abundance, bring prosperity!"

CANTO TWO

Chitrâpati Is Informed of the City Rumors

Chitrâpati, Mâdhavi's mother, was astounded to learn that her daughter and Manimekhalaï, her granddaughter, refused to take part in the dancing arranged during the festival in Indra's honor, celebrated under the auspices of the divine protectress of the vast continent of the jambu-rose-apple in order to thwart the influence of ill-omened planets and perfidious demons.

Chitrâpati had Vasantamâlâ called, Mâdhavi's faithful companion, whose long eyes were outlined in red, and enjoined her to go and firmly point out to her daughter the rumors running among the citizens of this magnificent and prosperous city, blaming her for not taking part in the dancing and music organized during the festival.

Troubled and surprised to learn that Mâdhavi wished to devote herself to the monastic life, Vasantamâlâ betook herself to the vast hall where in times past they had spent long hours together weaving garlands of flowers. There she found Mâdhavi and Manimekhalaï and, seeing Mâdhavi's delicate body made thin by fasting, she said tenderly to her, "Friend, equal to the goddess of fortune, whence this grief? Have you no longer any consideration for the city's inhabitants, both wise and mad? For girls like us, the life you wish to lead is a culpable breaking of custom."

4

Mâdhavi of the golden bracelets had studied all the arts practiced by girls of pleasure, and had reached unrivaled perfection. She knew both kinds of dance, dances suitable for the royal palace and those for the common public, poems set to music, the art of dramatic posture (*tukku*) to emphasize the rhythm of the poetic meter, the various musical rhythms (*tâla*), and how to play the harp (*yâl*) tuned according to th ᐟ various modes.

She knew by heart the poems chanted during the dances and had mastered the language of gesture (*mudra*), by which love (*akam*), virtue, and glory (*puram*) are expressed. She knew how to play the great drum and how to adjust the tightness of its skin to regulate the sound. She knew how to play the melodious flute, as also the art of playing ball, of preparing dishes according to the recipes of the best cuisine as well as the preparing of scented powders of diverse colors, the manner of bathing in the various seasons, the body's sixty-four positions in making love, the art of anticipating men's desires, of speaking charmingly, and of seeming reluctant (the better to excite her lovers), of writing elegantly with a cut reed, of arranging magnificent bouquets of flowers chosen for their form and color, the choice of dress and jewels according to circumstances, and the art of fashioning necklaces of pearls or precious stones.

She had also studied astrology and the art of measuring time, and other similar sciences, the art of drawing and painting, all of which, according to the books, forms part of the métier of an accomplished courtesan.*

Vasantamâlâ attempted to convince her. "For a girl destined by birth for art and pleasure to become an ascetic and mortify herself is an impious act. All the scholars and wise men will tell you so, and the entire population of the city condemns Mâdhavi without pity. To act in defiance of the laws of the city is no virtue. Renounce this behavior which dishonors us."

Mâdhavi replied, "Maid of the beautiful bracelets! When I learned the news of the terrible death of Kovalan, who was my lover, I survived. Life did not wish to leave

* A similar list is given in a commentary on the *Kâma Sûtra*.

my body. I thus lost the esteem of the people of this ancient city bristling with flags, and since then I have lived in shame.

"When honest women lose their husband, more precious to them than life itself, they burn up with grief and their breath becomes scorching like that of an anvil activated by the bellows of a forge. Incapable of controlling their sorrow, they waste away and die. Others mount on the pyre, casting themselves into the flames as though they were the fresh waters of a lake. If they are forbidden to do so, they destroy their beauty with mortification and fasting as prescribed for widows so that they may, in another life, live long and happily with their husband. These are the three ways in which honest women may end their life in this vast ocean-girt world.

"The virtue and faithfulness of Kannaki, the legitimate wife of my beloved Kovalan, was of another stamp. Her scented hair falling in disarray on her shoulders, unable to bear the grief caused by her husband's dramatic death, in her fury she tore off her radiant young breast drenched by the flood of her tears and, flinging it into the city, caused the conflagration of the Pandyas' famous capital. For Kovalan's daughter, Manimekhalaï, the monastic life seems to me more fitting than the vicious commerce of her charms and the base acts which are the courtesan's lot.

"Vasantamâlâ of the rare jewels, give heed! In the keenness of my sorrow, I came here to the retreat of the sages to prostrate myself before the feet of the great Aravana Adigal, who, free from all ties, has attained the knowledge of essential reality. When I recounted to him my distress at the dreadful death of the one I loved, he said to me, 'All beings born into this world know only growth, decline, and sorrow. Only those that cease to be reborn can attain endless happiness. Birth is the fruit of our attachments. It is by practicing self-denial that one is able to escape the inexorable cycle of reincarnation. Keep this in your heart.'

"The most wise Aravana Adigal then explained to me the nature of the four truths, which are: suffering, the causes of suffering, the cessation of suffering, and the method for being free from it. He then taught me the five rules of conduct (*shîla*), which are: the renunciation of lust, cruelty, drunkenness, lying, and the appropriation of others' goods.

"Return now and repeat what I have told you to my beautiful companions, whose long eyes are charged with kohl, and to Chitrâpati, my mother."

CANTO THREE

As the scent hidden in the bud is diffused when the flower blossoms, the destiny stemming from Manimekhalaï's actions in her former lives began to bear fruit as she heard Mâdhavi recall to Vasantamâlâ the distressing story which plunged all its listeners into deep sorrow.

It was the first time that Manimekhalaï had heard, brutally assaulting her ears, the account of the terrible fate reserved for her father Kovalan and his virtuous wife. With a troubled spirit, deeply moved, she shed such bitter tears that her beautiful eyes striped with red lost their brilliance. Her floods of tears flowed onto the garland of perfumed flowers she was weaving.

Seeing her face ravaged with weeping, Mâdhavi wiped her eyes with her beautiful hand to remove the tears. It was as though a lotus flower came to caress the moon.

To distract her from her grief, Mâdhavi then said to Manimekhalaï, "You are defiling that pure garland with your tears. Go now and seek a selection of new flowers to make another necklace."

On hearing these words, Sutâmati of the beautiful braided hair adorned with honey-scented flowers, who was weaving the garlands together with Manimekhalaï, expressed her concern.

"Seeing the tears streaming from the corners of Manimekhalaï's eyes whose beauty shames the flowers of the blue lotus, the god of love risks losing his arrogant assurance. Should he see that, in her despair, now that she has learned the tragic fate of him to whom she owes her life, she is preparing to renounce the pleasures of this world and enter a monastery, will he not throw away his now useless arrows, since the beautiful girl will no longer serve his intrigues? Save for those ambiguous beings for whom women have no attraction, no virile man subject to the forces of desire could resist her charms, nor even catch a glimpse of her without losing his reason.

"Mâdhavi of the rare jewels, I must explain to you how it is that I am here. Listen to my story."

The Story of Sutâmati

"Not far from the ocean, in a town called Champa, there lives the tribe of Kârâlar. Much sea produce is found at Champa. I am the daughter of a Brahman named Kaushika. I used to go everywhere alone, without the slightest fear and without imagining that anything unpleasant could happen to me. One day I went as usual to look for flowers in a public garden.

"There I was discovered by a Vidyâdhara, a spirit of the air called Marutavega, who had left his country beyond the Himalayas to take part in the festival in Indra's honor in the ancient city of Puhâr, which is protected by the goddess of fortune. His appearance was superb, without equal in the world of men. He wore a necklace of flowers and jewels encrusted with precious stones and golden ornaments. Apart from myself, many others would doubtless have succumbed to his charms. He abducted me, taking me with him up into the air. He took possession of me and made me the plaything of his pleasure. Then, one day, he became invisible and vanished, abandoning me in this city far from my own country. Because of this experience, I feel that Manimekhalaï, slim as a liana and covered with precious jewels, should not go alone to gather flowers in the gardens."

The Gardens of the City

The city is surrounded by many gardens. One called Lavanika-vanam, the garden of delights, is reserved for the amusement of those belonging to the royal family and

8

their companions. The walls of the enclosure may not be approached: the guards who stand watch arrest all trespassers. Within, there is a small lake, which can be filled with water and emptied by machinery.

Another pleasure garden, known as Oyyâna-vanam, is set apart during the festival of Indra for celestial visitors, who alone have the right to enter. This is why even the buzzing of bees cannot be heard there. Due to the power of the heavenly beings, all the trees are covered with masses of the rarest flowers which never fade. A demon with a noose in his hand guards the garden entrance. This is why it is useless to attempt to enter.

In the garden that bears his name dwells Sampati, the noble vulture who lost his wings, burnt by the heat of the sun when he tried to fly as high as it.

In the garden of Kavera, there dwells the famous ascetic, father of the river Kaveri, whose streams never dry up. This garden is guarded by old hags who attack those who dare approach.

None of these gardens is accessible to ordinary mortals, but there also exists another place, known simply as "the garden" (Upavanam). There, by the will of the Buddha, the benevolent, the compassionate, who by practicing a faultless asceticism dedicated his whole life to the protection of living beings, the trees are always in blossom.

In the midst of the garden, there stands a pavilion made of crystal panels, which insulate it from the noises of the world. Within stands a lotus-shaped pedestal, shining with the brightness of the marvelous rubies with which it is encrusted. On the pedestal are to be seen the miraculous footprints of wonder-working Buddha.

Flower buds placed on this pedestal open their corolla forthwith. Flowers in bloom laid there never fade, even after many years. Neither dare the bees approach these flowers to steal their honey.

This divine pedestal is the work of Mayä, the heavenly carpenter. It was built to remind men athirst for virtue, practicing severe self-denial, that only those actions accomplished for love's sake will one day be rewarded, while the privations without any particular aim self-imposed by some ascetics will have no effect.

"Mâdhavi of the rare jewels! Your daughter must

not seek to repair to any garden other than the Upavanam. Furthermore, excellent woman of choice ornaments,
it is fitting that I should accompany her when she goes
to seek her flowers."

The Street Scene

With Mâdhavi's agreement, Sutâmati, accompanied by
Manimekhalaï, more beautiful than a liana of flowers,
started off through the city streets clogged by innumerable wagons with their bells and drivers.

A filthy Jain monk, looking like an emaciated elephant, drew near to them. In his hand he held a loop of
cord from which hung a vessel full of water. Ceaselessly
he waved a fly-whisk. Living in a famous and ancient
monastery, he had renounced all modesty and clothing.
He walked hesitantly, fearing lest an imprudent movement might hurt some fragile insect indiscernible to the
eye, an offense to be expiated with a lengthy fast.

A drunkard, seeing him approach, hailed him,
"Holy man! Come here so that I may bow before your
lotus-like feet! Good monk! Hear my words! Your life
dwells in your body which is but filth, but you do not
suffer like those who live encased in hot clothes which
make them sweat. Come and share this sweet toddy liquor
made from good coconut palm juice! My guru taught me
that only those who get drunk on palm wine know ecstasy
in this world, happiness in their next life, and eternal
beatitude. There are no tiny beasts in the liquor secreted
by the generous spathes of the palm tree. You will not
have to risk being a murderer. Good monk! You are wise!
You will see that drunkenness clears your mind. But if
you find it more to your liking to fast rather than drink
an honest toddy, then go on your way!"

Thus the drunkard tried to convince a Jain monk
who practiced fasting and abstinence. Many there are who
let themselves be convinced by the words of drunkards.

Further on was one of those ascetics called Black
Heads (Kâlâmukha), who feign madness. This one wore
a round necklace of oleander flowers and another of ru-

draksha seeds (the emblem of Shiva's followers). Fixed on his tattered garments were twigs which he had gathered from the highest branches of the trees. His body was smeared with a mixture of ashes and sandalwood. He responded with insults and obscene or senseless words to those who addressed him. He wept, rolled about on the ground, wailed, uttered strange cries, prostrated himself, stood up, turned round and round until he became dizzy. He ran, then squatted in some corner where he stayed a long time without moving. Sometimes he tried to fight his shadow. Idlers watched him stupefied, moved to pity by his madness and wretchedness.

Others had gathered to watch the dance of the transvestites, called *pêdi*. This was the dance which once was performed by Kâma, the son of the hero Krishna in the main street of Chöe (Sonitapura), the capital of the cruel genie Bana. Kâma, under the name of Pradyumna, disguised himself as an invert and sought to free his son Aniruddha from the prison where Bana had confined him as a punishment for having seduced his daughter Usha. Krishna was the incarnation of the god Vishnu who, in the form of a dwarf, had measured the three worlds with his own paces. The boys who performed the *pêdi* dance wore curly beards, with long tresses of black hair. Their mouths were painted bright coral red and they showed their beautiful white teeth. Their large shining eyes were slightly underlined. They wore mother-of-pearl earrings. Their black eyebrows were arched like the crescent moon, their brow curved. Their hands with red-dyed palms were like the water lilies of Malabar. They had pretty little upraised breasts, a slim figure, and protruberant sex. They wore a short dress above the knee. Brightly colored designs decorated their shoulders and breasts.

Many visitors admired the stucco sculptures made by skilled craftsmen, representing all living beings, as well as the immaculate statues of the gods, similar to those that adorn the walls of the many-storied temples in the ancient city of Puhâr. The chatter of all these visitors made a ceaseless uproar.

In the long avenue where the festivals always took place, the women with their shining bracelets were celebrating a festival in honor of the young god Murugan. They made their children climb on the backs of toy elephants whose foreheads were marked with spots of color, harnessed to gilded wagons. They invited the passers-by to come and take part in the joyous feast of Murugan, son of the god Shiva seated in the shade of a banyan. The children's hair had been made to shine with oil, and their faces had been powdered with white mustard. Three rows of pearls were pinned to their hair as well as a jewel in the form of a crescent moon which prettily framed their tiny faces. The saliva which dripped from their rosy lips mumbling childish phrases fell on their ornaments representing the five weapons of the god Vishnu: the god's disk (*tâli*) was completely soaked. Around their loins the children wore a piece of cloth which left their sex uncovered. They had been given belts encrusted with diamonds that sparkled on their garments. They walked with uncertain steps which did not take them very far. A crowd surrounded them, amused at the sight of the feast of Murugan organized by the women.

Once upon a time, in King Virâta's capital the people assembled, protesting loudly at the sight of Vijaya (the hero Arjuna) when he appeared disguised as a eunuch. In the same way, a great number gathered around Manimekhalaï, saying, "A mother who allows a daughter so pretty that she needs no rouge to choose the arduous path of monastic life is a cruel and unworthy woman. When this too-beautiful girl enters the garden to gather flowers, the young swans that have taken up their abode there will not be able to move with a grace equal to hers, and the peacocks will be spellbound in their inability to rival the elegance of her bearing. The green parrots will vainly try to imitate the music of her voice." It was with such remarks that the townspeople expressed their surprise and indignation.

Manimekhalaï entered the garden led by Sutâmati for whom the Upavanam was a sacred place. There, the pedestal bearing the divine footprints of the Buddha is found. The ground was covered with a wonderful carpet of bright-colored flowers, carefully arranged by artist-gardeners to form designs. Among the trees and plants which flowered there were the dark-green *kurava*, marine oaks, wild lemons, laburnums, coral trees, acacias, scarlet ixoras, orange trees, golden jasmin, pandanus with low-sweeping branches, milingtonias, bamboo, *ashokas*, sacred fig trees of wide girth, golden-flowering pear trees, kinos, great champacs and red-flowering cotton plants, brilliant like fire. The two women soon set to gathering flowers.

CANTO FOUR

Manimekhalaï Enters the Crystal Pavilion

The trees and creepers of the Upavanam were so thick that when one entered it seemed that night had fallen. All the darkness of the neighboring areas appeared to have taken refuge there, fleeing from the attack of the army of sun rays laying siege to the garden.

The humming of the bees sounded like a harmonious flute and the chirping of the crickets called to mind the quivering of a harp (*yâl*). In the part of the garden where young trees had been planted they had grown so dense that, from its rising to its setting, the sun's rays were unable to penetrate: even the cuckoo was hardly able to open a path. A peacock was dancing, surrounded by a circle of female monkeys, constituting his audience. Sutâmati and Manimekhalaï lingered to watch this charming scene.

The water of the pool was as clear as crystal. At one end, covered by wide green leaves, the great white lotuses with their heady scent rose proudly above the brightly coloured water lilies. A royal swan sat motionless, majestic as a king. In front of him, at the water's edge, a peacock spread his tail, like a dancer come to make a show for a prince. A black mynah perching on a branch repeated the words of the song accompanying the dance in rhythm with the cry of the heron, whose powerful call sounded like a drum. Sutâmati drew the attention of her listless companion to the unexpected charm of the scene.

"Your beautiful face, still covered with the dust raised by the wagons driving along the public street, has lost its luster, like the perfumed lotus which appears soiled by the pollen falling from the flowers of the long-branched tamarisks growing by the edge of the pool.

"Look, what a sight! The red carp jumping amidst the flowering lotus recall your red-tinted forearms waving about to try and chase away the bees come to suck the nectar of your eyes, which they take for blue iris.

"A black fisher starling, spreading his magnificent wings, dived through the lotus, but without managing to hold his prey. When the fish fell back into the water, he flew away disappointed.

"Can there be a prettier sight?"

Prince Udayakumâra

Prince Udayakumâra was the son of a king whose white parasol was as bright as the moon.

When a ship finds itself caught in a storm, its helmsman, perched on the raised bridge in the poop, trembles with fear lest the main mast fixed at the vessel's center break off at the base, tearing away the ropes holding the sail, which, breaking loose and losing its tightness, begins to lash about with a furious flapping, finally tearing itself to shreds, so that the ship breaks adrift without any means of control, on an ocean whose waves splash and drive in all directions.

Like a ship in distress, the royal elephant called Kâlavega, overtaken by madness and having ejected his mahout, his trunk rubbing the wound left by the goad in trying to hold him back, rushed blindly through the city, heavy as a mountain, sowing panic in the streets of the bazaar and on the royal road blocked with wagons, drummers, beggars, and banners. Nothing could halt his advance. The supervisor of the elephants did not know what to do. Without hesitating, Prince Udayakumâra jumped onto his charger as fleet as air and reached the place

14

where the maddened animal was. He managed to master the menacing elephant in rut with admirable courage.

He returned along the main avenue, surrounded by his guard and chariots, holding the reins of his splendid chariot gathered into his fist in the form of a flower bud. It was only by looking at the necklace that adorned his breast that the people knew that this hero was not the god Murugan himself, but only a prince of the Chola dynasty, since Murugan wears a necklace of tamarisk flowers, which only blossom during the rainy season, while he was wearing a necklace of orchid-tree leaves, the symbol of the Chola dynasty.

In passing through the charming street where the women of pleasure dwell he noted a window wide open to the breeze in a house of several floors with gilded balconies. There, on a bed covered with a soft and scented carpet of flowers, easily visible from the road, he saw a young man, the son of a rich merchant, with a seventeen-string harp called a crocodile harp (*makara-yâl*) on his knees, holding in his arms a most beautiful girl with long scented tresses. The boy sat motionless, seemingly spellbound, like a figure in a picture painted by an artist's brush.

Udayakumâra, passing by in his chariot, was intrigued by this young man. "Hallo there! You with the girl! What is the reason for your amazement?" On hearing these words, the young man came down at once to the princely chariot, together with the girl with large young breasts. Having spoken the customary greetings and bowed before the king's son, who was wearing a necklace of flowers dripping with honey, he told him of the incident that had troubled his spirit.

"I have just seen Manimekhalaï, daughter of Mâdhavi the dancer, walking towards the flower garden. Her peerless beauty seemed faded, as when a bunch of flowers is closed in an airless coffer. The sight of her awoke in me the memory of the terrible punishment of which Kovalan was the victim. I was so troubled that when I sounded a chord on my harp, a wrong note destroyed the harmony of the mode I had been playing, causing me a terrible shock."

Udayakumâra, wearing a necklace of scented flow-ers, was enchanted to hear these words. He declared to the merchant's son that he was going to recall Manimek-halaï to her duty and would soon bring her back seated in his chariot. Then, like the moon which seems to race through the morning clouds, the Prince continued his way along the street lined with many-storied houses. He be-took himself to the entrance of the flower garden, whose great trees reached up to the sky.

Manimekhalaï, wearing only her simplest jewelry, heard the sound of the chariot's approach. In her am-brosia-sweet voice, she said to Sutâmati, "Prince Udaya-kumâra seems to be infatuated with me. Chitrâpati told Vasantamâlâ, who told Mâdhavi one day and, by chance, I overheard their confidences. I am under the impression that the sound my ears caught could be Udayakumâra's chariot."

On hearing these words, Sutâmati felt overwhelmed, like a peacock exhausted after his dance. She led Mani-mekhalaï, beautiful as a doll, to the crystal pavilion, made her enter, closed its doors, and fastened the locks. She then withdrew, remaining within five bow shots of the pavilion.

Having halted his chariot and ordered his escort to cease their uproar, the Prince entered the garden of a thousand flowers, radiant as the rising sun. As he walked, he admired the flowering trees and the artificial hills that had been constructed. Seeing Sutâmati, he said to her, "I know why you have come to this solitary place and that you did not come alone. The delicate maid called Mani-mekhalaï, with her young breasts just beginning, is now reaching womanhood. She has now reached the age when children stop mumbling confused words and express themselves properly. Her milk teeth have fallen, giving place to new teeth like rows of pearls. Her great eyes like red carp stretch as far as her ears to tell the wondrous secrets of the god of love. She is now ready to undergo the assaults of the males, who, under the effect of Eros' cruel darts, lose all restraint. Could you explain to me why this charming girl has left the monks' monastery to come here alone with you to this garden?"

When she heard the Prince's words, Sutâmati, whose long hair was adorned with sweet-scented flowers, felt helpless, as if she had been walled up in an underground place with no escape. Nevertheless, she replied to the Prince, "Is it truly a woman's place to recall the royal virtues of moderation, impartiality, and justice to you, the descendant of the great Chola king Karikâl, who from childhood took the appearance of an old man, so as to judge more wisely, and who weighed the arguments of plaintiff and defendant before pronouncing judgment?

"It is to the heir of such a noble line, wide-shouldered Prince, whose valor has been proven on the battlefield, that I now speak. Hear my words!

"Due to the effect of our past actions, we enter into possession of our body. It is the field on which we forge our future destiny. Stripped of its ornaments, it is but evil-smelling flesh, subject to age and decline, prone to the worst ills. It is the seat of all the passions. It is simply a vessel in which all the vices are, as it were, stored, always ready to loom into view. Anger and hate hide there like a venomous cobra curled up in its hole. It is the consciousness which it also contains that causes our anguish in the present, our fears of the future, our feeble efforts to free ourselves, and, finally, our despair.

"You, so proud of your rank, think of what this body contains. Regard it as though all its viscera were in full view."

But, before the wise words of Sutâmati could penetrate the Prince's ears, his eyes perceived Manimekhalaï, whose slim form, like a coral doll, shone in the crystal pavilion.

The Goddess Manimekhalâ Arrives at Puhâr

The beauty of Manimekhalaï, which astounded even the heavenly beings with bodies of light, rivaled Lakshmi, the goddess of fortune, when she danced the dance called *pâvaï* before the Asuras.

When the Prince glimpsed the girl's charming body through the transparent walls of the crystal pavilion, the god Eros, a crocodile on his pennon, let fly his five flower darts, inspiring him with irresistible desire.

He thought at first that the object he saw was a statue, the work of a sculptor of genius, but soon realized that the image was none other than Manimekhalaï of the dark eyes like blue lotus. He approached the pavilion, vainly seeking a door handle. Addressing Sutâmati, he said, "In this crystal pavilion are gathered a great number of statues and portraits. Your young friend, comparable to a liana, is hiding among the statues. Tell me what she looks like."

Sutâmati, her long hair decorated with flowers, answered, "Frankly, Prince, I must tell you that the beauty of your young body, rivaling Murugan, the god who dwells on heron (*krauncha*) mountain, has no attraction in her eyes, since, due to her past virtues, she is destined for the monastic life. Beneath the arch of her eyebrows, her eyes dart arrows whose effect is mortal, since she is protected by magical powers. She has attained true knowledge and the god of love has no hold over her."

The Prince thought to himself, "The virtues which Sutâmati attributes to Manimekhalaï may be sublime and her conduct irreproachable. However, no dam can long resist the water's extreme pressure. Nothing can check the power of desire." Turning to Sutâmati before quitting the garden, he said, "Honorable lady with lovely red cheeks! The people of this city in which so many rumors are circulating claim that a spirit of the air, a Vidyâdhara belonging to a cohort of heavenly spirits, abandoned you

in a monastery of pious Jains. May I know why you have
left the monastery to accompany Manimekhalaï to this
garden?"

"Prince with the heavy ankle-bracelets! Blessed be
your prayer rosary! May your spirit not let itself be led
onto the path of vice! Son of a king who reigns over the
vast ocean-encircled world, hear me, and I will explain
why I am here in Manimekhalaï's company."

The Story of Sutâmati

"I come originally from Champa (in Bengal). My father
was a Brahman sage, strict and austere, who kept the
fasts and carefully tended the ritual fires, thanks to which
the seasonal rains bring prosperity. I was still an infant
when my mother died. My father was in despair and his
sorrow grew still greater when I too was lost to him, on
the day when, by a sad fate, I was forced to submit to the
perverse assaults of Marutavega, a Vidyâdhara, who later
abandoned me here and disappeared.

"Pilgrimages are a duty for a Brahman. My father
departed one day with a group of pilgrims on a very long
journey to take a purifying bath near the sanctuary of
Kanya Kumâri (Cape Comorin), built in ages past by the
monkeys at the order of the hero Râma. He sought me
everywhere during this long periplus in the company of
the other Brahmans who knew the Sanskrit texts. One
day he came to bathe at the sacred spot where the river
Kaveri pours into the ocean. It was on returning from his
morning ablutions at the bathing-ghat that, crossing
through the city, he saw me and, with floods of tears, exclaimed, 'My child! How do you come to be here?'

"Although I was henceforth unworthy to live among
the Veda-chanting Brahmans, my father, because of his
immense tenderness towards me, did not wish to reject
me, and started going each day to beg for alms in front
of rich peoples' homes. One day, however, at the time
when he was going his round, a cow about to calve dashed
headlong against him and gashed open his belly. The
wound was wide, the animal's horn had caused his en-

19

trails to spill out, and he tried to hold them in, mixed with fat as they were, as though they were a scented garland of oleander flowers. Unable to go any further, and knowing that his daughter had lived there, he entered the monastery of the Jain monks, saying, 'O Jains! You are my sole refuge: save me!'

"The Jain monks, who are always fearful of pollution, drove us out with word and gesture, saying that neither my father nor I were the sort of people who could seek refuge with them. I had already upset them by coming to stay in their monastery when I first arrived in the city.

"In this sorry state, we walked, weeping and bewailing our lot, through the streets of the city, crying, 'Is there not a single charitable being disposed to perform a meritorious act to us, who wander without hope?'

"By good fortune, we then met a Buddhist monk called Sangha Dharma. With his beggar's bowl in his hand, he was going his midday round among the tall buildings. He was an ascetic and a sage. Despite the burning of the sun, his face shone with freshness, like the light of the moon. He wore a bright yellow robe. Noticing us, he said with compassion in his benevolent voice, 'What is then this misfortune which has struck you?'

"The sweetness of his voice refreshed our burning hearts. He placed his beggar's bowl in my hands and, without hesitating, lifted my father in his strong arms, took him to the monastery of the Buddhist monks and assisted him during the agony and suffering of death.

"It was with Sangha Dharma who had studied all the sacred books that we got to know the teachings of the *dharma*. 'The Buddha whom we venerate,' he said, 'was endowed by nature with all the virtues. He incarnates every perfection and, through the asceticism of many lives, he acquired experience of human problems. Without worrying about his own destiny, he dedicated his life to aiding all living beings and to guiding them on the righteous path of the *dharma*. By the very power of his faith, he succeeded in overcoming the might of Eros. I myself have renounced the use of words, except to celebrate his glory and promote the *dharma*.'"

Having terminated her discourse, Sutâmati added, "May prosperity go with you, noble Prince!"

"Woman of choice ornaments and skillful words! Now I know your story and understand that it is through Chitrâpati, her grandmother, that I shall be able to possess myself of Manimekhalaï, slender as a liana."

With these words, Udayakumâra departed from the flower garden, possessed in body and soul by his lustful desires.

With sweet-scented flowers in her hair, Manimekhalaï then opened the door of the crystal pavilion and rejoined Sutâmati. Her eyes like carps in her moon-shaped face were fixed on the departing, young prince. She said to Sutâmati, "Why does my heart, ignorant of love, feel drawn to this stranger who believes that I am without any real virtue, incapable of an honest life? He knows that I may expect no protection from the community in which I was born and believes that I can be bought if one pays the price. How is it that my heart is attracted by such a man, instead of being offended by the way in which he described me with such scorn? Can this be love? If it is so, may it be cursed!"

The two girls stood motionless, troubled, silent, when suddenly there appeared before them Manimekhalâ, the goddess of the ocean, who had come to Puhâr to amuse herself with the joyful din of the festival in Indra's honor. She had taken the modest appearance of one of the ladies of the city. She circled the crystal pavilion containing the Buddha's footprints, keeping it on her right and moving through the air without touching the ground.

Descended from heaven like a ray of light, Manimekhalâ, the solitary and distant goddess, endowed with immense wisdom and knowledge of all things past and future, letting her incurved tongue hang out, began to declaim the Buddha's praise:

"How shall I sing the praises of the only possessor of truth? The pure, the benevolent, the ancient, the glorious, who has destroyed the three sources of all ill: lust, anger, and error. He is the first of the heavenly beings, the possessor of all wisdom. Over him Eros has no hold. He is the blissful, the unique, the protector of all beings

whom he frees from those vices that are their mortal enemies. Not possessing a thousand tongues, how shall I sing
as is his due the praises of the feet of him who put in motion the thousand-armed wheel of the *dharma*?"

Having spoken thus, Manimekhalâ, the goddess of
the ocean, like a glittering jewel, descended to the ground
and stood near the two young women.

Evening Falls on the City

For lack of words to describe the splendor of the city of
Puhâr, more beautiful than a flowering liana, the poets
have compared it to a great lady. "The moats filled with
clear water, embellished with innumerable flowers, sound-
ing with the song of a thousand kinds of bird, form a ring
around her ankle. The surrounding walls, commanded by
towers, are her diamond-studded girdle. The gates, surmounted by staffs with flags flying, are her shoulders
laden with many necklaces. The temple of the tree of
abundance (*kalpataru*) and the temple of the thunderbolt (*vajra*) standing face to face, are her two superb and
provocative breasts. The vast palace, thousands of years
old, of matchless splendor, commanding the city, the residence of the Chola king who wears a necklace of orchid-
tree leaves, is her face. The full moon rising in the east
and the sun setting in the west are her earrings of silver
and gold."

It was the hour at which the women with glass
bracelets light a great number of lamps and place them
on the threshold. The musicians, skilled at playing the
harp, set their catgut strings to the notes of the *mullaï*
mode which is the one played at dusk. During their games,
the swan's companion had concealed herself in the heart
of a lotus which, unconscious of her presence, reclosed
its petals. The male swan then tore it open, destroying its
beauty, in order to free his partner, who sought refuge at
the top of a coconut tree hidden amongst the palms. The
herons, with their feet red like coral, arrived to hop around
in the vast pool. Calling with her sweet voice, the hen
anril bird informed her friend that evening was come and

the sun's departure nigh. The red-eyed cows browsing on the blue grass felt the milk leaking from their udders and, beating the dust rising from the thirsty earth, they headed mooing through the countryside back to their stalls, anxious to find their little ones. The Brahmans poured offerings into the flames of the hearth, which they revive every evening.

Like a widow whose husband is dead on the field of battle, who returns ghastly pale to her parents' dwelling, having lost all her joy in living, the shadows of the evening decked the great city, bewailing the sun's loss.

CANTO SIX

The Temple of Heaven (Chakravâla-Kottam) and the City of the Dead (Shudukâttu-Kottam)

The sun had disappeared and the last glimmerings of twilight had gradually vanished. The full moon rose gentle and fresh in the pure sky, spreading her rays like floods of milk flowing from a silver urn. The blemish that mars her beautiful face could be seen. It is when they are at the height of their glory that the faults of the powerful are remarked.

The goddess Manimekhalâ, who in her heavenly form is as brilliant as the lightning, covered with jewels and enveloped with rainbow-colored veils, had adopted the simple form of a townswoman in order to come and venerate the one who, sole among the immortals, gave the world the gift of his never-failing charity. She went to bow before the pedestal which bears his footprints. Seeing the anguished faces of Sutâmati and her companion, the good lady asked them the cause of their anxiety. Sutâmati told her of the Prince's words and the danger that threatened the graceful Manimekhalaï.

The goddess told her that nothing could arrest the force of the desire that drew the Prince to Manimekhalaï.

23

He had left the garden because it was frequented by ascetics. Manimkhalaï should not risk leaving the precinct by passing through the streets of the city, since he would doubtless attempt to force her to his desire. The goddess advised them to slip through the postern to the west of the garden and to spend the night in the sanctuary of the Temple of Heaven, the Chakravâla-kottam, where there dwelt many ascetics who observe strict rules. "That is where you must go," she told them.

Astonished, Sutâmati remarked, "That place is only called thus by you, lovely lady, and by that Vidyâdhara traitor, Marutavega. Everyone else in the city calls it Shudukâttu-kottam, the temple of the city of the dead." The lady with the precious jewels replied, "Although the night is progressing, I will explain the reason to Mâdhavi's daughter and to yourself.

"When this great city was built, peopled with many inhabitants, a vast plot of land surrounded with high walls was set apart for the dead. Four posterns gave access to it, opening towards the four cardinal points. Over the first of these entrances flies a bright-colored standard. This is reserved for the heavenly beings. They draw nigh in their flying chariots which await their return, suspended in the air, immobile as a painting. The walls of the next gate are decorated with frescoes, the work of skilled artists, representing rice paddies, sugar cane plantations, lakes, and groves. Another entrance, with an upper floor, appears naked and empty. Its walls are covered with spotless white lime, without ornament or decoration. In front of the fourth entrance there stands a great statue of stucco and clay, representing the demon-guardian of the cemetery, with thin red lips and furious stare, holding a pointed spear and a long rope.

"Only the friends of the dead dare to tread this terrifying place surrounded by ramparts. Others never enter. Within there stands a vast temple dedicated to the black goddess who dwells in the desert. Before its door is an altar on which offerings are left. The temple is surrounded by trees, whose long branches bow under the burden of the severed heads hanging from them. These are the heads of fanatical votaries, who sacrifice themselves to the goddess.

24

"In one area are brick monuments of various sizes, forming smaller or larger mounds, built by the rich families of those buried there. Among them are found the tombs of famous scholars and kings as well as those of holy women who have followed their husband onto the funeral pyre. These women belong to the four castes: Brahmans, princes, merchants, and peasants. Inscriptions commemorating those whose remains are housed in these monuments recall their name, status, way of life, and the circumstances of their death.

"Not far off can be seen the pillars in which dwell terrible spirits gifted with magical powers. Offerings are placed at the pillars' foot. On stone platforms reached by a labyrinth of narrow paths are built the huts where the watchmen sleep and take their meals. In their hands they hold a staff and a bowl for their food. Temporary shelters have been built near the cremation ground shining with rings of fire. A pillar of smoke rises constantly from this place, like a waving flag.

"Every noise expressive of grief resounds in these places, ceaselessly disturbing the peace. Night and day can be heard the comings and goings of those bringing bodies to be disposed of according to their custom. Some cast them onto a pyre, others abandon them on the very ground and go away. Some bury them in graves dug in the earth itself or else in narrow tombs sunk underground whose doors are then walled up. Others cover the corpse with a great clay urn fashioned for this purpose. From time to time echoes the crash of drums accompanying the funeral chant (*neytal*), which makes the hearts of those who hear it tremble, reminding them that sooner or later, they too will end in the cemetery. On certain days can be heard the continual murmur of the prayers of the monks who come to recite the merits of their deceased companions during their cremation. The lamentations of kin who have lost someone dear are also heard. To these sounds is added the barking of the long-muzzled jackals, the cry of the owls frightening those who soon must die, and the hooting of the screech owls, feeding on the flesh of the dead. Off and on bursts out the ill-omened cry of the vulture (*antalaï*) who breaks the skulls and crushes them, feasting on corpses' brains. All these sounds surrounding grief and death mingle to form a dull noise, recalling the bar formed when the heavy waves of the sea run into the river's current of sweet water.

"Very tall trees, myrobolam, *otuvai,* and albizzias (*ulincil*) grow in the cemetery, together with laburnums, jujubas, and huphorbias. In the shade of the wide-branched acacia are gathered the hordes of hideous famished demons who feed on human flesh. On the scraggy pines (*vellil*) perch the vultures, satiated and satisfied, having filled their paunch with meat and white fat. In the shelter of the mesgrits, the Kâpâlika, skull-wearing ascetics, cook food for offerings at all times. Under the great jujubas are gathered mendicant ascetics who collect skulls to make necklaces of them.

"In an isolated spot without trees are encamped those wretches who feed on the flesh of corpses. There they prepare their feast, filling an enormous cauldron with fat. Everywhere there are small cups lighted to serve as lamps and vessels containing the gruel to nourish the spirits of the dead. All around is waste ground littered with refuse, pots in which fire has been carried, broken coffins, rings of rope used to carry jugs, necklaces of withered flowers, broken vases, grains of rice, the remains of fried rice, dishes which contained all the ingredients necessary for the various funeral rites.

"After seeing saintly ascetics, the rich and powerful, young women just delivered, tenderly loved children, all seized by the god of death and abandoned in this field, without any respect for their age or rank, and seeing the pyres devouring adored bodies with their flaming mouths, how is it possible that there are people mad enough to amass riches and waste in pleasure the precious time they have to live, without bothering to do good."

The Story of Gotami

"One evening, a young Brahman called Shankalan entered the cemetery having mistaken it, on seeing its walls, for the gate into the town. While he was walking there alone, he suddenly found himself face to face with a sorceress

26

who danced on a stage as though in a theater. Her limbs were smeared with the ashes of bodies which once shone with beauty. A fire-blackened skull in her hand, she screamed with laughter. Her sparse hair framed her face like a dark cloud, her eyes seemed as big as carp, her nose like a gardenia bud, her lips red like the flowers of the coral tree, her white teeth shone like pearls. With no pity for the skull, she tore out its eyes and devoured them, and then began a lively dance on her cloven feet to the sound of a strange orchestra, with a spellbinding rhythm formed of mingled cries. The vocal ensemble was supplied by the howling of the jackals, making feast by devouring a corpse whose entrails had already been the prey of worms, reminding all those who had loved the living body that it was only flesh, bone, and blood. The prolonged cry of the harpies, who had torn off and devoured the sexual organs, which in life are veiled with a scrap of cloth, seemed like the piercing sound of the oboe in rhythm with the repeated barking of dogs, holding in their jaws tiny hands whose glass bracelets they crushed, and punctuated by the cries of the great white-headed and brown-bodied vultures, ever hungry, who devoured the young breasts, still anointed with sandal paste.

"Alone in the night, the young Brahman watched the scene and when the sorceress approached him, he fled terrified away. He had just the time to run to his mother and tell her that an evil spirit he had had the misfortune to see had taken possession of his soul, when he fell dead.

"The poor woman, whose name was Gotami, was blind, like her husband. Taking her son's body in her arms, she staggered towards the gate of the cemetery. Distraught with grief at the death of him who was her only support, with loud cries she called upon Champâpati, the city's protecting deity.

" 'Without consideration for two old people bowed with age and infirmity, a sorceress has seized my son's life, leaving us without protection. Goddess Champâpati! Is it not your duty to protect this city and its inhabitants from all ill? You watch over the public baths, the great trees under which the gods shelter, the flowering temple gardens. Had you then no duty toward my son? What did you do to defend him?'

"Golden-hued Champâpati appeared before her and said, 'It is almost midnight and in the deep darkness your cries of sorrow have called me here to this postern where demons prowl. Tell me! What has happened?'"

"Gotami spoke, 'I no longer have anyone to take care of me. My young son innocently entered the cemetery compound. There a horrible sorceress or some evil spirit took possession of his life. He lies here as though asleep. Look at him! I beseech you to restore him to life and take my own. Thus, he can look after my old blind husband. Take my life and restore his to him!'

"Hearing Gotami's words, the good and ancient goddess, moved to pity, tried to console her. 'Neither sorceresses nor demons can take your life. It is the child's fate, his chest crossed by the sacred thread, which has taken him, and it is because of his ignorance that life has left his body. Despite your great grief, you must resign yourself.

" 'None is unaware that the life leaving one body is transferred immediately to another, according to the actions, good or bad, performed in the previous life. To restore life to this body to deliver you from your great sorrow is not within my power. Do not grieve! Those who claim to raise the dead are liars, exploiters of grief, cruel people for whom killing is a meritorious act. Ignorant woman! Do you not see that masses of people would be ready to give their lives to save the kings of the earth, while in this very cemetery, hundreds of monuments speak to the memory of dead kings buried there? Cease cursing the cruelty of fate, which would lead you to hell, and refrain from asking me to do the impossible, since nothing can exchange your life for that of your child.'

"Gotami replied, 'The holy books of the Brahmans, learned in the four *Vedas*, state that the gods possess the power to accomplish whatsoever their faithful demand of them. You are a great goddess! If you refuse me the grace I have asked of you, I shall go instantly to put an end to my days.'

"Champâpati said, 'Mahâ-Brahmâ alone, the creator of the world, who exists beyond time, could have the power to restore to a body the life that has left it. If one of the innumerable gods who dwell in the heavenly spheres were able to grant you the miracle you request, I also could do it. See now my power!'

"She then made appear before Gotami the four groups of world planners (Arûpa-Brahmâ), the sixteen regents of the visible worlds (Rûpa-Brahmâ), the two luminaries, the sun and the moon, the droves of heavenly nymphs, the innumerable hordes of spirits (Asura), and the forefathers of the eight kinds of human being, the constellations moving in the sky, the twenty-seven houses of the moon and the planets, as well as all the spirits who could grant favors to those that called on them.

"When they were all gathered together, the goddess asked them whether they could grant what Gotami begged. All, with a single voice, repeated what Champâpati had already stated. When she heard the word of the gods who reign over the heavenly worlds, Gotami ceased her lamentations and resigned herself to her bereavement. She placed her son's body on the funeral pyre on the cremation ground and departed.

"The world of the spheres where the gods dwell is named Chakravâla. This is why the place where Champâpati's power was able to call together all the denizens of the heavenly worlds was henceforth called 'the temple of heaven' in memory of this event. Mayä, the skillful divine architect, built there a temple with clay and stucco in the image of the gods' dwellings. In its center is represented the world's axis, Mount Meru, surrounded by the seven mountain chains and four continents, and encircled by islands to the number of two thousand. On each continent the most noteworthy places are marked, together with the appearance of their inhabitants and the style of their houses.

"It is because the temple of heaven is situated not far from the walls of the city of the dead that people commonly call it the temple of the cemetery."

Mâdhavi's daughter had listened in silence to the goddess explaining to Sutâmati the history of the temple of heaven. She simply murmured, "Such is the fate of life on earth."

It was the middle of the night and the darkness was

deep. Sutâmati, whose feeble mind had hardly been able to follow the goddess's discourse explaining the nature of life and the fate of beings born into this world, had fallen sound asleep. Leaving her there, with the aid of a magic spell the goddess plunged liana-like Manimekhalaï into deep slumber and, lifting her in her arms, carried her one hundred and twenty leagues through the air southwards from there. She left her on the isle of Manipallavam in the midst of the sea and then disappeared.

Sutâmati's Awakening

Having left Manimekhalaï on the isle of Manipallavam, the goddess returned to Puhâr. She appeared before Prince Udayakumâra, who, troubled since he had seen Manime-khalaï in the garden and humiliated at not having been able to approach her, was spending a sleepless night in his luxurious many-cushioned bed, searching in his mind for the means to possess himself of her as soon as dawn should appear. The goddess spoke to him.

"King's son! When the royal scepter loses its recti-tude, the planets swerve in their orbits. If the planets change their course, the rains diminish, and when the clouds stay dry, all life ceases on earth. For this reason, all living beings depend on the virtues of the king who reigns over the world. Cast far from you this blameworthy desire which draws you to Manimekhalaï, since she is destined for the monastic life."

The goddess then betook herself to the flower gar-den and woke Sutâmati, who was deep asleep. She told her, "I am the goddess Manimekhalâ and I have come to this city for the festival of Indra. The moment has come for Manimekhalaï, like a tender liana, to follow the path traced by the Buddha. Thanks to my magical powers, I have carried the girl with her precious jewels off to Mani-pallavam, where no danger threatens her.

"Manimekhalaï, like a young liana, is adorned with the rarest virtues. She will return to Puhâr in seven days' time, having learned all the events of her former life. She will come disguised so as to be recognized by no one in this city, famous for opulence and pleasures, but to you she will reveal her true face. On the day of her return, tragic events will take place in the city.

"Run and tell Mâdhavi of my arrival here and of the spotless path for which her daughter has been chosen. Mâdhavi has long known me. Kovalan spoke to her of the goddess of the powerfully waved ocean when he decided that his daghter should bear my name. Then I appeared to Mâdhavi at midnight on an auspicious day. In a dream as clear as reality, I told her that she had brought into the world a child destined for a life of asceticism and renunciation, who would deliver the world from great distress and destroy the power of the god of the passions so completely that he would remain without strength and disoccupied. Remind her of this dream!"

Having said these words, the goddess rose into the sky and disappeared.

Midnight in the City

Sutâmati, troubled and anxious, listened to the confused sound of the thousand city noises.

Standing by their teachers, experts in language, dancing, harp-playing, music, flute, and drums, the young dancing girls, having terminated the shows given in their own homes, with joined hands made the gesture of obedience before their enlightened audience, who knew how to appreciate the language of gesture and the other aspects of the art of the dance. They now started getting ready to sleep, since midnight was approaching. The instruments which had accompanied them were still; the melodious strings of the harp, tuned to the notes of the various modes and made to vibrate by the delicate fingers of small bracelet-laden hands with red-tinted palms to accompany the voices of skilled girl singers, charming to the ear, being no longer in use, slackened with a groan.

The women who during the day had shown their

31

anger on learning of their fickle husbands' infidelities, their kohl-laden eyes red with fury, disdaining every excuse, now asleep on their scented couches scattered with flowers, clasped their husbands, all unawares, like lianas.

The young children with their uncertain steps who had spent the whole day trotting about on their tiny feet with their playmates, drawing along the little carts that served them as toys, running around and amusing themselves all the time, were now tired. The boys, wearing a golden pendant representing Vishnu's five weapons as a talisman, chattering quietly, were made to inhale the smoke of white mustard leaves placed on a brazier before falling asleep lying beside their nurses.

At the approach of midnight, the doves nesting under the eaves, the waders of the lakes, and the small birds hidden in the thickets or perched in the trees, no longer let a sound be heard.

The festival's amusements had ceased; the drums were silent; the ancient, powerful city now lay asleep.

Now and again, the call of the palace watchmen was heard, crying the hour in accordance with the instruments used to measure time.

The ever-hungry elephants, restless in their shelters, let out an occasional long trumpeting. The police, who protect the city from thieves, sounded their horns while making their rounds along the wide avenues where carriages move and in the narrow streets of the meaner quarters.

From far off could be heard the songs of the boatmen on their ships anchored in the harbor, getting drunk on beer and other liquor to appease their boredom. Their voices mingled with the rolling of the waves.

Sometimes there rose the joyful laughter of women who had given birth to a son, their period of ritual uncleanness after childbirth ended, feeling free of anxiety and surrounded by other women, going to bathe in the lake. They carried censers burning the dried leaves of margosa and white mustard, whose smoke keeps away evil spirits.

The king's guards ran noisily like a troop of tigers to the crossroads of the four main avenues, where the city's protecting genie dwells, shouting, "Our king will be victorious!" even though the king was threatened by no enemy.

To banish the risk of possession and various ills that threaten women recently delivered, to avoid sickness of the newborn and the dangers that menace women pregnant for the first time, the soothsayers stood before the trees which house the evil fairies, howling imprecations to frighten them.

All these noises mingled together in a confused sound which surprised the troubled spirit of Sutâmati, whose beautiful teeth were the color of the root of the peacock's feathers.

She fled from the flower garden, through the western postern in the enclosing wall. The darkness was so deep that the air seemed like a black-painted curtain. She reached the pilgrims' hospice, called Ulaka-aravi, situated in the enclosure of the temple of heaven, the Chakravâla-kottam, of which the goddess had spoken, whose great doors stood always wide open so that all could find shelter there. Still confused in spirit, she went and hid in a corner.

Then, to her great fright, a statue sculpted on the pillar in front of her began to speak. The statue, the work of the divine architect Mayä, was the dwelling place of a genie who revealed to his listeners the actions they had performed in their former lives, to the marvel of all. Hearing him speak, Sutâmati's great eyes, their lids burdened with kohl, grew dim with fear.

He said to her, "Ravivarma's adored daughter! Queen! Spouse of Durjaya, owner of much cavalry! One day you lost control of yourself and were killed by an elephant. You were the cause of the death of your elder sister Tara, who wore bright necklaces of flowers. Now you are Sutâmati, daughter of the Brahman Kaushika, of the land of Champa where the Karâlar tribe dwell. You came to this city with Marutavega and here have found again her who, in your former life when you were called Vera, was your elder sister Tara, today named Mâdhavi.

"Hear me! On the seventh day from today, just

33

before the middle of the night, Lakshmi, who was your younger sister in your former life and today is known as Manimekhalaï, will come here, knowing all about her previous life and yours. Do not worry about her absence."

Hearing the statue speak, the good Sutâmati with her modest jewels was terrified and stayed motionless until daybreak.

Day Breaks on Puhâr

The sun rose above the sea, chasing away the shadows of the night.

The policemen of the guard went back to sleep, and the citizens, still stretched out on their clean beds, began to awaken. Some, for no particular reason, sounded the conch, whose spiral winds to the right. The wise men gathered together to discuss important subjects. The elephants, their foreheads marked with red patterns, trumpeted their call. The cocks with their many-colored plumage raised their joyful cries. The horses, still shut in their stables, got up and began to paw the ground in their desire to go out. Birds of all kinds, perched in the trees, started singing. The cheeping of their little ones, nesting among the charming shrubs, became gradually louder. Here and there could be heard the clinking bracelets of the women, resembling blossoming lianas. The people placed the day's first fruits, pleasant to the eye, on the altars of the gods. At the entrance to the street of the bazaars, the merchants murmured their prayers, making offerings of flowers.

The sound of drums and other instruments gradually rose in the musicians' houses. Charitable people left good food on the threshold of their homes, to be distributed to the poor and needy.

The whole town awoke from its sleep to do its daily tasks.

Agitated like a peacock pursued by volleys of arrows, Sutâmati staggered as she made her way through the streets of the great city towards Mâdhavi's house, to recount to her all the happenings of the night, omitting nothing.

34

On learning what had happened and of the disappearance of Manimekhalaï, Mâdhavi was seized with great uneasiness, like a cobra who has lost the precious jewel which adorns its forehead. After making her report, Sutâmati remained prostrated, unable to move, as if all life had left her body.

CANTO EIGHT

Manimekhalaï Awakes on Manipallavam

While Sutâmati was worrying over her disappearance, Manimekhalaï, lying on a sandy flower-strewn beach, awoke from a deep sleep on the isle of Manipallavam.

The strand was littered with the shells in which fishermen sow pearls to reap a harvest. Here and there, the waves had left branches of coral and pieces of scented sandalwood. Further on, the ground fell away towards a lake bordered with tall orange-flowered *nâlals;* on the clear deep water the iridescent water lilies opened, whose honey the bees came to suck. On the lake shore, there grew an abundance of *punnaï* with bushy foliage, and violently scented pandanus. Their thick leaves excluded the sun's rays. The sand was so white that it seemed as though it were lit by the moon. Strewn petals covered it with a perfumed carpet.

Like a newborn child who with astonishment discovers a world unknown, where nothing remains of the familiar places and persons of its former life, Manimekhalaï looked around her dumbfounded. Only her black hair with its ornament-laden tresses reminded her that she had not left this world.

The sun rose, spreading his rays over the dark-sapphire sea. At first glance she thought that the shore must be the continuation of the garden, unnoticed during the night. She began to weep, calling her companion, "Sutâmati! Where are you hiding? Have you no feeling for my distress? I do not know whether I am dreaming or whether what I see is part of reality. My heart trembles with fear. Reassure me with a word, now that the darkness is finally dispelled. All this must be the effect of the magic of that strange woman who appeared to us covered with sparkling ornaments. I no longer understand anything and am afraid of being alone. Come back to me, Sutâmati, equal to the goddess of destiny!"

At the lake's edge, at sunrise, the waders stretched their wide wings. The grasshoppers took flight in their thousands. The many-colored aquatic birds gathered around the male swans, like kings in their majesty. Groups formed around them on all sides of the lake, like the armies of enemy princes ready to give battle.

Manimekhalaï explored the shore and the dunes seeking her friend, but without success.

The tresses of her black hair, to which some flowers were still attached, fell disheveled on her shoulders. She called out, wept, and cried in her despair. In her loneliness, she called her father to mind, remembering his tragic death.

"Inexorably the day arrives on which our guilty actions, the source of our destiny, begin to bear fruit and plunge us into torment. At just such a moment, you departed for a far country with Kannaki, your wife, with her charming body, wearing golden ankle-rings. Dear father! Your chest adorned with a magnificent jewel was ripped asunder when you suffered an unjust death by the sword of royal power."

Walking on, she arrived at what seemed to be a sacred pedestal, which rose three cubits above the ground, making a square block nine cubits wide. In the center was traced a circle made of tiny pieces of incrusted crystal. Within this circle was another square, in which was drawn a lotus flower. This sparkling pedestal adorned with rare stones had been raised by Indra, the king of heaven, in honor of the Buddha so that he could rest there when he came to preach a sermon. At his touch, the pedestal acquired a marvelous power: all those who approached it at once received a vision of their former life.

Dazzled by the splendor of the divine pedestal, two

minor kings from the barbarous country of the Nâgas (Nâga-nadu) on the eastern marches resolved to seize it. First one, then the other, they sought in vain to loosen it and, unable to renounce their ambition, enraged, they set against each other. Anger made their reddened eyes even more red. Fury troubled their minds. Having decided on battle, they marshaled their armies.

Suddenly the Buddha appeared before them. Sitting on the pedestal, he ordered them to cease fighting. "This pedestal," he said, "is made for me alone. None other has the right. Due to its matchless virtues, it is an object of veneration for sages and the powerful."

Amazed at the sight of the miraculous pedestal, Manimekhalaï, who had thought herself abandoned on some savage island, dried her tears and ceased her lamentations.

CANTO NINE

On Seeing the Divine Pedestal, Manimekhalaï Recalls the Memory of Her Previous Life

Filled with wonder at the sight of the divine pedestal, Manimekhalaï forgot her troubles. Her hands, their palms tinted like autumn leaves, joined unconsciously together before her forehead. Her sight grew dim and tears of joy fell like a shower of pearls from her reddened eyes onto her breasts.

Thrice she walked round the pedestal, keeping it on her right. Then, at the risk of breaking her frail body, she prostrated herself. Had someone been there to see her throw herself to the ground, as bright as a flash of lightning with her black hair like dark clouds, he would have believed he had seen a thunderbolt fall. When she rose, all the events of her former lives were present in her mind. Remembering the prediction of the sage Brahmâ Dharma, she invoked him mentally.

"Venerable sage! You know the ultimate truth of which the sacred scriptures bear unfailing witness. I see that all you predicted for me on the banks of the stream Kâyankaraï has come to pass.

"O Brahmâ Dharma, you who incarnate the right way! You were the brother-in-law of King Attipati, who reigned over Gandhara, the renowned country in the east (Pûrva-Desha), whose capital was Idavayam (Rishabaka). Thanks to him, order and virtue reigned in the land.

"One day as you taught Attipati the right path of the *dharma*, you revealed to him that in seven days' time an earthquake would shake the continent of the jamburose-apple (the whole of India) and would destroy the capital, which would have to be abandoned at once.

"You told him, 'O King! Soon the earth will start to tremble, spreading terror amongst all living beings. Your capital, situated in Nâga-nadu, with a territory four hundred leagues wide, will plunge down into the infernal regions and all will be destroyed.'

"The king had the news proclaimed in all the quarters of that vast city. He ordered the people to move away, leading their cows and domestic animals. He left Idavayam at the head of his mighty army and encamped for some time in an area shaded by great trees on the banks of the stream Kâyankaraï, before proceeding to Avanti, the great city in the north.

"On the very day and at the hour predicted, the kingdom's capital was no more than a heap of ruins. On receiving the news, the king and all his people came to prostrate themselves at the seer's feet, thanking him and singing his praises. You then taught them the *dharma*, which removes from us all evil and leads to everlasting happiness.

"In my former life, I was the daughter of a king named Ravivarma and of his highly-born wife Amritapati, whose tiny feet were tinted with essence of red cotton. They reigned over the great city of Ashotaram, whose noise like the boom of the ocean spread far and wide. They called me Lakshmi. Later, I was married to Rahul, born like the morning sun of the womb of Nilâpati of the precious jewels, daughter of Shridhara, king of Siddhapuram, and first wife of Attipati.

"One day while you were addressing the crowds on the banks of the stream Kayankaraï, I came with my dear husband to bow before you, whose fame knew no bounds.

"You spoke to me saying, 'In sixteen days from today, your husband Rahul will die of the venom of a serpent called *drishtivisham*, the sight of whom alone is fatal. You will follow your husband in death, climbing onto his funeral pyre.

" 'You know that all that comes to pass is but the fruit of our past actions. In this life you have not acquired the merit which will allow you to pass to a better world. You will therefore be reborn in a city of unrivaled luxury whose name recalls that of the daughter of King Kavêran (Kaveri-Pumpattinam).

" 'Girl of rare jewels! One day you will be threatened by serious danger. The goddess Manimekhalâ will then abduct you in the darkness of the night, and leave you on an islet in the sea to the south of the city.

" 'There you will see the divine pedestal of matchless radiance, on which reposed the Buddha, the physician who cures the sickness of being born and once calmed the fury of two uncouth and vigorous kings from the Nâga country and, after pacifying them, opened their ears to the teaching of *dharma* and closed them to pernicious ideas. He then taught the people the way of wisdom. At the very instant when, with joined hands, you bow before the divine pedestal, you will remember your former life and understand the meaning of what I am telling you.'

"When I heard of the imminent death of my husband Rahul, I was deprived of all courage and strength. I then begged you to reveal to me what would be my husband's next existence. You replied that the goddess who would carry me far from Puhâr to this southern isle would explain to me what had become of my husband. Will the goddess then now appear?"

Speaking thus to herself, Manimekhalaï, like a young liana, continued to shed tears.

Manimekhalaï Learns Magic Formulas

While Manimekhalaï wandered, burdened with sadness and doubt, the goddess, knowing that she had by now learned the circumstances of her former life and that she seemed ready to understand the path of renunciation, descended from the clouds. Holding a bouquet of flowers in her hand, she illuminated everything around her. Moving in the air, she spoke so as to be understood by the young girl.

"At a time when goodness was no longer to be found among living beings, when ears had become deaf to the teaching of the wise, when men had lost their sense of justice and the world was impoverished for lack of true knowledge, you appeared like a young sun rising after long darkness.

"I have come to bow before this pedestal, in which your invisible presence is felt, and in which you have deposited your power. I bow my forehead before your feet. Your image lives in my heart like a lotus in full bloom."

The goddess circled the pedestal thrice, keeping it to her right, and then, descending to the ground, she approached Manimekhalaï and ordered her to cease her lamentations.

Manimekhalaï came and prostrated herself before the goddess, saying, "Thanks to your goodness, I have been able to remember what happened in my former life, but I am eager to know what has happened to Rahul, who was my husband."

The goddess told her, "You may recall, Lakshmi, the events I shall now relate. One day in a garden, at the noon hour, you had a tender quarrel with Rahul.

"Unable to check his amorous desire, he lay down beside you and stroked your charming feet, trying to calm your resentment.

"While he was in this position, there suddenly appeared one of those wandering monks, called Charana,

40

who journey through the air. His name was Sâdhu Sakkara. He had been to the Continent of Jewels (Ratnadvīpa) to start the wheel of *dharma* moving there. Since it was noon, he had come down to earth in search of food. You were startled and embarrassed by his arrival. Rahul was highly displeased at the sight of this ascetic whose intrusion at the wrong moment had thwarted his desires. He rudely asked him what he wanted.

"Tying your hair adorned with choice flowers, trembling with dread, you scolded your husband, saying, 'Your tongue has lost a good chance of acquiring merit by not greeting an ascetic descended from heaven who, moreover, is a faithful worshiper of the Buddha, the prophet who has vanquished the inner enemies of man— lust, anger, and mistaken beliefs.' You then went and apologized to the holy man, begging him (although you were not followers of his creed) to do you the favor of accepting from your hands fresh water and modest food you could offer him, saying, 'We are your servants and obey your orders.'

"The sage accepted your offer and this act which remains to your credit will be taken into account at your next rebirth.

"In his new incarnation, Rahul is now the prince Udayakumâra, who yesterday pursued you in the city garden. The ties that united you both in your former life explain the attraction which draws you to him and the gentle feelings he inspires in you, despite yourself. But your present destiny is of another kind and this is why I have brought you to this island and let you see the pedestal. The best rice is not sown in soil that is arid, salty, or so sandy that it may be dispersed by the wind. Within yourself you bear the seed of the highest virtues and it is important that it be put to good use. I have many things to tell you.

"In your former life, you were the daughter of Amritapati, wife of Ravivarma, who reigned over the city of Ashotaram. You were called Lakshmi and you had two elder sisters named Tara and Vera who had both married Durjaya, king of the land of Anga (north of Magadha). One day, he took his two wives to visit the mountains of his kingdom and, on returning, stopped for a pleasant rest on the banks of the Ganges.

"There arrived to visit him the sage Aravana Adigal of pure knowledge, freed from all passion. Durjaya went immediately to greet him and enquire as to the purpose of his visit. The sage explained that he had come to worship the Buddha's footprints, impressed on the Mountain of the Vulture (Gridhra-Kuta), near Rajagriha, where in a former age the Buddha, standing on the hill, taught the *dharma,* so that all living beings could be delivered from the anguish of birth and death, and that the conflicts between the species which made them live in fear could cease. The sacred imprint of his lotus-feet, the mere sight of which frees us from lust and other vices, can still be seen on this mountain. This is why it is now called the Mount of the Lotus-feet (Padma-pankaja-malaï). All those who wish to attain wisdom come to worship it.

"In the company of Aravana Adigal, they all made the pilgrimage around the mountain and celebrated a festival in its honor. Thanks to the merits obtained by this act, the two girls who were your sisters in their former lives have gained the privilege of being near you once more. One has become your mother, Mâdhavi, and the other, Sutâmati, your faithful companion.

"Now that you know about your former life, girl adorned with a necklace of flower-petals! and now that you have understood the value of the *dharma,* it only remains for you to study the other doctrines so as to work out your own destiny. You must study the deceitful theories of the various religions. There is however a risk that their preachers, seeing a young woman adorned with bracelets, might be unwilling to accept you among their disciples and expound in front of you the most secret tenets of their doctrines. For this reason, I am going to teach you magic words, highly effective *mantras,* by which you can change your appearance and travel through the air."

The goddess thus imparted to her, observing the rites, the secret formulas, and then said, "On a day when the moon is full and the stars favorable, you will receive the initiation handed down to us by the Buddha, the ascetic without equal, who despised ordinary knowledge and by the strength of his own merit acquired the true knowledge. Bow now before the divine pedestal, source of perpetual prosperity, and return to your native city."

The goddess rose for a moment in the air, but descended again. "One thing I have forgotten to tell you, girl adorned with precious jewels! You are destined for the hardships of ascetic life, but the body of a living being is built of food and hunger is a pressing need. I will therefore teach you another magic word which you have only to utter to eliminate the pangs of hunger."

Having made her gift, the goddess disappeared into the air.

CANTO ELEVEN

Manimekhalaï Receives the Magic Bowl

When the goddess had departed, Manimekhalaï wandered haphazardly about the five leagues of the island, admiring the sandy dunes, the shady thickets, and the fresh pools full of bright flowers.

Suddenly she saw another woman approaching, who appeared to be a heavenly creature and who asked her, "Beautiful maiden with the brilliant bracelets! You seem alone here, like the survivor of some shipwreck. Tell me who you are."

"You ask me who I am! Do you mean in my present life, or in my other lives?

"Formerly I was Lakshmi, the beloved wife of a sovereign named Rahul. Now I am called Manimekhalaï, daughter of Mâdhavi, the dancer.

"A goddess, whose name I bear, took me away from my native city and brought me here, where, at the sight of the sublime pedestal, I suddenly regained the memory of my past existence. Lady more beautiful than a heavenly liana! May I know your name?"

Seeing that Manimekhalaï of the beautiful jewels remembered her former life, Tivatilakaï straightly told her, "Not far from this isle called Manipallavam, there exists another known as Ratnadvïpa. There on the summit of a high mountain named Samanta-Kuta can be seen the footprints of the Buddha, the incarnation of all virtues.

"For us, these footprints are like barks which allow us to cross the ocean of perpetual rebirth. A very long time ago, I came to venerate these footprints. Then, at the order of Indra, the king of the gods, I remained as guardian of this enchanted isle, far from all impurity. My name is Tivatilakaï (*dvîpa-tilaka*, the adornment of the isle).

"Listen to me! Only a chosen few who have amassed great merit and have never strayed from the path of the *dharma* which the Buddha taught are privileged to see the divine pedestal and worship it. When they bow before it with their hands joined, the remembrance of their past existence suddenly appears in their mind. These rare beings are the only ones worthy to receive the secret aspects of knowledge.

"Girl of rare jewels! Your previous life has been revealed to you. You are therefore among the chosen. Now listen to what I will teach you, O liana-like maid!

"Just in front of the famous pedestal is a lake of sweet water called Gomukhi, 'The Bull's Muzzle,' covered with water lilies of all colors and entwined with lianas which open when the heat of the day starts to lessen during the summer season.

"The Buddha was born on the longest day of the year, in the month of the bull (Rishabha), also known as Vaishakha (April 15–June 15), since the moon is then in the constellation of Vishâkhâ, the sixteenth of the twenty-seven asterisms, which initiate in the Pleiades (Kârtika, October/November).

"Each year on the anniversary of this day, by the will of Buddha, there emerges from the lake a magic beggar's bowl, called Cow of Abundance (Amritä Surabhi), which once belonged to Aputra.

"Today itself is the auspicious day and the fated

hour is now approaching. The magic bowl seems destined, girl of rare jewels, to find its place in your hands. Any offering placed in this bowl is multiplied to the extent of being able to feed all those that suffer misery and famine. Whatever amount of food is given away, the bowl is never exhausted. When you return to your native town, O maiden of the scented flower necklace, the sage Aravana Adigal will be able to tell you all the details of the bowl's history."

Like a young liana, Manimekhalaï listened to these matters with immense interest. She withdrew in recollection before the pedestal of ineffable splendor and then, in Tivatilakaï's company, went around the pool, keeping it on her right and, observing the prescribed rules, stood straight and still. The venerable magic bowl then suddenly emerged from the waters of the pool and came to rest in Manimekhalaï's red-tinted palms. The young girl, her wrists encircled with glass bangles, felt an immense joy on receiving the bowl, and began singing the praises of the Buddha.

"Blessed be the sacred feet of the hero who resisted the arrows of desire, forewent the delights of the heavenly paradise, and overcame the power of evil to lead men on the path of the *dharma*.

"Blessed be the Omniscient, whom thought cannot reach, the seer who opens our eyes, the possessor of true knowledge who teaches us the *dharma*, whose ear is deaf to slander, whose mouth has told nothing but the truth, who descended to hell to assuage the sufferings of the damned and delivered from their anguish the serpents of the underworld. To sing his glory passes the power of any words my tongue can tell. My body finds its only reason for living lying prostrate before his sacred feet."

When Manimekhalaï had finished chanting the glory of the Buddha, the Immaculate One, seated in the shade of the pipal, Tivatilakaï spoke to her of the suffering that hunger can cause and the merits of those who seek to appease it.

"Hunger is the most hateful of maladies. It degrades the most noble beings. It is the cause of all crime and kills all human feeling. It wipes out acquired knowledge, drives away modesty and shame, reduces glory and splendor to the dust. It forces the best of men to beg humbly, standing before the door of strangers, with their wives who once wore jewels on their breast. I cannot find words of sufficient praise to recount the merits of those generous beings who dedicate themselves to delivering man from the curse of starvation.

"I am now going to tell you a story which reveals to what point hunger can degrade human beings.

"At a time when the rains had failed, when the grass and trees were dried up and the earth had become hard and scorched, so that all living things were gradually dying, Vishvamitra, the sage skilled in the *Vedas* who had renounced his position as king in order to lead an ascetic life, wandered from one end of the earth to another during this time of famine, finding nothing to eat so as to survive. He came upon a dead dog and decided to eat it in order to appease his hunger. According to custom, he offered the gods, beginning with Indra, the god of the rains, the first fruits of this strange meal. The king of heaven forthwith appeared before him, calmed his pangs of hunger and made abundant rain fall. Life prospered once more and the harvests were abundant.

"Perhaps you have already heard this story?

"Food offered to those capable of providing it for themselves is really only a kind of exchange made under the pretext of charity. Only those who distribute food out of pure charity, expecting no return, are protectors of life in this world, which is but a temporary assembly of atoms.

"You must now return to your city and attend to the destitute who suffer from starvation. You now know the true nature of the *dharma* and have acquired true knowledge. You are on the path which will allow you to come to the aid of all living beings."

Manimekhalaï replied, "When in my former life my husband died, poisoned by a serpent the mere sight of which causes death (*drishtivisham*), I followed him onto the funeral pyre and was burned alive. At the very moment when I lost consciousness, I remembered the day

46

when, at noon, I had offered food and water, to a mendicant monk named Sadhû Sakkara. I believe it was this thought, at the very moment of my death, which made the magic bowl that allows hunger to be appeased come into my hands.

"On that part of the jambu-rose-apple continent called India, there are many fortunate people who profit from the fruits of the virtues sown in their past existence. But in front of their beautiful houses stand crowds of miserable beings, clothed in torn rags, tortured by hunger, protected by nothing from the sun's burning rays or from the rain. Standing there humbly before the rich man's door, desperate, without refuge, they pay dearly the price of the errors of their past lives.

"At the sight of her baby, a mother's breasts secrete sweet milk for its nourishment. In the same way, I hope that at the sight of the poor who despite the rain and the sun's heat roam in search of something to appease their hunger, the magic bowl will secrete unlimited amounts of good food."

Tivatilakaï said, "I had forgotten one aspect you are right to recall. This magic bowl will only be filled in the hands of those whose charity, the fruit of their past virtues, is sincere. Your desire to feed the poor is a grace that your merits have obtained for you, and I think you understand that it is the result of that good deed you performed in your former life."

Manimekhalaï prostrated herself at Tivatilakaï's feet and then, holding the wonderful bowl in her lotus-like hand, she venerated the Buddha's sacred pedestal. Having circled thrice around it, she then repeated the *mantra* which gave her the power of flying and returned through the air to Puhâr, where she appeared to Mâdhavi and Sutâmati, her companion. They were worried by her absence, since this was the seventh day foreseen by the goddess for her return. At the sight of her daughter, Mâdhavi regained her peace of mind.

Manimekhalaï greeted them saying, "In my previous life you were my two sisters Tara and Vera, the daughters of Amritapati, fortunate queen, and of Ravivarma, and wives of King Durjaya, the owner of many

horses. Now you are my mothers and I bow before you.
May the austerities you practice in this body be profitable
and free you from passion. Women with slender bracelets! It is from Aravana Adigal that you too will learn
the secret of your past lives. I have brought with me the
magic bowl called Cow of Abundance, which once belonged to Aputra. Both of you must worship this divine
bowl."

They thus decided to betake themselves to the great
ascetic whose name is spotless and together departed for
the place where he dwelt.

CANTO TWELVE

Visit to the Ascetic Aravana Adigal

After several efforts, Manimekhalaï finally discovered
where the venerable Aravana Adigal was to be found.
His hair was grizzled and his body enfeebled with age,
but his voice was still firm and alert.

Manimekhalaï, whose long hair seemed like a black
cloud scattered with flowers, went thrice around the sage's
dwelling, then, prostrating herself before him, she recounted what had happened since the moment when she
went to the flower garden on the outskirts of the city:
the advances of Udayakumâra, the appearance of the
goddess, and how she had been conveyed to the isle of
Manipallavam; the discovery of the Buddha's sacred pedestal which had given back to her the memory of her
former life; the goddess's revelation of the actual incarnation of Rahul, her husband in her previous life, as well
as the news that her sisters Tara and Vera, after their
tragic death, had now become Mâdhavi and Sutâmati
of the beautiful hair and had found her once more.

"The goddess told me, 'Girl like a liana in flower!
It is from the lips of Aravana Adigal that you will learn

their story.' Then, after teaching me some magic words, she disappeared."

Manimekhalaï also told the sage of the sudden appearance of Tivatilakaï and how she had procured for her the magic bowl of Aputra, telling her that only Aravana Adigal could recount to her its history as well as the past lives of her mother and her companion.

She explained that she had come back to Puhâr on Tivatilakaï's instructions.

The great sage showed a growing interest in Manimekhalaï's account. He told her, "May fate be kind to you, girl of the golden bracelets! I can, indeed, tell you the story of these two women.

"Not only on the day when the full moon is in the sixteenth house, in the month of Vaishakha, but also on many other occasions have I gone to the mountain of Gridhra-Kuta to venerate the footprints of the Buddha, who purifies us of our faults. As I was making a pilgrimage one day, I met in an orchard King Durjaya wearing ankle-rings as a mark of his great deeds. He then reigned over the city of Kacchatam (Champapuri) in the Anga country (in Bengal). I asked him, 'O King, endowed with a mighty army, are you full of strength? Hero! do you and your two wives lead an exemplary life?' On hearing these words, the king told me sobbing the tragedy of which his wives with their bright jewels had been the victims.

"A few days before, Vera, the younger queen, who was drunk from too much wine, imprudently and without precaution approached an elephant which had just been captured in the forest for training, and was killed by it. The elder of the two queens, Tara, maddened with grief at the loss of her sister, killed herself by jumping from one of the palace's high terraces.

"I did my best to console the king, telling him that his misfortunes were the result of acts committed in his former lives, and I left the place. And now I find these two princesses once more at Manimekhalaï's side, in the form of Mâdhavi and Sutâmati, like actors who have changed their appearance in a play.

"Manimekhalaï, adorned with a necklace of scented

flowers! You have the rare advantage of knowing your former life and of having glimpsed the path of the *dharma*. This is why I am imparting my thoughts to you with such emotion.

"The three precious teachings left us by the Buddha, the most virtuous of all beings, have not yet been spread abroad as they ought. The royal path leading to wisdom and eternal happiness has become impracticable, over-grown with thorns and weeds, while the path of vice, leading to great misfortune in future lives, is wide open with crowds rushing along it. This is why most beings remain chained to the endless cycle of death and birth. The noble way preached by the Buddha appears veiled by a fog like that which sometimes hides the red morning sun. All know that the bright sun must have risen in the east, but their eyes cannot see it. It is the same with the Buddha's teachings, which remain a dead letter since no one puts them into practice.

"It is not possible to make all the water of the sea pass through a hole pierced in a pearl to make a neck-lace. Nevertheless, a few drops may filter through this narrow orifice. I have no hope at all of drawing the mass of human beings in this vast and prosperous world to the way of the *dharma*, since they are incapable of doing so. However, the advice I can give may influence some of them.

"One day, all the inhabitants of the heavenly spheres (*Chakravâla*) foregathered in the paradise of light (*Dutita*)—the ninth of the thirty-one spheres form-ing the fourth of the worlds where the gods dwell—to supplicate the Great Spirit to make the world better. The god promised them, 'Like the morning sun which rises and spreads its light, banishing the darkness of the night, the Buddha will descend from the paradise of the perfect (*Tushita*) and will be incarnate in the year sixteen hun-dred and sixteen (of the ancient Dravidian era). Like a flood which removes the mud of the fens, his teachings will penetrate all ears, charm all spirits and be accepted and practiced by all.'

"When the sun appears, the sun-stone (diamond) reflects its light. When the sun that is the Buddha arises, he drives away darkness and confusion of spirit. The sun and the moon shine in a pure sky, the moving stars are placed in beneficent conjunctures, and the rains arrive at their proper season. The trade-winds blow in the right direction, the harvests of pearls and coral emerge from the depths of the ocean, the cows, having fed their calves, make the basins overflow with their richest milk, prosperity extends to the four corners of the earth, and the satiated birds forgo their migration. Men and beasts abandon their aggressiveness and live in harmony, freed from fear. Demons and evil spirits cease to torment them. No longer is anyone born hunch-backed, dwarfed, dumb, deaf or deformed like a beast or misshapen mass devoid of human faculties.

"All beings born in this age will receive from his mouth the teachings of the *dharma* and will be freed from the cycle of birth. Never shall I forget, throughout all my lives, my happiness in worshiping the master's feet, seated glorious in the shade of the pipal: life after life, I have sought to lay my praises at his feet.

"Girl like a young liana! The two women who accompany you come together with you to venerate the sage seated under the sacred fig tree who possesses all knowledge, are with you as a reward for the merits they earned when, on the mount of the vulture, they worshiped the lotus-like footprints of the Buddha who has freed them from the faults they committed in their lives. Delivered from the ties which fate imposes, they too will start on the bright path which leads to *nirvâna*.

"Manimekhalaï, young liana! You now possess the magic bowl, Cow of Abundance, which contains the substance of life. You must now go about the world to put an end to the pains of hunger suffered by living beings. There exists no more meritorious act towards gods or men than to assuage the pangs of hunger."

While he was speaking, Manimekhalaï remained standing before Aravana Adigal holding the magic bowl in her hands.

The Story of Aputra

"Manimekhalaï of the beautiful jewels! I am going to tell you the remarkable story of Aputra, the first possessor of the bowl Cow of Abundance, which today is in your hands.

"In the city of Benares there lived Abhanjika, a Brahman who taught the *Vedas*. His wife Shali had committed some unforgivable faults for a woman of her rank. Fearing the chastisement meted out to adulteresses and in the vain hope of purifying herself, she decided to depart on a pilgrimage to go and bathe in the sea at the holy place called Cape of the Virgin (in the extreme south of India). She was pregnant and seemed to have forgotten that ritual bathing in the sea is forbidden according to Brahman custom to women in such a condition. One evening during this long journey, while the other pilgrims were asleep, she gave birth at the roadside to a baby boy whom she abandoned without pity in a palm plantation, out of sight of the passers-by.

"A cow passing nearby, hearing the cries of the hungry infant, drew near, licked its whole body, and then, for seven days, fed it with her milk, protecting it from all harm.

"A Brahman named Ilam Bhuti, a learned interpreter of the sacred scriptures, who lived at Vayanagoda, by chance passed by the place with his wife. 'This baby cannot be the cow's child: he will therefore become my son.' Joining his hands together, he thanked the gods for having given him a son, for his marriage was barren, and entrusted the child to his wife, saying, 'A beautiful man-child is born to us to continue our family.'

"On returning to his village, he integrated the child into the family clan, looked after him, protected him, and gave him an education worthy of a Brahman. When he was the right age, he handed him the sacred thread and taught him to chant the *Vedas*, which the child learned perfectly, without ever committing a mistake in pronunciation.

"One day it came to pass that another priest of the village decided to offer a great sacrifice for the undeclared purpose of eating the flesh of the victims. Entering the place adorned for the sacrifice, the boy saw a cow, protesting like a gazelle taken in a net who fears the arrows of the murderous huntsman. Seeing the cow lamenting, her horns entwined with garlands of flowers, the young boy, moved to tears with pity at the cruelty of men, formulated a plan to steal the cow and hide her somewhere in order to deliver her from her cruel fate. He hid in a corner and, during the night, untied the cow and led her far from the village along stony paths where passers-by are few.

"The group of Brahmans, accompanied by brutal peasants, set out to seek the boy and captured him together with the cow. 'You stole the cow dedicated to the gods and fled by tortuous paths. No wellborn man would commit such a crime. Your behavior proves that you are of low origin. Repent, if you wish to escape the punishment you deserve!' They then set to thrash him with sticks.

"When the cow saw that they were ill-treating the boy, she rushed at the head Brahman and disemboweled him with her horns, tearing out his intestines. She then fled at top speed towards the forest, thus escaping such cruel people.

"Aputra then addressed all those who were assembled there, saying, 'There are vast commons set aside for the cattle. Abundant grass grows there without requiring any man's work. Out of kindness to us, the cows that go and graze there feed us from our birth with their creamy sweet milk. Why do you therefore do evil to such innocent and generous animals? You Brahmans who know the ancient *Vedas*, heed my words and forgo any action which makes other living beings suffer. What have you to say?'

"'You have understood nothing of our acts and twist the meaning of the *Veda* verses which were taught us by Brahmâ, sprung from the navel of Vishnu, the greatest of the gods, who in his right hand holds the resplendent golden disk which is his weapon. You are but the son of a cow, a dunce! You are not really a man, stupid boy! And you are incapable of grasping the meaning of our actions.'

"To the words of the Brahmans trying to humiliate him, Aputra replied that the *rishi* Achala was also the son of a cow, that the sage Shringi was born of a hind, that the *rishi* Vrinchi had been begotten by a tiger, and that Keshakambala, respected by all the sages, was the son of a jackal.

" 'Are all these sages now despised by those of your caste? Quite the opposite! You venerate them with respect. You Brahmans learned in the four *Vedas!* According to your holy books, is it then a defect to be born into a family related to cows?'

"One of the Brahmans in the gathering then declared that he was aware of the young man's origins.

" 'One day on one of my journeys, I met a Brahman woman called Shali, who looked emaciated and exhausted, having left her family to go on a pilgrimage on foot to Virgin Cape, so as to worship the goddess Kumâri according to the Vedic rites. I enquired of her origins and of the reasons for journeying so far from her country. She then recounted her story. "I am the wellborn wife of a Brahman of Benares who teaches the *Vedas* to students. I lived in an unsuitable way for the wife of a Brahman. Betraying my husband, I went beyond every tolerable limit. I then decided to depart and go to bathe on the sacred stairs of Virgin Cape. Fearing to go alone, I joined a group of pilgrims who were hastening to go there.

" ' "About ten leagues from the town of Korkaï, where King Pandya reigns, I was delivered during the night by the roadside of a child which I abandoned, not far from a village of cowherds, in an isolated orchard where it would not easily be found. I then continued my journey. Is there some way in which I can one day be forgiven for such a crime?" she asked weeping.

" 'This boy is the son of Shali, the outcast Brahman woman. I have not divulged this tale till now, believing it was to no purpose, but now that he has by his actions revealed his low birth, consider him untouchable.'

"On hearing the Brahman's tale, Aputra smiled in irony. 'Do you not know then, from what caste were sprung the greatest teachers of the *Vedas*? Do you not know that the two greatest sages, Vasishtha and Agastya, who composed the Vedic hymns, had been begotten by the elder god Brahmâ on the heavenly courtesan Tillottamâ. You who wear the sacred thread across your breast, dare you state that my assertions are false? This being the case, with what do you charge my mother? What was Shali's offense?'

"Speaking thus, he stood proudly with a scornful smile. The council of Brahmans who chant the *Vedas* decided however that Aputra was unworthy to live among them. His adoptive father, Bhuti, and his mother, drove him from their dwelling. He was henceforth considered a malefactor, a cow-thief, and in all the villages where Brahmans lived, only stones were thrown into his beggar's bowl.

"No longer having any means of subsistence, Aputra therefore departed for the rich city of Madura in the south. There he installed himself in the vast precinct of the Temple of Lakshmi, the goddess of fortune.

"Each day with his beggar's bowl, he begged before the splendid dwellings of the rich inhabitants of this great southern city. Afterwards, he distributed what he had managed to gather to the poor, the blind, the deaf, the infirm, the orphans, and the sick, keeping for himself only the remains. He then went to sleep having only his beggar's bowl for a pillow on which to rest his head."

 CANTO FOURTEEN

The Vengeance of Indra

The holy man continued his tale.

"Aputra lived in this manner for many years in the temple court without anything happening of note. But one night, during the cold season, a group of people who seemed hardly able to drag themselves along drew near, despite the darkness, to the corner where he was sleeping. They woke him, begging him to give them food as they were dying of hunger. Aputra was dismayed at not being able to relieve their suffering, since he had no other resources but the meager ration he had obtained for himself by begging.

"Suddenly, shining with light, the goddess of learning (Chintâ/Sarasvati), inspirer of knowledge, appeared before him. 'I know your good deeds and wish to free your charitable soul from its anxiety. Arise! Take this bowl and your desires shall be fulfilled. Even should the whole land be devastated by famine and all its stores exhausted, this bowl will always be filled with the most exquisite food, in such large quantities that the recipients' hands will hardly be able to bear its weight. This magic bowl will never fail so long as it remains in the hands of one who deserves such a gift.' The goddess then gave Aputra the vessel she had brought.

"Aputra prostrated himself before the apparition. 'Sovereign lady of the heavenly worlds, worshiped by all who live on earth! You who reign over our minds, who in the form of language preside over all knowledge and illumine the temple of the arts, your benevolence alone can save us from misfortune!'

"That night, Aputra was able to appease the hunger of those who despite the late hour had come to waken him in the hope of a meal. From that day on, he saved thousands of lives, tirelessly distributing mountains of food. The temple court was invaded by crowds of men, animals, fowl, and other creatures, whose uproar was like a flock of birds on a tree laden with fruit.

"The news of the merits of Aputra the charitable finally reached the dwelling of the king of the gods. The white carpet on which his throne stood began to shake.*

"The god took the form of an old Brahman bowed with age, supporting his enfeebled limbs with the aid of a stick and moving with uncertain steps, and presented himself before him.

* The gods mistrust the powers which may be acquired by men who are too virtuous.

"Having decided to seduce Aputra who had become the real protector of all living beings over a vast area of the earth, the god said to him, 'I am the king of heaven. I know your merits and have come to visit you to give you the reward for your inexhaustible charity.'

"Aputra was a simple and innocent boy. He broke into such violent laughter that his sides ached. Mocking Indra, he said, 'All the pleasures that the paradise of the gods has to offer are without attraction for those that follow the *dharma*. Those charitable souls who take care of living beings and protect the unfortunate, or practice asceticism and free themselves from all ties, are not to be found there. Valiant king of the gods! I desire nothing from you. My only ambition is to distribute food, thanks to this magic bowl, to all those that come to me suffering from the pangs of hunger. My reward is the joy I can read on their faces. Sovereign of celestial beings! I have nothing to do with the feasts, sumptuous clothes, heavenly girls and other pleasures which you could offer me.'

"Faced with Aputra's scorn, Indra, whose body is covered with a thousand eyes, felt violent resentment. Seeing that Aputra had mocked him because he possessed the magic bowl, he decided to make the bowl useless by freeing the world from hunger.

"For twelve years the rains had failed to appear in the country where the Pandya reigns and many people had died. Returning to his paradise, Indra sent heavy clouds over the earth, that sucked up the water of the sea and made such abundant rain fall that the earth began to smile and produce several harvests each year. Prosperity became so great that no creature in the world lacked anything and none knew any longer what it meant to suffer hunger.

"The noise of the crowds that gathered on the public square where Aputra stood gradually ceased. At the same time, profligates appeared in search of adventure, loafers or delinquents thrown out by their families. All these people amused themselves, laughingly held parties, and gambled and spent all their time in futile conversation.

"Aputra understood that there was no longer any

room for practicing charity. He therefore left the temple court where he had been living and wandered from village to village seeking poor people to feed. The villagers brusquely sent him on his way. He was like a king whose state and riches have been devoured by the ocean, who finds himself alone, abandoned by all.

"One day he met some travelers disembarking from a ship coming from the isle of Java (Shavakam), who greeted him with respect and told him that in their country the rain had not fallen and many had died.

"Since Indra's intervention, Aputra had no longer been able to find anyone to whom he could distribute the produce of his magic bowl. He felt like a girl who has failed to find a husband and who feels herself growing old without being of use to anyone. He decided to depart for Java, joining a group of travelers who were leaving for that distant island, and with them embarked on a great ship. During the voyage, the ship was overtaken by a violent storm and had to settle her sails, putting in at the isle of Manipallavam for a day.

"Aputra went ashore. During the night, however, the wind dropped and the captain, believing all his passengers were on board, gave the order to leave. Aputra found himself alone on this desert island. His bowl, thanks to which he had been able to satisfy the needs of all the living beings on earth, now fed only himself. Deeply frustrated, he was seized by great despair. He had lost his chance of feeding all those that suffered hunger. To possess a magic bowl without being able to use it seemed intolerable to him. He decided to give up life itself rather than stay alone and useless on this desert island with a miraculous bowl in his possession that no longer served anyone but himself.

"Bowing before the bowl with respect, he threw it into a pool named 'Bull's Muzzle' (Gomukhi), instructing it to emerge from the waters once a year and if on that day someone should be present desirous of protecting life according to the way of charity and the *dharma*, to place itself in his hands.

"He allowed himself to die of hunger and had already been several days without food when I arrived and asked him the reason for his despair. He told me his story before leaving this life.

"Like the sun which disappears in the west to be born again in the east, Aputra left his body at Manipalla-vam, taking with him his passion for feeding living beings, and was reborn forthwith as the calf of a cow belonging to the king of Java who reigned benevolently over his people."

CANTO FIFTEEN

Sequel to Aputra's Story

"Gracious maiden, slim as a liana! Now hear what was Aputra's destiny.

"The good cow that had protected him for seven days when Shali, his mother, abandoned him in an orchard, had been reborn on the high white mountain, the Dhavala-malaï, on the island of Java, in the comfortable dwelling of a famous ascetic called Manmukhan. Her hoofs and horns were lacquered with gold. All the people of the country came to worship her and praise her beauty. Without even having calved, she produced a great abundance of milk, which she generously gave away to mankind.

"The *rishi* Manmukhan possessed the vision of past, present, and future events. He informed those around him that this cow would give birth to a hero-protector of life and that, thanks to his beneficent influence, the rains would henceforth be abundant, the earth's fertility increased, and the duration of life prolonged. Although conceived by her, the child would not be the fruit of her womb, but would come forth from a golden-shelled egg.

"Aputra had left his previous life, without suffering any ill, on the isle of Manipallavam, with the hope of being reborn in this world in order to carry out his charitable work. At the moment of his death, he thought of the cow who had caressed him and fed him with her milk for the first seven days of his life. As a reward for his virtues, admired by the heavenly beings, he obtained rebirth in the womb of the same cow so as to be able to accomplish his unique destiny in that vast region of the earth known by the name of the jambu-rose-apple of the sweet fruit.

"Hear, Manimekhalaï, the description of the wondrous signs which accompanied his birth! It was in the spring, during the month of Vaishakha, when the sun, wandering through the signs of the zodiac, installs himself in that of the bull. And the moon, of its twenty-seven houses (divided into two groups of thirteen), was situated in the middle one, the predominant fourteenth, which is also called Vishâkhâ. This coincidence is the same which presided at the birth of the Buddha, the great sage who taught seated in the shade of the pipal.

"Although it was not the rainy reason, a heavenly dew mingled with flowers started to fall on the earth. All the ascetics who reside in the Temple of Heaven, the Chakravâla-kottam, were struck with amazement at the appearance of such happy portents. Not understanding their cause, they betook themselves to the oracle of the pillar, who often gave them explanations of what occurred.

"The statue revealed to the holy monks that Aputra had left this life on the isle of Manipallavam, to be born forthwith on the isle of Java to carry out his destiny of saving innumerable lives. The genie recommended them to go and learn the rest of the story from the sage Aravana. So it was that the statue rid itself of the job and left me to do it. Hear my words!

"At that time, the king who reigned in Java was Bhumichandra. Long worried at having no heir, he had come to take counsel from the sage Manmukhan. The holy man entrusted to him the precious boy born of the cow, who was thus raised in the palace and, when he was grown, inherited the crown and became king. Today he wears necklaces of jewels and flowers."

Having told her the story, Aravana confided to Manimekhalaï that the offerings to Indra during the sacrifices had probably been insufficient and that the king, who must govern with equity, had perhaps failed in his duties, since, although the abundance of the Kaveri's waters allowed the earth to be irrigated even in times of drought, a period of famine had fallen on this once-prosperous land.

"Maiden with pretty jewels! To keep the magic bowl by which poverty can be annihilated without using it would be a sin. What would we say if the gods had kept for themselves the ambrosia obtained by churning the thousand-waved ocean without profiting the world by it after surfeiting themselves?"

Manimekhalaï, Mâdhavi, and Sutâmati took their leave of Aravana Adigal, thanking him respectfully, after which Manimekhalaï, dressed as a Buddhist nun, began to wander through the streets of the city.

Seeing this poor beggar-woman, the young people of the town, stupid and loud-mouthed, together with those dissolute persons who ruin themselves with pleasures, the profligate and those looking for fun, felt pity for her fate, saying, "How is it possible that Manimekhalaï, whose hair was entwined with sweet-scented flowers, who disappeared after seducing the heart of Udayakumâra, now roams the streets of Puhâr with a beggar's bowl in her hand?"

The Emperor Pradhyota once seized by treachery Udayana, king of Kausambi, city of many flags, despite his powerful army. He kept him imprisoned, and his minister, the Brahman Uki, while attempting to free his master, took the appearance of a madman attacked by frightful diseases. Seeing him wander through the streets of Ujjaïna, the people, moved with pity, surrounded him displaying their commiseration, as they now did for Manimekhalaï.

Far in the north, beyond the Himalayas, lies the Golden City (Kanchanapuram), where the genies of knowledge, the Vidyâdhara, live. It is there that Kaya-shandikaï was born. During a journey to visit the lands of the south, she halted one day on Mount Podiyil on the bank of a stream in order to rest a little. Since that moment, as a result of the curse of an ascetic, she has been afflicted by the hunger sickness and her insatiable appetite has caused her intolerable pain, obliging her to move ceaselessly. Seeing that ravishing liana, Mâdhavi's daughter, roaming the streets bordered with houses of pleasure, Kayashandikaï reminded her that in order to make it fruitful the first alms thrown into her bowl should come from a woman of irreproachable virtue and generous heart.

"Girl like the incomparable lotus-flower, which surpasses all the other flowers of the pool in beauty! Of the virtuous wives who due to their merits have acquired the power of making the rain fall in due season, the most virtuous is the worthy lady Atiraï, whose reputation is without equal. Here is her house. Your first alms must come from her hand."

CANTO SIXTEEN

Atiraï's Alms

The daughter of the genies of knowledge, Kayashandikaï, like a flowering liana, told Manimekhalaï Atiraï's remarkable story.

"Maiden of the splendid jewels! Listen to my tale! Atiraï's husband, Shaduvan, was a depraved man. He abandoned his home and his wife with her beauteous jewels to go and stay with a courtesan who lived on her charms. Thus he gradually squandered all his wealth on gaming, betting, and other vile pleasures. When he was at the end of his resources, his lover preferred men better provided and threw him out as an intruder, insulting him with scorn.

"Not daring to return to his wife without the means of living, he decided to depart for distant lands in the hope of acquiring new riches by trading. He embarked on a ship chartered by some merchants, but during the voyage, overtaken by a storm, the vessel was dashed to pieces in the midst of the gloomy ocean. Shaduvan, grasping a piece of the mast and thrust by the waves, finally reached shore at the foot of a mountain where he was captured by the Nâgas who live naked.

"Some other passengers, hanging onto fragments of the ship, had also survived, and some returned to Puhâr. Not knowing the fate of the other passengers, the latter were reported missing. Shaduvan's name was mentioned among the dead, since they believed he had gone down with the ship in the midst of the wide sea of bursting waves in the darkness of the night.

"When she heard the news, the noble lady Atiraï resolved to die in order to rejoin her husband, more precious to her than life, wherever his unhappy fate had led him. Weeping, she prayed her kin to prepare her funeral, but they refused to build her a pyre in the cemetery so that she could be burned as is customary for widows.

"Convinced that Shaduvan had drowned at sea, Atiraï herself dug a large hole in the cemetery which she filled with dry wood. She then lit the fire and entered the flames, invoking her husband's name.

"But the flames touched neither the bed on which she lay nor the robe that covered her body. The sandal paste with which she had anointed herself and the flowers that adorned the tresses of her raven hair lost nothing of their fresh color.

"In the midst of the flames which caused her no harm, Atiraï seemed to be the goddess of fortune, with her bronze complexion, seated on her sweet-scented lotus.

" 'What curse has fallen on me that the fire, which destroys all things without discrimination, refuses to touch me! What can I do? Alas!' Convinced she had committed some terrible sin, she started to sob. A disembodied voice was then heard descending from heaven, saying to her, 'Put away your grief! The husband who is so dear to you, driven by the waves, has reached the shore of a mountainous country where the Nâgas live. He has remained there, but his stay will be short. He will embark on a ship belonging to the merchant Chandradatta, who trades beyond the seas, and will return to you.'

"Atiraï, her eyes laden with kohl striped with red lines, was thus delivered from the grief which had made her weep so many tears. She withdrew from the pyre, fresh and light, like a woman returning from bathing in a pool. She went home and henceforth dedicated her life to good works, thinking thus to hasten the return of her husband, dearer to her than the pupils of her eyes. She soon became an object of envy among the exemplary women who, due to the powers acquired by their virtues, could make the rain fall whenever its need was felt.

"On reaching the island, Shaduvan was exhausted after struggling so long in the sea where the clouds come to draw their water. He painfully climbed along the sheer side of a mountain which plunged into the sea, and, reaching a tree hanging to a rock, he fell deep asleep. The cruel inhabitants of the country, who live naked without clothes and are known for their ferociousness, discovered him and woke him with their shouts of joy. They said, 'This man has come here alone, with no companion. His well-covered body will make us an excellent meal.'

"During his journeys, Shaduvan had had the chance to learn their dialect. Forthwith he spoke a few words. Surprised at hearing their tongue spoken, the savages kept at a distance without harming him and spoke warily.

" 'Noble Lord of rare strength, hear us! Our chief lives nearby. It is better that you go and present yourself to him.' Accepting their invitation, Shaduvan followed them to the Nâgas' guru, whose dwelling was a cave. He found him seated naked on a bed of boards, with his wife at his side, as naked as he. They could have been a bear and his companion. They were surrounded by small vessels in which palm-wine was fermenting. Other pots contained morsels of tainted meat. Whitened bones were scattered on the ground, spreading a fetid smell. Speaking to the chief in his tongue, Shaduvan managed to impress him favorably. The chief invited him to sit next to him in the shade of a tree with dense foliage and questioned him as to why he had come.

"Shaduvan explained that he had come from the sea with its mighty tides.

64

"The chief then said, 'This worthy man has undergone great tribulation without food, in the midst of the sea. He is very weary and deserves our pity. Tribesmen! Give him a girl for his pleasure, some of our strongest palm-wine, and as much meat as he desires.' Overwhelmed by the barbarous customs of his host, Shaduvan refused his benevolent offer. 'Your words,' he said, 'hurt my ears. I can accept nothing of what you offer.'

"Furious at Shaduvan's refusal, the chief said to him, 'Is there anything more desirable for a man than girls for his pleasure and sustenance to feed him? If you desire something else, explain!'

"Shaduvan replied, 'The sages who have attained a higher vision of things do not use inebriating drink and avoid destroying life. In this world, we can see that everything that is born has to die and whatever dies is born again. Life and death are phenomena similar to the states of sleeping and waking. Those who have accomplished meritorious acts are reborn in a better world and sometimes know the delights of earthly paradises, while those that committed evil deeds descend into the infernal world where they undergo unspeakable tortures. Such is reality, and this is why wise men give up intoxicating liquor and refuse to feed on the flesh of living beings. These are the facts you should consider.'

"The Nâga chief laughed loudly and replied with scorn, 'You claim that when life has left a body, it survives in other forms and is transferred elsewhere? Explain how life can leave a body in order to enter another!'

"Not at all worried by the chief's question, Shaduvan answered, 'Hear me without anger! As long as it is inhabited by life, the body perceives things by touch, taste, smell, sight, and hearing. It no longer feels any sensations, however, when life has left it, even if cut into pieces or grilled on the fire. It must therefore be admitted that in death something leaves the body, and everyone knows that, on leaving one place, one must inevitably be in another. You may have this experience when in your dreams your spirit is carried far away, leaving the sleeping body behind. So it is that on leaving a body, life goes far away and enters the destined body according to the results of its actions in its previous life. You must reflect on these things.'

"His eyes red like fire, the Nâga chief then prostrated himself at the feet of Shaduvan the merchant, considering him a sage, and asked him, 'If we cease to drink palm-wine and to eat meat and fish, how can we maintain this life which, according to you, resides in our body? Explain to me the principles of your religion so that we can observe its rules for the rest of our lives.'

" 'Since you show goodwill and seem resolved to lead henceforth a life more consonant with the rules of the *dharma*, there are some counsels I would give you. For example, when a ship sinks and the shipwrecked, escaping death, reach your territory, avoid putting them to death and seek to protect their precious lives. Moreover, give up killing living animals and feed only on the flesh of those that die of old age.'

"The chief of this ancient tribe, which belongs to the lowest castes, then promised Shaduvan, 'We shall henceforth observe the rules of life suitable for what we are. In the past, we have made feast, devouring the bodies of the survivors of the very many ships that have been wrecked in the sea not far from our shores. We have plundered all the goods they carried, their cargoes of precious aloes and sweet-scented sandalwood, their bales of cloth, their precious objects—gold, diamonds, and rubies—and other booty of shipwreck. You may take all these things away. Anything among our possessions which is of some value to you is yours.'

"When a ship belonging to a Puhâr merchant named Chandradatta stopped over not far from the shore, Shaduvan climbed aboard laden with all the precious goods given him by the guileless chief of the Nâgas. He returned to Puhâr and now leads a regular life with his virtuous wife Atiraï, in his beautiful house. Many are the meritorious acts they have performed, both one and the other."

Having finished her tale, Kayashandikaï said to Manimekhalaï, "Honest girl, like a flowering liana! It is from the hands of Atiraï, of irreproachable virtue, that you must now receive the first alms which will make your magic bowl fruitful!"

Manimekhalaï then presented herself in front of Atiraï's house and stood motionless like a figure drawn in a picture without colors or decoration. Atiraï circled around the beggar-woman several times, from left to right as a sign of respect, pronouncing words of greeting which brought hope to all those able to hear them. "May the curse of famine disappear from the world!"

She then filled to the top with choice food the magic bowl called Cow of Abundance, so that the whole world could be delivered from the suffering of hunger.

CANTO SEVENTEEN

Manimekhalaï Establishes Herself in the Hospice

Like endlessly growing riches accumulated by honest means, the food placed in the magic bowl by Atiraï multiplied without ever running out. Its possessor could thus, at will, amply feed a mass of poor people, whose hands gave way under the burden of the exquisite viands distributed to them.

Marveling, Kayashandikaï watched the scene. She prostrated herself before Manimekhalaï, addressing her with this prayer: "Good mother! With your charity could you not calm the hunger which tortures me and which nothing can sate? Listen to my tale!

"At the time when the god Vishnu by his powers of enchantment became incarnate in the form of Râma the Charming, the army of monkeys tore up some mountains from their seat and together with all the divine beings threw them into the sea to make a ford to cross the strait separating India from the isle of Lanka. But, as the result of an ascetic's curse, these mountains disappeared without a trace into the belly of the vast ocean.

My belly is like the ocean. It engulfs mountains of food without ever appeasing the appetite which gnaws me. I know that my misfortune is due to my past errors. Take pity on me and deliver me from hunger!"

Manimekhalaï took from the bowl a fistful of rice which she placed in the hands outstretched. As soon as she had eaten it, Kayashandikaï found that she was freed from the burning which gnawed her entrails. She prostrated herself at Manimekhalaï's feet and began to tell her adventure.

"Far away in the north (near Mount Kaïlasa in Tibet), there is a region of dazzling whiteness whose capital is called Chedi. There a people of genies called Vidyâdhara, the Genies of Knowledge, lives. I was born in this mysterious capital, the Golden City of rare splendor. My husband Kanchana dwells there. Desirous of knowing the world, one day my husband and I came to visit the southern lands and to admire the fertile slopes of Mount Podiyil in the kingdom of the Pandya, where the river Tamrapani has its source. We sat down to rest for a few minutes on a beach of fresh sand that an impetuous torrent had heaped up on its bank. My husband moved away for a moment to go and admire the prosperous countryside, which resounds to the sweet murmuring of countless brooks.

"Fate decreed that at that moment a religious named Vrishchika, a sacred thread crossing his breast and his long tousled hair falling on his shoulders, arrived to bathe in a pool filled with flowers, whose perfume spread far and wide. He was dressed in a loincloth of tanned bark and held in his hand a jambu-rose-apple fruit, as big as the black fruit of the palm tree. He placed it carefully on a teak leaf and went to bathe.

"I was strolling vainly about and, unfortunately, did not see the fruit, which I crushed with my foot.

"Vrishchika returned, anxious to eat his fruit. He saw me crush it with my foot and exclaimed: 'This fruit comes from a heavenly strain of jambu-rose-apple, which only bears fruit once in twelve years. Whoever consumes the fruit is freed from the necessity of eating for twelve years. The vow of abstinence which I observe will now force me to fast every day for the next twelve years.

" 'You have destroyed the fruit which I had hoped to feed on today. As a punishment, you will forget the magic formula which allows you to fly through the air and will henceforth suffer from the sickness known as elephant's appetite. You will no longer be satiated till the day when, after twelve long years, I can finally eat of the fruit of the divine jambu-rose-apple.'

"It seems that the moment of my healing has now arrived, for today you have put an end to the curse that has pursued me since the fatal day on which I crushed the fruit of the jambu-rose-apple and the holy man departed, looking so weary and hungry.

"So, afterwards, my husband returned. He was dismayed to learn of the cruel chastisement inflicted on me for having inadvertently, stupidly placed my foot on a fruit. My husband, whose beauty is radiant, immediately understood the nature of the sickness that afflicted me. He said, 'Due to your stupid carelessness and as a result of an ascetic's curse, you are from henceforth affected by an incurable disease. Let us now return home through the air without delay.'

"I had to confess to him that the magic word I had to pronounce in order to rise into the air had slipped my memory, and that I was suffering atrociously from a hunger which burned my entrails.

"He brought me sweet fruit and all the wild vegetables he could gather. Devour them as I might, my hunger remained inextinguishable. He was disconsolate at the idea of having to separate from me and with deep emotion had to resign himself to depart. He then gave me these instructions:

" 'In the vast continent of the rose-apple (of which India forms a part), in the beautiful Tamil country there is a city whose inhabitants have acquired the greatest merits in their former lives. They are prosperous and peace-loving and seek to help the misfortunate by satisfying their needs without demanding anything in exchange. It will take you a long time to reach there on foot, but you must bear the fatigue of the long journey and establish yourself in that city.'

"Following his instructions, I arrived in Puhâr and that is why I am here now.

"Each year, during the festival of Indra, my husband comes to this town, full of compassion for my misfortune. He counts the years, waiting for me to be freed from the curse that weighs on me. He tries to console me and then has to leave me once more. Today, you have delivered me from the inextinguishable hunger which has tortured me so long. I throw myself at your feet and implore you to let me return to my native land.

"There is a place here called the Temple of Heaven (Chakravâla-kottam), where many ascetics live, free of all ties, who seek to assuage the misery of the world. Near the temple stands the hospice, a public building whose door stands ever wide for all to find a refuge there, without considerations of caste, religion, or place of origin. The hospice is now filled with those who wait for someone to feed them. Some have come from very far, suffering famine. Many of them live in misery, having no one to support them.

"O maiden whose hair is divided into two carefully smoothed braids! It is there you should go to employ the Cow of Abundance properly!"

Having spoken thus, Kayashandikaï departed through the air for her native land.

Adorned with her beautiful jewels, Manimekhalaï then betook herself through the streets lined with tall houses to the hospice, around which she circled thrice from left to right as a mark of respect. Alone, she penetrated the temple, after dedicating herself in thought, word, and deed to the ancient goddess Champâpati, worshiped by all the city's inhabitants as well as by strangers. Following this, she went to render homage to the statue of the genie which dwells in a large pillar and reveals to people the effects of the acts committed in their former life.

Like the sullen clouds accompanied by thunder and lightning which bring beneficent rain to the thirsty forest, where even the bamboos burnt by the sun's rays have become black, Manimekhalaï with her beautiful jewels appeared, holding in her hand the Cow of Abundance, before the people suffering from the pains caused by hunger. She invited all those present to draw near and

70

join in the meal which she took from Aputra's inexhaustible bowl.

In the great city, where each day brings new riches, from the hospice could be heard the sound of thousands of jaws regaling themselves on the choice viands produced by the magic bowl.

CANTO EIGHTEEN

Udayakumâra Visits the Hospice

When she learned that her granddaughter Manimekhalaï, dressed in monastic garb, was roaming the streets like a pauper, a beggar's bowl in her hand, and living in the hospice for the destitute, Chitrâpati felt a pang as sharp as though a burning firebrand had been plunged into her flesh. Haggard, she rushed out, swearing that she would force the guilty one to return to the way of life of their community.

"Once already, after the death of Kovalan, my daughter Mâdhavi, weary of life, tried to seek refuge with ascetics like Aravana Adigal.

"She wore the dress of the bonzes and became an object of scorn for the whole city. Those who sought to understand her were also covered with ridicule. We do not belong to those aggressively virtuous women, born to noble families, who at the death of their husband despair and, cursing the life that will not leave their body, throw themselves into the flames of the funeral pyre as though they were plunging into the cool waters of a pool.

"It is our privilege to eat from all hands. We are like the *yâl*, the lute, which when one musician dies is forthwith passed on to another. We are similar to the bee that plunders the perfumed pollen from a flower and when she has exhausted it passes on to the next. When luck abandons a man, the goddess of fortune breaks all her ties with him. We are like the goddess and reject a lover who has lost his riches.

"To wear an ascetic's habit and practice mortification is not in keeping with the ethics of our profession. The idea that Manimekhalaï, born into our family, can transform herself into a nun is ridiculous and contrary to the good standing of our whole corporation.

"That delightful liana called Manimekhalaï, daughter of Mâdhavi the courtesan, is now pubescent. She has reached the age of her blossoming.

"She deserves from henceforth to be the delight of the bee Udayakumâra who reigns over the world to the satisfaction of all. I must recall her to her duty and give her bowl to some other beggar come to ask her an alms. I want to see her very soon seated in the gold-plated chariot of Udayakumâra who has tender feelings towards her.

"If I do not succeed in accomplishing this mission, I deserve to suffer the fate of those that are thrown out of our caste, who are led around the dance floor with seven bricks on their head before being cast out, after which they are for ever excluded from public meetings."

Having made her vow with troubled spirit and deep sighs, and concocting skillful words to say to the prince, she departed on foot, her beautiful face shining with beads of perspiration. Followed by a small group of companions with slender bracelets through the streets traversed by fast carriages, she made her way to the prince's dwelling.

This dwelling was a palace of crystal, blinding bright. Its columns were of coral, its perfect walls covered with gold. The dais of brilliant pearls was supported by wonderful statues. Before the palace there was an open esplanade, covered with fresh sand strewn with flowers, which resounded to the buzzing of bees.

Udayakumâra was there, seated on a throne which stood on a lion-shaped pedestal. He shone with glory. Standing on either side of him were two women waving fly whisks of yak's tail, whiter than the foam of the waves. Chitrâpati prostrated herself before the prince's noble feet, saying the customary greetings suitable for people of her kind.

On seeing her, the prince began to laugh, showing his beautiful teeth, and asked her whether, in her opinion, the ascetic life practiced by Mâdhavi and Manimekhalaï was not somewhat contrary to the proper order of society.

Chitrâpati said to him, "Manimekhalaï of incomparable beauty was conceived by Mâdhavi as the result of an exceptional love affair. Her beauty, now in full bloom, is famous in all lands of the vast continent known by the name of Bhârata. She has now reached puberty and deserves to be courted. She is like a flower that starts to blossom so that a bee named Udayakumâra can suck its honey. That is why I have rushed here. This flower called Manimekhalaï is now in the travelers' hospice near the waste land, not far from the cemetery of the old town surrounded by high walls. Prince! Your sword has never failed to destroy all those that oppose your will! Your desires must be fulfilled!"

Udayakumâra felt restored to life, like someone who has been thrown a plank while struggling among the waves after his boat has broken to pieces. He judged that he could confide in Chitrâpati.

"When I saw Manimekhalaï for the first time in the crystal pavilion of the Upavanam flower garden, I thought she was some new work by a skillful sculptor, and I was getting ready to leave the place when I suddenly realized that the statue was alive. Her crossed arms compressed her charming young breasts which pointed slightly upwards. Her lips shone red as coral; her teeth were like rows of pointed-cut pearls. I felt a mad desire to drink the nectar secreted by her mouth. She smiled a little as if to arouse a new passion in my life.

"Her long eyes like black carp to which the somber petals of the blue lotus do not deserve to be compared, whose keenness surpasses a pointed spear, reached as far as her ears to inform them that Manimekhalaï's heart was not indifferent.

"I stood there fascinated by this vision and since then this girl, so like a coral doll, whom I glimpsed through the windows of the crystal pavilion, has taken possession of my heart and it is her memory that prevents life from leaving my body.

"That night as I lay unable to sleep for thinking

of her, just before midnight a woman appeared to me, whose body shone like gold, commanding me to hold my scepter with equity and to renounce Manimekhalaï since she was destined to lead the life of the ascetics. I do not know whether it was a goddess or some other creature from the spirit world. I really do not know who this woman is whose apparition left me in such great confusion."

Chitrâpati listened with satisfaction to the prince's utterance. Smiling at his simplicity, she said, "My lord! Why should you worry about things you have heard in a dream? Such hallucinations do not deserve to be given any importance. The passion that has seized you would destroy the mind of even a heavenly being.

"Mighty prince! Skilled in demonstrating the power of your sword! Have you never heard tell of the misadventures of the gods, who are not immune from the attractions of illicit love. The god Indra was victim of his burning desire for Ahalya, the wife of the sage Gautama. As a result of the curse pronounced by the sage, his whole body is now covered with eyes. Agni, the god of fire, was overwhelmed by violent desire on seeing the haughty wives of the most powerful Seven Sages when he discovered them bathing in a pool in the Himalayas, well-known for the sacred herbs that grow abundantly on its banks. His wife, Svâha, then took the appearance of each of these women in turn, and gave herself up to the desire of the fire-god, who was thus able to consummate a passion difficult to satisfy otherwise.

"Wives of noble blood have no other god but their husband. They must not cast lustful eyes on young men. For their whole life, their chastity is severely guarded, both while they are still virgins, and when married, and even during their widowhood when their husband is dead. But above all, it is their feeling of duty that exercises such absolute control over these noble women. Manimekhalaï does not spring from one of these proud families. The courtesan's role is different. They must attract men with their charms and bind them with their arts. My Lord, do they not play an essential part in a properly organized society?

74

"The women of our sisterhood must show themselves on the stage, publicly exhibiting their talents in music and dancing, and charm men with the beauty of their bodies so that the god of love, whose bow is made of sugar cane having as string a swarm of bees, can shoot his flower darts at all who attend the display. The girls' long eyes, like agile carp, weave threads into a noose to catch their prey. They take possession of men's hearts and enthrall them. Taking home those they have snared with the sweet music of their cajoling voice, they squeeze all their money from them, abandoning them when they have nothing more to give, like bees which leave the flowers after taking all their honey. Is it not a king's duty to maintain social order, to see that custom is observed and prevent confusion between the roles and duties of the various castes? I must therefore look to you to bring my daughter back to the path of duty and to stop the scandal which her behavior risks provoking."

Udayakumâra, till then undecided, suddenly changed his attitude. He mounted his chariot drawn by swift horses and betook himself to the hospice where Manimekhalaï of the beautiful jewels was to be found. Like the goddess in the desert feeding the horde of demons, Manimekhalaï, as pretty as a doll, was distributing abundant food to a mass of people whose appetite was like a devouring fire.

Udayakumâra was unable to understand why this perfidious girl having beleaguered him and stolen his soul, should have chosen such an austere kind of life, letting her beautiful body become arid with fasting, and begging in order to live. Having lost all reserve due to the heat of his passion, he drew near to her in order to speak, even though it is forbidden to address a woman alone. Taking courage, he said in a firm voice, "My good girl, can you explain to me why you are disguised as a nun?"

Manimekhalaï reflected, "In my former life, this man was my husband, my dear Rahul, who loved me tenderly. It is therefore proper for me to greet him humbly." She bowed before him, trembling and troubled at heart, thinking, "Although in so doing I am not observing the reserve which propriety imposes and risk his seizing my glass-braceleted wrists, I cannot refuse to reply to one who in another life was my husband."

She said to him, "If the aperture of your ears had been open to the ascetics' wise counsel, you would understand that the day on which I realized that the human body is the dwelling place of all kinds of anguish, afflicted by defects such as growth and decline, suffering and sickness that end in death, I chose to renounce the pleasures of this world and dedicate myself to assuaging the misery of living beings.

"Is there any advice that a woman can give to men, who like male elephants kill their opponents in combat? This is the answer to your question. It is for you to choose the most suitable path."

As soon as she had answered the question of the prince, more skilled in handling the sword in battle than in speech, Manimekhalaï, as graceful as a liana, left him and entered the narrow sanctuary of the old goddess Champâpati, senior of the heavenly beings, murmuring to herself, "Who can ever predict the behavior of men?"

She worshiped the goddess, whose flower necklaces never fade, prostrating herself before her. After so doing, she uttered the magic word that the goddess had taught her, which allowed her to take on the appearance of Kayashandikaï, the wife of the Vidyâdhara. In this form she returned to Udayakumâra, the beggar's bowl in her hand.

The prince, wearing a necklace of flowers, looked at the woman who appeared to be Kayashandikaï. He then penetrated Champâpati's sanctuary, saying, "Through some feat of magic, Manimekhalaï has disappeared, leaving her beggar's bowl in the hands of Kayashandikaï, a woman who suffers from the sickness known as elephant's appetite. I am unable to find her in the Temple of Heaven. She may be standing still among the innumerable statues that fill the temple. I will now stay at your feet as long as necessary, to supplicate you to grant me the favor of revealing to me her whereabouts.

"Sovereign of the heavenly beings! I can describe her to you! The mouth of Manimekhalaï is red like coral, surrounding the whitest of teeth. Her long eyes are like red carp, and are unburdened with fard. Her eyebrows are like bows stretched by several strings to increase their strength. She uses her attractions to lead her victims according to her desires as an elephant trainer uses his sharp goad with bent back point.

"Having surrounded herself with a protective net, with skillful words spoken with her voice as melodious as the sound of the lute, she captured the wild elephant and reduced it to her mercy. After this, her face shining like the moon, she entered your temple, which I refuse to leave without finding her. Prostrate before your image, I take my oath upon it. My fate is in your hands!"

 CANTO NINETEEN

Manimekhalaï Has the Prison
Transformed into a Monastery

When the prince with his necklace of scented flowers had taken his oath, after bowing thrice before the sacred feet of the ancient goddess Champâpati, he was challenged by a spirit which dwelt in a fresco drawn by a skillful painter.

"Prince with the flower necklace! Your hasty resolution has made you commit perjury before Champâpati, sovereign of all beings, since you cannot fulfill your oath."

Caught unawares by this mysterious voice, the prince's resolution was shaken. His spirit and senses were confused like those of a person who has been shut up in a sealed and windowless room. He began to reconsider. "The apparition of the goddess recommending me to bear my scepter with righteousness and to renounce Manimekhalaï seems like a premonitory dream. The fact that Manimekhalaï, whose pubis resembles a cobra's hood, goes about with a magic bowl in her hand allowing her to appease the hunger of innumerable persons, is a strange phenomenon indeed. The voice of a genie issuing from a picture to warn me of my perjury before the sacred feet of the goddess Champâpati is also a very miracle."

He then decided that he must elucidate all these mysteries as soon as he had discovered the secret of Manimekhalaï's disappearance and, still blinded by his passion, he departed for his palace.

The sun had vanished. The departing prince seemed pursued by the shadows of evening advancing behind him like an enormous drunken elephant, whose brow was the twilight, the moon his ivory tusks. The heavy odor arising from the masses of flowers where the bees gathered honey recalled the sweat oozing from his temples. The muffled sound of the drums echoed like his heavy paces. Little by little, the city was shrouded in the darkness of night.

The fashionable men of the town, seated with their glass-braceleted mistresses, all began to play the seven-stringed harp, called the crocodile harp (makara-yâl). They continuously sounded the fifth string, which stimulates the fires of desire. This sound pierced the heart of the prince fleeing through the night and exacerbated his passion. His breath was burning like the blacksmith's anvil on which the wind of the bellows is directed.

Manimekhalaï had realized that in her true form she would continue to be exposed to the prince's efforts to possess her. For this reason in Champâpati's sanctuary she took the appearance of Kayashandikaï of the green bracelets, well known throughout the city to be afflicted by the elephant's insatiable appetite.

In this form she left the temple, holding the Cow of Abundance in her hand, and began to wander from place to place, wherever she thought she would have some chance of finding people suffering from hunger. The sages teach us that begging is the most noble of professions.

One day, during her peregrinations, Manimekhalaï arrived at the city's central prison where all those who had committed serious offenses against the royal power were incarcerated in punishment for their crimes.

Entering the closely guarded place of punishment, she was deeply shocked by the prisoners' sad state. Speaking to them with sweetness and compassion, she at once began distributing to the hungry the exquisite viands

which came from her bowl so abundantly that their outstretched hands gave way beneath the weight.

The prison guards marveled to see her appease the
appetite of so many with the contents of a simple bowl
which she held in her hands. They decided that they must
inform the king about the strange behavior of this girl, as
graceful as a liana, and of the existence of this magic
bowl which produced unlimited amounts of food. They
betook themselves immediately to the palace.

In the Royal Gardens

The king had married a princess called Shirthi, a descendant of the famous king of the genies, Mahâ-Bali, whose
bow was unfailing, who in ancient times had solemnly
with the rite of poured water made a gift of his territories
and other goods to Vishnu, and who had taken the appearance of a dwarf and then, growing to gigantic size,
covered the earth with a single stride.

Together with the queen, the king had gone for a
rest in the royal gardens, full of flowers. He was amused
to observe a peahen and her mate who, drawing themselves up and flapping their wings, were admiring a snow-
white swan swimming in a pond. "They remind me of
Kannan (Krishna)," he said, "dark as a blue diamond,
with his lover Nappimaï and his fair brother Baladeva, as
they danced in the main square of the city of Dvaraka,
carpeted with a smooth layer of cow dung."

In a grove he remarked a konku tree and a mango
growing one next to the other, on which a peacock was
perched. A green mango hung above a konku flower, resembling a lump of cream on a golden plate. "It makes
me think," said the king, "of a beautiful woman feeding
her parrot with cream on a golden dish."

In the inner part of the gardens, a jewel-encrusted
swing had been installed for the games of the limpid-eyed
maidens. They were highly amused to see that a monkey
had installed his companion there.

Further on, the king noticed a tall bamboo with a
tuft of leaves on its slender dark trunk beside a white-

flowered kadamba, and compared them to Kannan (Krishna) with his brother Baladeva always faithfully standing by him. He at once invoked the names of these gods and saluted them joining his hands laden with heroes' bracelets.

Like the god Indra, sovereign of this vast world, the king liked to surround himself with experts and artists who could appreciate the art of the pure dance, which does not illustrate a story, as well as mime, by which all human passions can be expressed without words. He had gathered to his court learned men expert in dramatic art, musicians who could play every musical mode on the harp, drummers skilled in developing rhythm, composers who could coordinate the melodies of the flute with songs, and ensembles which practiced choral singing.

In his service there were also assistants expert in the arts of pleasure, who could repair broken pearl necklaces, remove sandal paste dried on the skin, massage the body with unguents and perfumes, weave rich garlands of red water lilies, anoint the hair with scented oils, and present gold-framed mirrors in which beauty could contemplate itself.

The groves were smiling with the flowers of the scented-leaved wild lemon, golden jasmine, champakas, Arabian jasmine, and giant gardenias. The king told the queen the names of the trees and flowering shrubs. There were a great number of mongooses trotting along on their short paws, long-eared hares, bounding hinds, and pet sheep, who came running up when the king called them by clapping his hands.

The pleasant season which precedes summer had come, cooled by the soft southern breeze. The king, always accompanied by the god of love whose bow is made of flowers, strolled about and enjoyed himself in this garden, where machines drew water from the wells to feed the fountains and artificial cascades flowing on the stony tiers with a clear sound.

There were flower-covered arbors, crystal pavilions, wide ornamental lakes, grottoes wth small pools, and a thousand nooks sheltered from indiscreet eyes.

Having spent the day's end joyously with the queen,

the king, whose riches equaled those of the whole Indian continent put together, came and sat in his audience hall, whose splendor astonished all those who had the chance to see it.

It was the work of the best craftsmen from the cool Tamil country, together with sculptors from Magadha, skilled in working rare stone, goldsmiths from the Maratha country, blacksmiths from Avanti, and Greek (Yavana) carpenters. The tall columns were fashioned of blocks of coral, their wooden capitals supporting beams encrusted with precious stones from which fringes of white pearls hung here and there. The dais was of cloth of gold, magnificently worked. The floor was not as usual covered with a layer of cow dung, but had been lined with gold plates.

The prison guards had the king informed of their arrival by one of the palace officials and, having been duly authorized, they entered the golden hall. From a distance, they greeted the king according to custom.

"O Manvankilli of the mighty arm and stainless parasol! Protector of our lives! On the banks of the stream Kariyaru, with the aid of the young prince, your brother, who wears a necklace of ebony leaves and whose long arm holds the spear, you conquered the two kings Chera and Pandya who, in the hope of aggrandizing their states, had sealed an alliance in the city of Vanji, in their folly believing that they could overcome the Chola king in combat. Wearing palm-leaf necklaces, they set out to march with their army, which included elephants, their wide ears like winnowing sieves, chariots, horses in great number, and valiant warriors armed with long swords. Then, as booty of war, you seized their white parasols and standards embroidered with the bow and the carp, the emblems of the vanquished.

"Long life to the greatest of kings! May you reign in prosperity for many ages! Hear now the news of which we have come to render an account.

"For some time a strange woman has been roaming the city streets, seeming weary and emaciated, suffering from the sickness called elephant's hunger, which gives rise to an inextinguishable appetite. Today she entered the well-guarded prison, glorifying your name and fame.

81

In her hand she held a humble beggar's bowl, from which she brought out vast quantities of food that the bowl seems to produce endlessly. With it she fed to repletion the crowd of wretches who encumber the place.

"Long life to the king! May he protect the world for many ages to come!"

"Let the woman come here!" said the king with benevolence. When the guards led her before the sovereign, she said only, "Long life to the king, wearer of a superb ankle-ring!"

The king asked her, "Woman, devoted to the ascetic life and its severe privations! Who are you and where did you find the bowl you hold in your hand?"

The woman, adorned with modest jewels, who was Manimekhalaï under the appearance of Kayashandikaï, replied, "Long life to the great king of the scented necklace! I am a woman of the race of the Vidyâdharas, come without authorization to dwell in this ancient city, famous for its festivals, wandering here in disguise.

"May the king live long!

"May the rains fall in their proper season!

"May the earth's fruitfulness increase and the king enjoy great revenue!

"May he never commit injustice!

"This beggar's bowl was given me by a heavenly being who dwells in the city's hospice. He possesses magical powers and cured me of elephant's fever which causes inextinguishable appetite. By its means, I can give back strength to those whose bodies have been weakened by hunger."

The king then said to her, "Young woman, similar to a liana! What can I do for you?"

"I desire only that of your benevolence you will have the prison demolished and in its place build an abode open to all those who observe the rules of the *dharma* and whose spirits are inclined to virtue."

According to the desire expressed by the strange woman, the king had the prisoners freed and transformed the place into an abode set apart for monks who could give wise teaching to the people.

Having replaced the prison with an abode for

saintly men, the king henceforth reigned over a country where there were no more criminals.

CANTO TWENTY

Udayakumâra Is Cut in Twain
by a Sword-Blow

The king was touched by grace in listening to Manimekhalaï's generous words. The prison was destroyed and its inhabitants, freed from an anguish like that of hell, all became honest citizens. They felt like those who, having led a miserable existence, are reborn in a noble and prosperous family as a reward for their virtues.

As promised, a temple of the Buddha, the inspirer of true faith, truth, and wisdom, was built in place of the prison, as well as a place of retreat for those seeking spiritual progress, together with a kitchen and a refectory.

Udayakumâra was informed of the audience granted by the king to Manimekhalaï and of the promises made her by the king of faultless fame that the prison would be destroyed and a building set aside for ascetics and monks raised in its place. He continued however to lay his schemes.

"Of small import to me are the townsfolk's reprobation and the king's anger. I will go and take Manimekhalaï at the hospice door. I will seize her and force her to mount my chariot. She will have to explain to me the origin of her magic powers. I will listen to her discourse, for which she has a remarkable talent." He then betook himself to the travelers' home where Manimekhalaï was busy feeding a great number of poor.

In his distant country, Kanchana, Kayashandikaï's husband, was reflecting. "Twelve years have now passed since, as a result of the errors committed in some other life, my spouse was the victim of a curse pronounced by the famous ascetic Vrishchika near a stream bordered

83

with rushes on the slopes of Mount Podiyil, whose crest is lost in the clouds.

"The effect of the curse must now be ended, but nevertheless my spouse Kayashandikaï has not come back to me."

Worried and anxious, he descended to the ancient and splendid city where he had left her and started searching everywhere, at the crossing of the four avenues where the genie's statue stands, in the gardens where flowers are grown, in the monks' monasteries, in the various public squares, and in the shade of the great trees. Suddenly, he saw Manimekhalaï with her pretty upward-pointing breasts in the appearance of Kayashandikaï, devoting herself to appeasing the pangs of hunger of the poor and misfortunate.

He drew near to her with familiar gestures and, speaking tenderly, asked her, "What is that curious vessel in your hands which allows you to feed so many people? Is it a magic object offered by some heavenly being which has thus freed you from elephant's appetite?"

Manimekhalaï regarded him with indifference and, with none of the affectionate gestures he was expecting from her, continued on her way. Passing near Udayakumâra, she pointed out to him a very old white-haired woman, taking the opportunity to give him a sermon.

"Look Prince! Her hair, once like black sand, is today the color of white sand. See her brow, which once shone like a crescent moon, now yellow and wrinkled, having lost its brightness. Her eyebrows, formerly like bows which bring victory, now resemble dried-up shrimps. Her eyes, which were like blue lotus, today ooze a repugnant fluid. Look at her nose, like a gardenia bud, dripping a pus-like liquid. See her teeth, that looked like fine rows of pearls, and now appear like disorderly watermelon seeds. From that mouth, once red like the silky cotton flower, today is exhaled a noisome odor like a putrid wound. Look at her ears, which were as charming as fresh bamboo shoots, now like pieces of dried meat. Her breasts, whose beauty attracted many a glance, now hang sadly like empty water skins. Her shoulders, once straight like young bamboo, droop, covered with wrinkles like coconut rind. Look at her emaciated furrowed fingers with their prominent veins: the skin no longer reaches her nails. Those thighs, formerly like banana trunks, are dried up like the bark of the marine pine. Her ankles, once like unfailing quivers whence leapt the arrows of desire, are now wasted away, letting the bones and veins appear. These feet, which were like tender leaves, now resemble dried coconuts fallen from the tree. Look well at this sad sight and reflect! Perhaps you are aware that the human body, attractive as it may appear to us due to its form, the quality of its skin, the clothes, jewels, and ointments with which it is adorned, is but an illusory appearance handed down to us by our ancestors."

Since her appearance was still that of Kayashandi-kaï, Kanchana the Vidyâdhara, who wore a shining sword, thought to himself, "When I approached her, she looked at me as though she did not know me, and refused to listen to my tender words. She has stopped to talk with this stranger, this prince who wears a necklace of honey-smelling flowers, to lecture him about ethics. But her smile allows her white teeth to be glimpsed between her coral lips, and the look in her eyes like water lilies shows she is enamored. It is because she has become his lover that she has stayed here instead of returning to me."

Filled with rage and hate, he entered the hospice where Manimekhalaï lived, hiding like a cobra who draws back ready to spring, skulking in an ant hill.

The prince had listened patiently to Manimekhalaï's discourse, but had no intention of renouncing his passion for her. He thought, "This can only be Manimekhalaï of the red-tinted hands and wrists encircled with glass bracelets who with the aid of her magic power, in the appearance of Kayashandikaï holding the bowl in her hands, has come to sow doubt in my heart. Why did she draw away from that stranger who approached her in the darkness near the hospice, speaking familiarly to her, and who seemed so astonished and furious?"

Udayakumâra decided to return later to this place, taking advantage of the darkness of the night in order to study the matter more thoroughly and assure himself that he was not mistaken. He therefore departed for his residence while thinking out his strategy, having as his sole accomplice in his plans the god of love, whose vehicle is the sweet evening breeze, whose banner depicts a fish, whose bow is made of sugar cane, and whose arrows are flower buds.

Intoxicated by his passion and heedless of all prudence like a tiger making an elephant his prey, he left the palace alone at midnight, when the whole town was asleep. He passed through the door of the hospice and entered the common-room where Manimekhalaï of the beautiful jewels lived, without realizing that he was entering an anthill in which a cobra of terrible venom was hiding. He walked slowly without making any noise, but everyone in the hospice had noted his arrival due to the smell of the sandal paste with which his body was anointed.

The Vidyâdhara, wearing a necklace of full-blown flowers, was already hidden there, convinced that Udayakumâra had come solely to make love to Kayashandikaï. Like a furious cobra who spreads his hood and shows his venomous fangs, he left the corner where he had been hiding and advancing cunningly behind Udayakumâra, who was wearing a necklace of flowers in which the bees were buzzing, he struck him on the shoulder with his sword, cutting his body in twain. Anxious to depart immediately through the air together with his wife, he approached the place where Manimekhalaï was, still in the form of Kayashandikaï.

Suddenly, the statue sculpted on the highest pillar, the work of Mayä, the architect of the genies, called him: "O Vidyâdhara Kanchana! Do not approach her! Do not approach! She is Manimekhalaï in the form of Kayashandikaï. Listen to the tale of the terrible accident of which your wife was victim, as she returned to you through the air after being cured of the sickness of the elephant's insatiable appetite.

"Those who journey through the air must not fly over that part of the Vindhya mountains where is situated the sanctuary of the goddess Durga, known as Vindhyavâsini. If a living being passes over that region, the goddess, furious at the affront, seizes its shadow, draws it down to earth and devours it. That is what happened to

Kayashandikaï, who inadvertently flew over the sanctuary and became the goddess's prey.

"None should ever debase himself by lusting after women not intended for him. O Vidyâdhara Kanchana! Do not feel remorse for what you have done. You have been the instrument of the chastisement Udayakumâra deserved for the perverse deeds of his former life. However, you have rashly committed a cruel murder. This deed will pursue you and one day you will have to pay the price even if you did it out of ignorance."

Hearing the words of the statue sculpted on the pillar, Kanchana, deeply disquieted and disconsolate at the turn of events, fled zigzagging through the air, pursued by remorse for his crime.

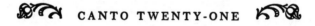 CANTO TWENTY-ONE

The Predictions of the Statue on the Pillar

Manimekhalaï, who was sleeping behind the tall gate of Champâpati's sanctuary, to the west of the statue's pillar, awoke hearing the words addressed by the genie to the Vidyâdhara. Thus she learned of Kayashandikaï's drama and of the tragic death of the prince, whose spear till then had brought victory.

Startled, she rose and, forgoing her disguise, took her natural form and approached the prince's body, wailing and lamenting.

"Beloved! When in our past life you died of the poison of a serpent that kills from afar, I followed you and climbed onto the funeral pyre, where my body was destroyed by the flames. When I saw you again in the flower garden, I was unable to chase my desire for you from my heart, which is why the goddess Manimekhalâ came and conveyed me to the isle of Manipallavam. There, thanks to the sacred pedestal of the Buddha, the sublime ascetic, free of all passion, the goddess revealed to me the story of my former life and the ties that had bound us. It was then that I understood the reason for the attraction I felt for you in this life.

"I took the appearance of Kayashandikaï to keep you from committing a grave fault and I tried to make you understand that it is not possible to escape the cycle of birth and death, that virtue alone can bring us peace, and that our blameworthy deeds are the cause of all our ills. It was my evil fortune that the faults committed in your former life came to maturity and now you lie dead under the keen sword blows of a furious and irresponsible Vidyâdhara."

The genie dwelling in the statue on the pillar then called Manimekhalaï, her long eyes striped with red, saying, "Approach not the prince with his flower-petal necklace! Approach him not! Not only in his former life was Udayakumâra your husband and you his tender wife. This relationship has been yours through innumerable lives. Henceforth you possess the knowledge that will allow you to escape the interminable cycle of birth. Do not be troubled by the grief caused you by the prince's death."

Surprised at the genie's words, golden-skinned Manimekhalaï, like a flowering liana, asked him, "Are you truly the genie that resides in this place who, without ever lying, unveils things hidden? I bow before your blessed feet. Can you reveal to me the nature of the crime for which my husband Udayakumâra has twice deserved to lose his life amidst atrocious suffering, once by the poison of a serpent that slays from afar and today by the sword of a jealous Vidyâdhara, each time leaving me trembling and disconsolate? Grant me this boon and explain it to me!"

The statue's heavenly voice replied, "O Manimekhalaï of the long eyes striped with red and of the magnificent jewels! Hear my tale!

"On the banks of the stream Kâyankarai there lived a sage called Virama Daruman who calmed unquiet spirits with his comments on the teachings of the Buddha, the great prophet exempt from all sin. You and your husband Rahul had come to prostrate yourselves before him and had requested him to let you prepare his meal the next morning to which he graciously consented. It was evening and you spent the night in profound joy.

"The next day your cook, who was late, slipped in his haste and dropped the dish he had prepared to be served to the great sage, adorned with all virtues, who abstained from inebriating drink, from lying, lust, cruelty, and stealing. Although he had acted with no evil intent, Rahul in his fury cut the poor cook's head from his body with a single blow of his sword. This evil deed has followed you since then: you with your tender body and hair strewn with sundry flowers and your husband Rahul.

"Those that claim that the gods can forgive cruel deeds committed on the living are ignorant. An evil deed though accomplished with the desire to do good will always pursue its author, since the consequences of our actions are ineffaceable. When the fruits of our actions have ripened, terrible dramas come to pass in our lives. Often such a moment only arrives in some future life. The crime committed by your husband in his former life is the origin of his present misfortune.

"Pretty maiden, as lithe as a liana! I must warn you that, troubled by the circumstances of the prince's death and relying on the report of the monks who dwell in the Temple of Heaven, the king will soon throw you into prison.

"The queen, when she hears of it, will have you released to keep you under her control as a slave-companion. Mâdhavi will go and throw herself at the feet of Aravana Adigal to explain your misadventure to him and, following the sage's counsel, will go with him to the queen and obtain your freedom.

"Prostrating yourself in gratitude at the feet of Aravana Adigal, you will then go to the isle of Java (Shavakam) to visit Punya Râja, who in his former life was Aputra, and now reigns over a rich kingdom. When you have exchanged some pious discourse, you will return through the air to the isle of Manipallavam. Punya Râja will join you there, crossing the ocean by boat.

"Having learned from Tivatilakaï the events of his former life, Punya Râja will return to his kingdom. You, who are like a liana in flower, will then take the appearance of a respectable male monk and, leaving the island, will take yourself to the great city of Vanji.

"It is in this immense city that great numbers of representatives of the various religions are gathered to expound their doctrines.

"There are some who affirm that creator of all forms of life is a personal god who reigns over the world. Others think that the supreme being, himself without form, created all forms. Yet others affirm that only through the practice of self-denial and mortification, inflicting cruel suffering on our body, can we free ourselves of our bonds and tread the path that leads to a world of everlasting delight. There are also others who say that the world is merely the result of combinations of chemical elements. You must listen carefully to the questionable lucubrations of the practitioners of these various creeds.

"O Manimekhalaï, with your necklace of scented flowers! You will hear the statements of those who affirm with authority that there are no gods, that the dead are never reborn, and that it is doubtful our virtuous deeds can acquire us merit. With your experience of transmigration and of the retribution of our sins, you can tell them the tale of your own life and expound to them the extremely precise data you possess on such matters.

"Daughter with shoulders straight as bamboo! The philosopher who believes that matter made of the five elements alone is real will tell you that when the goddess Manimekhalâ conveyed you to the isle of Manipallavam you were unconscious and have lived with an illusion, taking your dream for reality. You will refute his statements, irreproachable girl like a liana in flower! explaining to him that the only justification for suffering in this world is that it is the consequence of our past errors and this is the only reality, and you must advise him to abjure his digressions. For the time being, that is what I see for your future.

"I also wish to explain to you, since it surprises you, why figures painted in a fresco or images modeled in clay or sculpted in stone or wood, should sometimes have the power to speak.

"For this magnificent city of matchless splendor, where chariots with waving pennants race through the streets, the high walls assure external protection. It is in order to protect the people from domestic danger that skilled craftsmen with masterly calculations fashioned images of the gods in wood, stone or clay, or painted them on the walls, so as to trap the heavenly powers in them. The images were then placed in the temples, at the foot of ancient trees, near the stairs used by the people to come and bathe in streams or pools, in public buildings, or in the shade of the sacred trees at the city's center. The divinities thus represented are present in the images, in the places assigned to them. This is why the perspicacious know that through these images one can communicate with the divinities they represent.

"Many inhabitants of the heavenly worlds, even more ignorant than men, let themselves be caught. I had a very dear companion called Chitrasena. I do not know who informed the city painters of our friendship. They drew and painted our images down to the smallest detail in all those places where we went together for amusement as if they had followed us everywhere, spying on our games. They then consecrated the images with flowers, incense, and holy words, and invoked our names until their tongues were weary. Thus was he captured as also was I who am imprisoned in this statue which I cannot leave.

"I have described to you the events of your future with exactitude, so you must have faith in my words."

Manimekhalaï assured him that she would not make the mistake of doubting the words of a genie. She prayed that Tuvatikan would reveal to her the sequence of her future lives up to the day when she could finally attain liberation.

Tuvatikan told her, "Excellent woman, graceful as a liana! I can reveal your future to you. Listen to my tale! You must leave Vanji to go to the magnificent city of Kanchi, surrounded by high walls. When you learn that due to the failure of the seasonal rains Kanchi has lost its brilliance and that many of its inhabitants have died and many others fled, you will take from Champâpati's sanctuary the magic bowl called Cow of Abundance, the remedy that saves lives, and will depart for Kanchi, where Aravana Adigal, Mâdhavi, and Sutâmati will have gone before you.

"At Kanchi, under the protection of the master Aravana Adigal, you will abandon your male clothes and return to your own form with your pretty bracelets.

"Thanks to the magic bowl that replaces the seasonal rains as a means of sustaining life, you will save many from death and will accomplish other miracles.

"When you recount to Aravana Adigal all you have learned at Vanji about the beliefs of the various religions, he will say to you, 'Manimekhalaï! Young liana! I have spent many lives propagating the *dharma* and will not leave this town before the rising of the sun of the Buddha's religion, spreading light by its supernatural power. I shall continue to teach the importance of mortification (*tapas*), the moral law (*dharma*), and the effect of our actions (*karma*)—the causes of our destiny. I shall also reveal how people can be freed from the interminable chain of birth and of the illusions that unsettle the mind, as well as the means of attaining the perfect happiness of *nirvâna*. You and your mother have led exemplary lives. May your virtues be consolidated and accompany you always!'

"When you have accomplished all the good you are capable of, without ever straying from the path on which Aravana Adigal will guide you, your present life will reach its end in the city of Kanchi. During your next lives, in which you will henceforth always be a man, you will be reborn in a high-ranking family of the Magadha country and, never ceasing your charitable works, you will dedicate yourself to destroying the errors that darken men's minds. Having become the Buddha's chief disciple, you will teach the *dharma* and, freed from all earthly ties, you will attain *nirvâna*.

"Girl with the charming brow! Hear me once more! It was due to her knowledge of the problems of your present existence and of the circumstances of your former life, in which you served the best of food to the ascetic Sâdhu Sakkara, that the goddess Manimekhalâ (who once saved the life of one of your virtuous ancestors while he was struggling in the sea) came to find you in the Upavanam, the garden of flowers, to convey you to Manipallavam."

Having learned all these things from Tuvatikan, the honest Manimekhalaï, adorned with beautiful jewels, emerged from her sea of distress. Knowing the limits of her lives to come, she felt freed from all anguish, like a fawn freed from the net with which the huntsman had captured her.

At this moment, the sun god arose from the waves, rousing the world from sleep, and the day appeared in its glorious splendor.

CANTO TWENTY-TWO

Manimekhalaï in Prison

When the sun's divine orb rose in the sky, scattering the darkness of the night, the faithful who had come to worship the statue of the pillar and the great goddess Champâpati in her narrow sanctuary discovered the prince's body hewn asunder. They went immediately to inform the monks who live in the Temple of Heaven.

Learning the tragic news of Udayakumâra's death, the monks sent for Manimekhalaï, like a young liana, to ask what she knew of this event. She told them all that had happened, omitting nothing.

After hiding the prince's body in a secluded spot and confining Manimekhalaï, they betook themselves to the palace entrance. There, having asked the guards for an audience of the king, they presented themselves in the audience hall, pronouncing the customary greetings.

"May the royal parasol, like the moon shining so high in the midst of the sky, spread the coolness of its shade over the world! May your scepter and the spear you bear protect your subjects from all ill! May your disk crush all obstacles! May you O king, live in happiness all the years granted you by the gods!

"Not only nowadays have regrettable events taken place in the city. In the past, many have met with a deplorable and merited end because, drunk with desire, they pursued honest women with their advances and cast lustful glances on those holy girls dressed in the orange robe of nuns. You are sovereign of the world!

"When the god Vishnu, incarnate in the form of Parashurâma armed with his war axe, resolved to destroy the princely order of the Kshatriyas, the goddess Durga (whom we worship under the name of Champâpati) warned Kantan, the king then reigning over the Chola country. She enjoined him not to agree to do combat, but to leave the city and live in hiding until the peril was passed. In order to supervise the administration of the realm during his absence, the king sought to find someone who was not exposed to the same risks as himself. He decided in favor of Kakanda, his natural son by one of his courtesans, who was therefore not noble, but was nevertheless possessed of magnificent courage. His name already made enemies tremble throughout the whole rosewood continent and he was ever the victor in battle.

"Sending for him, the king spoke kindly to him.

" 'Since by birth you do not belong to the princely order and cannot therefore reign as Chola, Parashurâma will not attack you. I therefore entrust the government of the country to you until the day when, by the grace of the sage Agastya of divine powers, I can return.'

"The king changed the name of the city of Kaveri-pumpattinam, calling it Kakanda after the new sovereign's name. He then departed in disguise and Kakanda reigned for many years over the Chola kingdom, according to the instructions he had received from his father.

"It chanced one day that King Kakanda's son caught sight of a Brahman's wife called Marudi as she was returning home after bathing in the Kaveri's clear waters. Struck by her beauty, seeing her alone and taking her for a woman of easy virtue, he made amorous proposals to her, inviting her to accompany him. Marudi was abashed, aghast at his unexpected offer.

"She cried, 'In this world made of solid atoms, chaste wives have power even to control the rain and never do they provoke men's desires. How has my image come to be enshrined in a young man's heart? What have I done to deserve it? Have I committed some sin? I no longer feel worthy to tend the three sacred fires of my Brahman husband, whose breast is crossed by the sacred thread.'

"Speaking thus, instead of returning home, she wandered panic-stricken through the streets to the square where at the crossing of four avenues there stands the statue of the city's protecting genie. She called on him, complaining of her misadventure.

" 'I do not think that I have failed in my duties to my husband. How can I suddenly have found a secret place at the bottom of a stranger's heart? I embarked on marriage, believing I was one of those women of such great virtue that they have the power of making the rain fall in case of need. I do not understand what sin I can have committed to deserve what has happened to me. Genie! Always vigilant at the crossing of the four avenues! I have heard the sages of the city tell that you bind with your rope those given to evil courses, even if they act in secret, and that you then devour them. Have you relinquished your task, since you do me no harm?' Speaking thus, she began to weep loudly at the statue's feet.

"The famous genie then appeared before her, saying, 'Young woman, similar to a liana! It appears you have not understood the meaning of the divine bard's* words when he says that the rain clouds obey the orders of those women who, even if they do not worship the gods, start their daily tasks only after venerating their husband. In your life, you are used to believing in legends and delight in ridiculous stories. Your devotion to the gods consists mainly of attending the festivals where the drums whose hides are stretched by thongs sound, to listen to the music and watch the dancing. Furthermore, you worship gods quite other than your husband. Do not therefore delude yourself, good woman! You do not have the power to com-

* Tiruvallur, author of *Tirukkural*, the famous work in Tamil composed about 55 A.D.

95

mand the clouds nor to reduce to ashes the heart of strangers who are enamored of you. But you must change all your habits if you want the rain to obey your orders. The rope I bear will not be used to bind you nor my weapons to punish you, as I do with those women who let themselves behave as they please. You need not reproach yourself for the prince's misconduct. The law gives the king seven days to do justice and chastise criminals. If he fails in his duty, it becomes my task to punish the guilty. Young woman like a liana! Do not worry! In seven days from now, King Kakanda, when he learns of his son's misconduct and if the latter has not ridden himself of the desire that you inspire in him, will put him to death.'

"Thus spoke the infallible genie and, as he predicted, when the king learned of the prince's misconduct towards a Brahman woman, he struck off his head with his own hand.

"Lion among kings! With riches to govern the whole earth bound by the ocean! Hear further!

"In the good days of old, there lived in this city a young man of rich family, named Dharmadatta. He had a cousin, the daughter of his maternal uncle, whose name was Vishakaï. Both one and the other were of such marvelous beauty that they seemed like two statues lovingly carved by a god, better than the work of the most skilled craftsman. Being cousins, they had a deep affection for each other and behaved like the most united of young couples. Rumors started to spread in the city, suggesting that they had carnal relations and wished to marry according to the Gandharva rite* without bothering about legal marriage ceremonies.

"Saddened by these rumors, Vishakaï of the shining brow, pale as a drawing that has not yet been colored, left her house and betook herself to the pilgrims' hospice to ask the statue of the genie sculpted on the pillar what he could do to free her of the calumny caused by the rash gossip of the townsfolk. The heavenly genie, praising Vishakaï, publicly announced that she had committed no sin, either in intent or deed, saying, 'Vishakaï's virtue is

* By mutual consent.

96

irreproachable. She can make rain fall in case of need.'
In appearance, public opinion was calmed, but Vishakaï
herself was not satisfied.

" 'If the divine statue had not to the public astonishment made known that my virginity was spotless, doubt
would always have haunted the obtuse spirit of the people
of this city. It is only in my next life that I hope to become the wife of my beautiful cousin. In this life I do not
desire an amorous relationship with him and I vow never
to take a husband.' Explaining her virtuous resolution to
her mother, she entered a monastery.

"Deprived of the object of his love, Dharmadatta
then left Puhâr with his father and mothers* after thanking the statue of the pillar for having delivered them from
such an obsessive worry. They went to Madura, a city famous for the number of its scholars.

"Dharmadatta, faithful to his love for his cousin
Vishakaï, her braided hair mingled with open flowers,
vowed never to have relations with other women.

"He acquired a considerable fortune by way of
trade, showing an impeccable honesty in all his dealings.
He became influential and respected and was granted by
the king of the country the title of *Etthy* and the golden
flower which is its insignia. He attained the age of sixty
years as a dignitary of the realm and was the head of
many prosperous enterprises.

"One day he met a Brahman, who said to him, 'You
are an important man, encumbered with riches. But you
have neither wife nor son. Neither your good deeds nor
your good fortune will serve you to reach paradise.** It
is now time for you to return to your native town and
think of the future.' Struck by these words, Dharmadatta
came back here, bringing all his goods, to the great detri-
ment of the city of Madura.

"O king who reigns over this land! When she heard
the news of his arrival in town, Vishakaï, wearing narrow
golden bracelets, left the monastery where she had been
living and, showing no shame before so many witnesses,

* His father's wives.
** Only a son can perform the rites that open the gates of
heaven.

97

came to meet the merchant in all innocence, saying, 'We are no longer even able to recognize each other. The beauty of our bodies which inspired us with desire is now faded. You are now sixty years old and my hair, once divided into five carefully smoothed plaits, is now turning grey. Our youth and our desire have now left us. Inconstant man! Never in this life shall I be able to prostrate myself before your feet as wives do! Only in some future life shall I be your woman, obedient to your desire.

" 'Youth passes, beauty tarnishes, adolescence flies away. The importance given to riches does not last either. It is no son who will open us the way to paradise. The only thing that accompanies us beyond life is the good we have done during our present existence.'

"Having spoken thus, she exhorted him to employ his goods for works of charity. Dharmadatta then showed his cousin Vishakaï all he possessed and, letting her assist him, henceforth used his fortune for good works. He performed so many generous deeds that their number exceeded the stars that shine in the vasty sky.

"Cleansed by the intervention of the genie of the pillar of the stain with which public rumor had sullied her, the good Vishakaï, aging, but still a virgin, was returning home one day in the company of some other women through the crowded streets where many flags were flying. It came to pass that one of the princes, the elder brother of the one who had been put to death for his deplorable conduct towards Marudi, saw Vishakaï and, captivated by her gracious appearance, wished to express his feelings for her. To this end, he raised his arms to his head in order to remove the garland of flowers he was wearing around his hair and throw it around Vishakaï's neck with the intention of compromising her in public. But, by the power of Vishakaï's perfect virginity, his arms remained fixed and could not be lowered.

"When King Kakanda was informed of the misadventure of his son, whose hands, reaching up to the garland of flowers around his knot of hair, could not be lowered due to the lustful thoughts he entertained toward Vishakaï, he fell into a violent rage and, without considering the grief of his son's death would cause him, he beheaded him too with his sword.

"You are our master, O king! May you live always for the world's good, for thousands of years to come!"

The king of boundless fame, having listened patiently to the monks, said to them, "Monks! You have chosen the best of lives and have often given me the wisest of counsels. I now wish to know what you were alluding to when you began your discourse by saying, 'Not only nowadays.' Have similar evil deeds been committed now? Be so good as to illuminate me."

One of the monks then started speaking, beginning with the words, "May your scepter, O king, remain unsullied!

"In this ocean-girt world, the sages who know the final truths have recommended that five kinds of blameworthy acts should be avoided: drunkenness, lying, stealing, cruelty, and lust. Those who practice chastity can easily free themselves from these other faults, as shown by the experience of the ascetics who practice severe disciplines and have totally renounced sexual pleasures. O king, reigning over the vast world! Men who are unable to check their lustful desires are one day certain to meet with terrible suffering in the infernal world.

"The daughter of Chitrâpati, Mâdhavi, whose great eyes are striped with red, unable to bear the grief caused by the misfortune of her handsome lover Kovalan, has long taken refuge in a Buddhist monastery. Her daughter Manimekhalaï, who is still very young with her breasts just starting and who still prattles childishly, has also decided to renounce the world and lead a life of abstinence, eating only food obtained by begging, wandering from house to house of both rich and poor. She has now installed herself in the hospice on the outskirts of the city.

"Without consideration for her way of life, your son Udayakumâra, impelled by his extreme desire to possess her, followed her everywhere like a shadow. For this reason, he foolishly entered the hospice during the night. In order to avoid his approaches, Manimekhalaï, who was there, had taken the appearance of Kayashandikaï, the wife of a Vidyâdhara. Nevertheless, even under this disguise he pursued her with his attentions. The real Kayashandikaï had but recently resided in this place. Her husband, a Vidyâdhara, bearer of an invincible sword, had been looking for her and arrived at that very moment. He believed the prince had come to see his wife. Then raging fate manifested itself and the hour of doom arrived.

"O king, whose white parasol resembles the full moon! Cruel chance had gathered together in the same spot and at the same hour your son and Manimekhalaï, under the appearance of Kayashandikaï, as well as the Vidyâdhara with the invincible sword.

"As Udayakumâra approached the young woman in the darkness, the Vidyâdhara, Kayashandikaï's husband, furious at the thought that the prince had come to see his wife, clove the prince's body in twain with the sword he held in his hand, within the very hospice itself."

Having spoken thus, the monk fell silent, after pronouncing once more his sovereign's eulogy.

The king, bearer of a high and splendid crown, showed no grief on learning of his son's tragic death. With a glance, he called the captain of his army, on whom he had conferred the title of *Sholiye Enati,* and said to him, "This Vidyâdhara, an ordinary man, deserves our gratitude for having inflicted the proper punishment on the debauched prince, thus absolving me of the duty of doing it myself. Women's virtue and the laws decreed by the sages can only be guaranteed by the king's efficacious protection. I am the descendant of the famous sovereign who crushed his son under his chariot's wheels to punish him for his faults. However, before news of my son's misconduct spreads among the other kings, have a pyre built for the cremation of his body and have the dancer's daughter put in prison."

These orders were carried out.

Manimekhalaï Comes Out of Prison

Vasantavaï was a very old woman with long braids of grey hair. She lived in the king's house, since it was her privilege to teach the sovereign, the princes, and the women of the royal household the ancient ways and customs of the people of the country. She it was who had to present the king with the people's condolences on the occurrence of a sad event.

At the king's orders, she betook herself rapidly to the queen, whose long eyes were striped with brilliant marks, to try and calm the distress of her troubled mind. Without warning, she ran into the apartments of the splendidly bejeweled queen, who was weeping and bemoaning herself. Standing, without prostrating herself before her, she said, after the usual greetings, "To die in bed of old age, like a common man, is an unworthy death for a Chola. It is his duty to die gloriously in combat, protecting his people and earning the hatred of his vanquished enemies. Should it happen that a prince dies of sickness, his body is slashed and lain on a bed of holy herbs, to affect the belief that he has died a hero in battle. And they shout, 'May his spirit attain paradise where the kings reside who have subdued their enemies in the fight!'

"I do not know how I can explain to the people that your son died neither defending the fatherland nor in conquering enemy territory, and that his amorous adventures alone caused his end. It would not be seemly for you to show your sorrow in the king's presence, who must serve as an example to all the people." Having spoken thus, the old woman went away.

Obliged to conceal her grief and hide her tears, the queen, her hair carefully smoothed and divided into many tresses, decided to resort to intrigue to avenge the death of her son by making Manimekhalaï suffer. Without revealing her plan to anyone, she went to the king, saying,

"A man whose heart could be troubled at the sight of a female ascetic whom no normal male would have pursued was certainly not suited to become heir to the kingdom. Manimekhalaï has overcome Kâma, the god of love, bearing in his long arms a bow of sugar cane. She has resolved that her young body shall not serve men's pleasure. King, whose scepter is the symbol of justice! You must not let such a noble creature wilt in prison."

The king replied, "A king has no sons except those whose wisdom and conduct are without blemish. A king does not acknowledge other children. If you accept this rule, the girl with the beautiful jewels may be released from her sad imprisonment."

"Let this girl like a liana be entrusted to my care," said the queen, "and, should she desire to continue her wanderings, a beggar's bowl in her hand, then nothing shall hinder her."

The queen, whose hair spread a delicious scent, had Manimekhalaï found and returned with her to the palace.

The queen's plan was to drive her mad by giving her draughts that disturb the mind, and thus to make her the laughingstock and victim of all the city's inhabitants. Despite these draughts however, Manimekhalaï, who possessed the knowledge of her past and future lives, retained a lucid mind and did not for one instant forget what she had learned.

The queen then summoned a young man of humble origin, filling his hands with gold coins, and charged him to lead Manimekhalaï astray, pressing her young breasts against his strong chest, so that he could boast of it publicly afterwards.

The ignorant boy was shown into the dark chamber where the young girl was shut up. As he approached her, Manimekhalaï, knowing that this was an evil trick of the queen's, silently pronounced a magic formula which transformed her into a boy. When the young man wished to abuse her, he was somewhat confused by the contact and thought to himself, "No male has the right to dwell in the queen's harem. I do not wish to be ensnared in some strange intrigue for which this queen, who has so generously paid me, will doubtless end in hell." Frightened, he decided to leave the city and fled.

Desirous of putting an end to the life of this wretched girl, whose attractions has caused her son's terrible death, the queen locked her up in a bathouse, with neither window nor air, on the pretext that she had an incurable disease and refused to take food. Manimekhalaï, however, knew the magic formula that can suppress hunger. Her body was not weakened by her fast and remained youthful and charming. Faced with all these miracles, the queen with her superb jewels began to tremble with fear and to regret her behavior. She went to see Manimekhalaï and threw herself at her feet, saying, "Girl like the goddess of fortune! It was because I was unable to bear the sorrow caused by my son's death that I inflicted these torments on you. I now see that you are a saint. Forgive me for my evil behavior."

Manimekhalaï replied, "Gracious lady, like a liana! In my former life, my husband, Prince Rahul, fruit of Nilâpati's womb, died poisoned, victim of the venom of a cobra of the Tittivitam species, which works from afar. Unable to bear life without him, I followed him onto the funeral pyre. It is this same Rahul that, in this life, has become your son Udayakumâra. You weep for the prince's death, but where were you at the time of his previous decease? What is the object of your grief? His body, or rather the life that animated it? If it was his body, why did you allow them to take it to the cremation ground? If you weep for the being that lived in that body, we have no means of knowing in what living being he has been able to be reborn, according to the merits he acquired. The only thing you can do, O bracelet-laden lady, is to transfer your affection to the whole mass of living beings, knowing that your son's soul has been transferred to one of them.

"I can explain to you, Great Queen, that it was due to the grave fault committed by your son in his former life that he deserved to become the victim of the sword of Kanchana the Vidyâdhara. It was for having killed a poor servant in an access of rage, who, slipping in the kitchen, had spilled on the ground all the dishes prepared for a dinner of honor, that he lost his life the first time through the serpent whose glance is death, and that yet again, as Udayakumâra, he perished under the sword blow of an enraged Vidyâdhara.

"Valiant lady, like a liana in flower! You ask how I know all things, which is why I wish to tell you what has happened to me."

Omitting nothing, Manimekhalaï then explained to the queen all that had come to pass from the moment she entered the flower garden, the Upavanam, up to the words of the statue on the pillar, which had unburdened her mind and dissipated her doubts. She then continued her discourse.

"Excellent lady of the marvelous jewels! Is it not strange that you, the mother of him who was my husband in my former life, wished to drive me mad by making me take poison. Since I obtained the vision of my future life, however, I can also perceive the things of this world. When the stupid boy of low origin approached me in the dark, I transformed myself into a man. I was finally able to escape your perifidious designs due to a magic formula I know that allows me to live without food. I can, at will, take on any appearance I choose and travel through the air. I did not use these powers to escape you since I desired to free you from your great grief and deter you from base deeds, for, in this life, you were the mother of him who was my husband in my former existence.

"Lady! Rid yourself of this useless sorrow that has clouded your mind and driven you to commit blameworthy acts. The virtues of kings must be without stain. Listen to the tales I now will tell you.

"In a land where the royal scepter had lost its righteousness and the citizens were corrupt, it came to pass that an upright woman, whose married life was reproachless, was repudiated by her husband, together with the child she carried in her womb. She departed, abandoning the child at the wayside, and led a degraded life, offering her body to all comers. The child was saved by a Brahman, whose breast was bound by the sacred thread, who raised him without revealing his origin to his neighbors. The child grew and it came to pass that he had amorous relations with a woman met by chance, whom he then found was his mother. When he realized what a terrible sin he had unknowingly committed, he killed himself.

"A young hind on the point of giving birth was wandering in the forest in search of water to quench her thirst. A huntsman passing by shot his arrow with such force that the animal's belly was torn asunder and the little one fell out. The huntsman approached, hearing the cries of the newly-born fawn lamenting and shedding tears. He was seized with horror on seeing this innocent being escape alive from the gaping entrails. Unable to calm himself and dismayed by his cruel deed, he too ended by taking his life.

"Queen, whose long eyes seem like lances! Have you perhaps already heard these stories?

"Proud lady! Has it never happened that during elephant fights you see men, intoxicated through having drunk too much palm-wine, rashly draw near, with their staggering steps, to these enraged animals and perish, pierced through by their tusks?

"Those who always seek to deceive others do not escape the sad fate reserved for them!

"Lady with shoulders as supple as reeds! I need not remind you of the fate awaiting those who prefer lying and stealing to the hard work of the fields to assure their livelihood. Nothing can be done to save those unfortunate people who cannot forgo the five vices, soure of all ills, which are lust, drunkenness, lying, stealing, and murder.

"Lady! The education we have received does not lead to true wisdom. The wise are those that know how to check their emotions and forgo vengeance. In this vast world, only the life of those who are generous and try to assuage poverty is fruitful.

"Lady of peerless bracelets! Those who have understood the nature of the world and who have a happy future before them are benevolent to all beings, dedicating themselves to assuaging suffering and feeding the hungry."

Thus, by her discourse, Manimekhalaï poured the

pure water of wisdom into the queen's ears and extinguished the flames which burned her entrails caused by grief for her son's death.

From the sorrow that had clouded her mind and awakened her hate, her spirit was gradually released, as water, clouded by mud, becomes clear again when pieces of soap-root are cast into it. She fell at the feet of Manimekhalaï, who, unable to bear seeing her humiliated before her, lifted her up and, bowing in turn, complimented her, saying, "It is not meet for you to bow before me, since you were the mother of the prince who, in another life, was my husband. Moreover, you are the queen of this country, and it is unfitting that a mother-in-law should prostrate herself before her daughter-in-law, or a queen humiliate herself before one of her subjects."

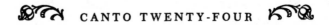

CANTO TWENTY-FOUR

Manimekhalaï Visits Aputra

Chitrâpati, the dowager of the courtesans, who had given her support to the Prince's lewd designs on Manimekhalaï, was terrified when she learned of his unhappy end under the Vidyâdhara's sword blows. Extremely worried by the possible consequences of her intrigues, she ran and threw herself at the queen's feet to try to have Manimekhalaï released from prison.

She explained to the queen, "The wives of the hermits, whom Indra, the lustful king of heaven, had seduced, gave birth to heavenly nymphs. One hundred and twenty-one of these nymphs, whose charming pubes resembled a cobra's hood, came in ancient times to live in this city. Five of them had been exiled for their inaptitude in mime when they danced in the audience hall of paradise. A further one hundred and four, guided by Jayanta, Indra's rebel son, had come down to earth to hear the preaching of that most famous sage, Agastya.

The nymph Urvasi, of incomparable beauty, who had incurred the wrath of Indra, bearer of a crown adorned with precious jewels, also came to take refuge in our world. It is from her that my family descends. Since the very beginning, none of us has ever had to face such serious problems as I am facing now.

"All the townspeople were indignant to learn that my daughter Mâdhavi, disconsolate at the death of a lover who used to pay daily for her amorous services, had suddenly decided to renounce the world and take refuge in a Buddhist convent (*vihâra*). And now Manimekhalaï, whose job is to dance in the theater for the public pleasure, is creating yet another scandal, wandering from house to house, a beggar's bowl in her hand, begging for alms. Such behavior is contrary to the rules of good society. Prostitutes are not born to play at being devout folk. These girls have become a public byword and are a source of discredit for our whole corporation. I do not know how to hide my shame. Manimekhalaï, who has already caused the prince's death, risks drawing misfortune on the entire city. We must not forget that, since the time of King Killi, this town has lain under the threat of disaster.

"During the pleasant season that precedes the great heat, King Killi, whose high and brilliant crown was adorned with precious jewels, had come to relax in the shady groves protected by the high dunes along the sea, beyond the salt marshes which the waves come and caress. Walking in this secret garden where none but he could go, he thought himself alone to breathe the flowers' exquisite perfume, when, to his astonishment, he suddenly perceived in that place a woman of incomparable beauty.

"Struck at first blow by Eros' five darts, the king, unmindful of all his duties, succumbed to the attractions of this creature. The season was pleasant, the surroundings charming. The fragrance of the ashokas, mangos, blue water lilies, the thick-petaled lotus, and all the spring flowers perfumed the air, and the young woman herself was of dazzling beauty.

"Unable to control himself, the king, without knowing who she might be, possessed this woman who had

107

come alone to offer herself to him. When he clasped her to him, his eyes delighted in the beauty of her limbs, his ears echoed to her sweet words, his mouth tasted the savor of her saliva, and his nose breathed the perfume of her body. He trembled at her touch and he, who had so often been amused at the sight of kings' backs fleeing from his invincible spear (whereas a true knight never shows his back to an enemy), now stooped before a woman and rendered her all the small services she desired of him. Then, at the end of the month, she suddenly vanished without trace.

"Disconcerted by her disappearance, the victorious monarch, who had given himself to her unreservedly, had her sought everywhere, saying, 'Where could she be hiding, this woman so like a young liana?' Then it was that a Charana appeared before him, one of those mysterious Jain ascetics who possess the power of moving beneath the earth, in the air, and on the waters.

"The king greeted him, standing respectfully before him and, after rendering him the customary honors, said, 'Holy man! A woman, more precious to me than life itself, has vanished. Would you not help me to discover where she could have gone?'

"The Charana replied, 'For the moment I do not know where she is, but, since I have vision of events past, I knew of her existence.

" 'This charming woman is the daughter of Vasamayila, the wife of Valaivanam, the valiant sovereign of the Serpent People, the Nâgäs, over whom he reigns with equity, whose lance is invincible and who is victorious in all his combats. When their daughter Pilivalaï was born, the astrologer predicted that she would become pregnant by a king of the dynasty of the sun, who would be the first to caress her young breasts.

" 'Never again will you see this woman like a liana in flower. Her son will return to you alone. Waste no time therefore in futile regrets, but think rather of celebrating the festival of Indra as soon as possible, for, if you neglect to do so for one single year, this town will at once be overcome by the sea. Long ago the goddess Manimekhalâ predicted that when the festival of Indra ceased the ocean would rise and swallow the city. Since that time the town has always lived in fear of the curse that lies on her. Your kingdom will meet with ruin if ever you neglect this festival. Hasten then and prepare this famous festival, since otherwise you will see your magnificent city swallowed up by the waves.' "

Chitrâpati continued, "Queen! If the girl who bears her name is for some reason in distress, Manimekhalâ, the great sea goddess, could well reappear, which is what I fear."

Having terminated her discourse with the usual compliments, Chitrâpati requested the queen to deliver Manimekhalaï to her so that she could take her back home.

In answer, the queen said, "Manimekhalaï left your dwelling when she realized the sad condition of a prostitute's life, a degrading life where nothing counts but palm-wine, lying, endless eroticism, carnivorous cruelty, and intrigue, all things which the wise prefer to renounce. For this reason, she chose to dwell with you no longer, but to abide under my protection."

Whilst this discourse was taking place, Mâdhavi, who had learned from Sutâmati of her daughter's misfortune, felt troubled in mind, like water in a pool that becomes muddy when clay is thrown into it. Her body trembled like the branch of a tree shaken by a violent wind. Dragging Sutâmati along, she ran to Aravana Adigal, her last hope, and with him they went to the queen.

On seeing them, the queen and all her court, together with Chitrâpati and Manimekhalaï, arose and came forward to receive Aravana Adigal with the respect due to him. He blessed them with the words, "May true wisdom dwell among you!"

Her arms laden with bracelets, the queen led Aravana Adigal to the high seat set aside for ascetics. She washed his feet and rendered him all the proper honors. Then, after speaking his praise, she said, "Venerable Master! Only a happy portent can have incited your unsteady feet to fetch you to my abode. May your body, the dwelling place of your ever-agile spirit, last you yet for many years, despite the ravages of age!"

"Good Queen!" replied the sage, "as a reward for

past merits, I was born in this body, now emaciated by the rigors of asceticism. I am now declining like the setting sun.

"All beings born into this world pass through birth, growth, sickness, old age, and death. The marvelous experience of release is reached only by those that understand the nature of this world and of the twelve links (*nidâna*) of this chain whose bonds determine the state of existence. These twelve links are: ignorance (*avidyâ*); intelligence (*buddhi*); consciousness (*chit*); name and form (individuality); the five senses and the mind, the organ of thought; perception (the relationship between the senses and their organs); sensation (experience of pleasure and pain); desire; attachment; the entry into existence; rank (birth in a particular species of being); decline and death.

"It is the deeds, whether good or evil, accomplished in former lives that cause a soul to be incarnate in a particular race of beings, during which life its former deeds gradually come to fruition. Those who fail to understand that all our unhappiness derives from these bonds, these limits that determine what we are, will after death know only the sufferings of hell.

"Ignorance means the failure to understand the *nidâna* and a form of mental confusion that leads us to take man's beliefs for eternal verities, without reference to reality, as in the case of the hare's horns.*

"Many are the spheres existing in the three worlds, and many are the kinds of beings found there. The possibilities for individual forms of existence are limitless and may be classed in six categories: humans; spirits; gods; Brahmâs (creative principles); Nâgäs (serpents, genies of the underworld); and demons (evil spirits). According to their merits, beings are lodged at birth in the embryo of one or another of these six kinds of beings and, in due time, when their past deeds reach maturity, they gather their fruits and live for a time in suffering or delight.

"Excellent woman with elegant bracelets! The ten kinds of fault that cause our downfall are of three orders:

---

* A classical example in logic for any theory that does not take account of facts.

deed, word, and thought. Murder, theft, and lewdness belong to the domain of deed; lying, slander, cruel words, and useless verbosity belong to the domain of word; covetousness of others' goods, anger, and perverse theories belong to the domain of thought. These are the faults that cause all our misfortunes, and this is why the wise avoid them.

"Those that choose to err along the paths of vice are reborn as beasts or demons, unless they find themselves in hell, where their obtuse spirits will endure terrible sufferings.

"Good conduct consists of avoiding the ten faults I mentioned, in observing the five prescribed rules, in preserving integrity and in employing life's short duration in acts of charity.

"Those who keep firmly to the path of righteousness will be reborn as human beings, or among the higher beings, as genies or gods, or sometimes even as Brahmâs, and then enjoy the fruits of their good deeds.

"You women who surround the queen! Take care to observe the rules of the *dharma*, preserving a spotless virtue, and be benevolent to all living beings. As for you, Manimekhalaï, with your teeth like rows of pearls! You already know the secret of your former life. If you return to me when you have studied the teachings of the masters of the various religions, I will then explain to you the multiple paths of knowledge."

Having spoken thus, the venerable Aravana Adigal rose to leave.

Like a young liana, Manimekhalaï went and prostrated herself at the feet of the great ascetic, the prophet of the *dharma*. She then addressed the queen and the women of her court, as well as Chitrâpati, Mâdhavi, and Sutâmati, exhorting them not to forget the teachings of the great ascetic and to preserve the city from all danger by leading an exemplary life.

She added, "As for myself, if I remained here, I would always in the mind of the citizens be the image of the god of death who brought about the prince's unhappy end. I have therefore decided to depart and visit Aputra's kingdom, after which I shall once more go to venerate the

Buddha's sacred pedestal on the holy isle of Manipalla-vam. Then I shall go to the great city of Vanji and dedicate myself to good works in memory of the virtuous Kannaki. Do not worry about me or about the difficulties I may encounter in such a life."

She saluted them all, telling them how sweet their affection had been to her.

When the sun vanished beyond the horizon, she left the palace like a flash of molten gold through the air. After thrice circling over the Chakravâla-kottam, the hospice, Champâpati's sanctuary and the splendid pillar where the genie dwelt, she traveled through the air on the paths of heaven to the outskirts of the city where reigned Aputra, as Indra's descendent. There she landed to rest in an orchard of flowering trees, where the ascetic Dharma Shrâvaka lived. She bowed before the holy man and asked him what town it was and who was the king.

The ascetic replied, "This city is called Nâga-puram, and the king who reigns there is the virtuous Punya Râja, son of Bhumichandra. Since the day of this king's accession, the somber clouds that roam the sky have always poured down generous rain. The soil is fertile and its fruits abundant. All who live in the city are free from the diseases that install themselves in the body and make it suffer."

The famous ascetic who resided in the flowering garden then recounted to her the story of the king who always wears a magnificent necklace of flowers.

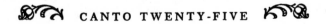 CANTO TWENTY-FIVE

Aputra Returns to Manipallavam

In the meantime, King Punya Râja, together with the queen and his court, had gone to pay his respects to the Preacher of the Faith, Dharma Shrâvaka, in the garden where he had elected to live and to hear his godly teachings. The holy man gave them a long exposition of the nature of the *dharma* and of the vices to which it is opposed. He then spoke of what is eternal or temporal, of suffering and its causes, of transmigration, life after death, and of the means of attaining release. He mentioned the twelve *nidâna*, the factors of existence, and explained how everlasting peace is obtained after release. Finally, he talked to them of the nature of the Buddha, the supreme teacher.

The king noted in the company a girl of remarkable beauty, who kept herself apart, holding a beggar's bowl in her hand. He thought she must be one of those persons over whom the god of love's darts have no power and he asked who the creature was that listened so raptly to the holy man's teaching.

Wearing a long robe, the symbol of his rank, the master of ceremonies bowed before him and said, "O king, wearer of a pollen-laden necklace of flowers! In the vast rose-wood continent, there is no being whose merits equal those of this girl. I heard of her when I was sent on an embassy to seal our friendship treaty with the Chola king, Killivelavam. I reached Puhâr by vessel after an ocean crossing. Then it was that the sage Aravana Adigal told me the mystery of this girl's birth. I spoke of it to you on my return. This must be the very same person, come from her native town."

Manimekhalaï then addressed the king. "The prosperity and great riches you enjoy in your present life are the reason why you have not remarked that it is your beggar's bowl, called Cow of Abundance, that is now in my hands. It belongs to the order of things that you have no remembrance of from your previous life, but it seems you are not even informed of the circumstances of your present life, in which you were born of a cow's belly. You will not understand the reason for this birth and the bonds between us until you have thrice circled, from left to right, the Buddha's pedestal, which is to be found on the isle of Manipallavam. This is why, O king with the necklace of scented flowers, you must take yourself to Manipallavam without further delay."

Like a young liana, Manimekhalaï then rose into the air and vanished on the spotless paths of heaven.

Before the sun had disappeared over the western horizon, she redescended from the sky on the isle of Manipallavam, and walked around it on its wave-caressed beach. She then circled three times from left to right the pedestal encrusted with the purest jewels that bears the footprints of the Buddha, the great ascetic, free from all human bonds. Prostrating herself, she once more clearly relived the events of her former life and remembered the episode of the flying monk Sâdhu Sakkara, and the words that the sage Brahmâ Dharma had spoken when the king of Gandhara took leave of him on the banks of the river Kâyankaraï, where a great crowd had gathered to hear the words of truth from his mouth and receive his advice.

Addressing the courtiers accompanying the king who was on the move to the city of Avanti, the sage, letting the stick of his tongue strike the drum of his mouth, had proclaimed, "People of this land! You must renounce the vices which dim thought, result in suffering, and cause you to be reborn in your next life as beasts, evil spirits, or denizens of the infernal world. A life of virtue alone will allow you to be reborn amongst the inhabitants of heaven, as human beings, or even Brahmâs, the Regents of the world. Dedicate your lives, therefore, to accumulating good deeds!

"A great sage whose knowledge is free of all wrong belief is to be born into this world to deliver it from all the ills with which it is afflicted. Those who shall have the incomparable joy of listening to his teaching and of living according to his counsels will escape the anguish of the birth cycle."

Meanwhile, he exhorted them to follow the path of the *dharma* without wasting time, and to employ the days of their lives fruitfully, before the god of death, whom nothing can stay, should reach them.

Manimekhalaï remembered that after hearing the wise counsel of Brahmâ Dharma, she and her husband prostrated themselves before him and sang his praises. It was then that he announced the sad news of Rahul's imminent death through the venom of a serpent the sight of which distills poison and predicted that she would follow him onto the funeral pyre.

During her previous visit, Manimekhalaï had asked the fairy-guardian of the isle to explain to her why the god Indra, long before the birth of the Buddha, the Illuminated One who possessed knowledge of all things, had built this miraculous pedestal of rare splendor, and why the pedestal had permitted her to know the secret of her previous life, the cause of her death, as well as the destiny of her soul on leaving her body.

The fairy had replied to her question, "This pedestal has never allowed any but the Illuminated One, who possesses knowledge of all things, to rest on it. Moreover, Indra never worshiped it before it bore the footprints of the Illuminated One, the Incarnation of the *dharma*. Indra had it built with a view to his coming and it was at his order that the pedestal revealed the secret of their former lives to those that came to worship it." These words remained fresh in her memory, as though they had been spoken that very day.

While recalling these things, Manimekhalaï had walked many times around the pedestal in the ritual direction. Then, after prostrating herself before it, she waited.

While Manimekhalaï was waiting on Manipallavam, the king, leaving the holy man's hermitage in the garden of flowers, had regained his palace. Returning through the town, he mused on his strange birth, with a cow for mother and the ascetic Manmukhan for father, and on the odd way in which, thanks to the ascetic's magic, he had avoided all contact with the animal's entrails, protected inside an egg made of gold leaf, after which King Bhumichandra, who was childless, had adopted him as his son. It had been his adoptive mother, Amara Sundari, who wore precious circlets on her wrists, who had told him the truth of his birth and the reasons for which he found himself on the throne of Java.

He felt deeply humiliated and saddened on learning the story of his previous life and the way in which his mother had abandoned him by the wayside. He then began to muse on the mystery of birth and on the connection between the deeds accomplished in his former existence and the enviable position he occupied in his present life.

Until that day, he had reigned without a care, surrounded by great luxury, and had availed himself of all life's pleasures. The kings whose suzerain he was had long since laid up their arms and awaited the favor of an audience.

He spent a good deal of his time in watching the pretty dancing girls and in listening to the most beautiful music, performed according to the best rules of art and song. After his amorous sport, he bowed before the queens' tiny lotus-feet, with precious rings around their ankles. He admired the refined designs traced in saffron inks on charming breasts, and the skillful head-dresses of flowers woven into waving hair. Voluptuously he drank the ambrosia secreted by mouths behind rows of teeth like jasmine buds. He liked to practice all kinds of erotic games with women drunk with pleasure, touched by the red corners of black eyes shining in a moon-like face, whilst Kâma, the god of love, bent his sugar cane bow to shoot ceaseless flower bud arrows. When a woman did not respond to his advances, he put his pride into seducing her and became the slave of his own passions.

All this suddenly appeared without attraction to him, and Punya Râja, wearer of the precious crown adorned with jewels that had ornamented the brow of all his forefathers since time immemorial, began to reflect. While all the assembled kings patiently awaited his pleasure, he thought that the time might have come for him to renounce the splendor of his present life and detach himself from worldly pleasures. "Manimekhalaï was the source through which the germ of knowledge, sown by the ascetic Dharma Shrâvaka, penetrated my ears and in ripening has now illuminated my mind."

When he realized the change that had come about in the king's mind and had heard his discourse, the minister Janamitra requested an audience and, after prostrating himself at his feet and wishing him long life, he spoke. "Forget not, O Great King, that in the time of my former sovereign lord, your father Bhumichandra, until

116

the day when by the grace of a holy man he obtained you as his heir, this land of yours, of which this superb city is the capital, had suffered drought for twelve years. Many men and animals had died. Such was the famine that mothers were reduced to devouring their children instead of feeding them.

"It was during this time of great distress that you appeared like a benevolent cloud in the scorching summer. You are a privileged being and it is for our good that you wear the royal necklace made of a single row of flowers. You were born here and since your birth the seasonal rains have never failed. The land is fruitful and gives abundant harvests. None has suffered any more from the pangs of hunger and all bodies are strong. If you renounce the throne and give up your power, your whole people will become orphans and will lament, crying for you as a child cries for its mother.

"If you cease to reign over the world, the people, separated from you, will find themselves without protection. The living beings that depend on you will come to the end of their happiness and you will bear the responsibility for all the dangers that threaten them. In your desire to enter a better world, are you not acting selfishly, seeking only your own good, your own salvation, when you are going to cause misfortune, distress, and death to your subjects? That is not the *dharma* taught by the Buddha, the noblest of immortals who, without worrying about his own life, dedicated himself to the defense of all living beings. That is why, Great King, your decision seems contrary to your duty and to the true *dharma*."

Having listened attentively to his minister's counsel, the king replied, "For the moment I cannot resist my intense desire to go and worship the Buddha's pedestal on the isle of Manipallavam. For the period of one month, it will be your duty to assume the responsibilities of administering the realm, protecting the queens, and overseeing the palace officers."

The king summoned shipwrights, responsible for building vessels, and commanded the crews to prepare several ships. Then, descending to the shore where the sparkling tidal waters move, he embarked on a vessel which took him, without stopping elsewhere, straight to the isle of Manipallavam.

As pretty as a flowering liana, Manimekhalaï, who knew all the secrets of the island, saw the fleet bearing the king. Happy to see him, she went down to the strand to greet him. Taking him with her, she went around the island, from left to right, along the beach pounded by the waves and bordered with honey-scented flowering shrubs. She then led him up to the Buddha's miraculous pedestal, through which each may know his former life.

The king walked around the divine pedestal of the *dharma* in the ritual direction and worshiped it. He then received the vision of the events of his previous life, like one who discovers his own face in the mirror held in his hand.

The king exclaimed with astonishment, "I now know what my former life was and feel delivered from all my anguish. You I invoke, O Goddess of Knowledge, beauty without equal, since it is you who in southern Madura, cradle of the prosperous Tamil land, made me the gift of this inexhaustible bowl when on a dark night of ceaseless rain, strangers came to me in the almshouse, begging me to find them food, and I was desperate at being unable to come to their rescue. You then said to me, 'Forget your anguish! Were the whole land to suffer famine, this bowl will never dry up. Arise and receive this bowl from my hands.' In giving me Cow of Abundance, you transformed my life. Henceforth, whether I am reborn in this world, or amongst the gods of Brahmâs, Regents of the Universe, the care of protecting all living beings will always be mine. Brilliant as crystal! Beautiful as a doll! You belong to the tribe of heavenly beings. You it is who teach men the secret of language which permits them to attain knowledge. In each of my lives I will remember your incomparable splendor, O divine creature, and will worship you! You transcend the world of the gods and Brahmâs. Words cannot tell of your greatness!"

Having invoked the goddess, the king, together with Manimekhalaï, made his way south-west. They went and sat in the shade of a great bay tree at the edge of a pool with trembling waves, called the Bull's Muzzle (Gomukhi).

Tivatilakaï, the fairy-guardian of the isle, then appeared before them, delighted to see Aputra again, in the company of Manimekhalaï of the beautiful ornaments. Approaching them, she spoke to the king. "Exceptional man! You came here in your previous life, bringing with you a divine bowl called Cow of Abundance, which allowed you to assuage the pangs of hunger of great multitudes. The people who abandoned you when their vessel put out to sea again came back after some time looking for you on this island. Dismayed by what had happened, they put an end to their days by fasting on the very spot where you had left this life. You can see the skeletons of these nine noble merchants (*chetty*) who stayed here as well as those of their servants who, having been kept by them in life, repaid their debt by loyally following them in death.

"In the shade of the great bay tree covered with magnificent flowers, you may find, half-hidden by the sand that the moving tides have left on the beach, the remains of the body you left when you renounced life, before dwelling in this new body that today is yours.

"But when you let yourself die, you made yourself responsible for the death of those who, taken by remorse, returned here, and I am astonished that you, their murderer, should today be a king."

She then addressed Manimekhalaï. "Young and frail creature! You are the one that now owns this divine bowl, this Cow of Abundance, worthy of worship. While you are sheltered here, the magnificent city of Puhâr is being swallowed into the belly of the ocean. I will explain why. Pilivalaï, the daughter of peerless beauty of the king of the Nâga country (Nâga-nadu), having been delivered of the son she had had of a king of the dynasty of the Sun, came piously to make the round of the isle, carrying her newborn son in her arms. She wished to venerate the precious pedestal of the *dharma*, built by the king of the celestial worlds.

"Here she met the *chetty* Kambala, a merchant in woolen rugs, who had also stopped over at the island to venerate the pedestal. Learning that he was returning to

Puhâr, she entrusted the child to his care, praying him to consign him to the Chola king, and explaining that he was his son. Honored and delighted by this chance of taking the little prince to the king, the merchant took charge of this child of rare beauty, wearing green bracelets. Bowing, he immediately left the shores of Manipallavam. In the darkness of the night, however, the boat was shipwrecked not far from the coast, and no one knew what had happened to the child.

"On reaching Puhâr, the survivors informed King Vadivel Killi of the pointed spear of the loss of the young child. Made desperate by the disappearance of his son, the king fell into a state of feverish agitation, like a cobra that has lost the jewel which adorned his forehead. He had him sought for everywhere, in the sea and among the coastal plantations, without taking an interest in anything else for a very long time. He forgot that the fatal moment of Indra's festival was at hand. That year the festival was not celebrated and, at this omission, the city's protectress, the goddess Manimekhalâ, lost patience and allowed the curse to be accomplished. The furious ocean swelled up and the magnificent city of Puhâr was swallowed by its flood.

"When the tall waves, rising in rage, began to invade the superb city, Indra, the king of the heavenly worlds who bears in his long arm the fiery weapon called lightning (*vajra*), left the town forever, and Killi the king, wearer of the crown that his ancestors possessed since time immemorial, had to flee alone, abandoning all his possessions swallowed up by the sea.

"Forewarned in time, the sage Aravana Adigal and Mâdhavi departed on foot with Sutâmati and went to take refuge in the city of Vanji.

"This information I received from the goddess Manimekhalâ, the divine protectress of the immense ocean, whom the whole world worships. You will learn more from Aravana Adigal when you reach Vanji. Now that you know both your past and future lives, he will tell you how the goddess once saved one of your famous ancestors from death by drowning when his vessel broke up in the midst of the waves. He was a rich merchant who later performed so many good works that he earned the reputation of being the most generous man of his time."

Having spoken thus, the fairy-guardian of the isle of Manipallavam vanished.

Realizing that he had caused the death of so many good men who had graciously offered him a place in their ship in his former life when he was Aputra, the king was deeply moved. With the aid of Manimekhalaï, he dug in the sand under the bay tree and there discovered the skeleton of what had been his body in his former life. All trace of flesh or tendon had disappeared, but the bones had remained in place and were so brilliantly white that they might have been coated with white paint. Without moving the skeleton, he built over it a tomb of white mortar.

Perceiving his perturbation at the sight of this form that had been his, Manimekhalaï, rising into the air, called out to him. "King! Wearer of a garland of bright flowers! What did you come here for, and what is the reason for your anguish? I went to seek you far away in your own land and brought you to this island solely to allow you to learn about your former life and enable you to reign with greater charity, establishing your fame over your great island as well as over the four continents and the myriads of smaller islands surrounded by the ocean. If the kings who govern this vast world follow the way of the *dharma*, there would be no more problems, since the common people would no longer commit any offenses. If you wish to know what the *dharma* is and how to follow the way of wisdom, listen carefully to what I am going to tell you and forget nothing!

"There is no higher virtue than charity, which consists of making sure that no living being lacks food, clothing, and a place to live in safety."

The king replied, "O girl with the charming brow! I will try to apply these principles in my realm and in other lands. I will essay to follow the path of charity you have described. By revealing my former life, you have made a new man of me. I cannot bear the idea of leaving you."

Manimekhalaï consoled him, saying, "Let not your mind be troubled and overcome by regrets. Your kingdom

121

suffers in your absence and with loud cries begs for your return. The time has come for you to reembark and return to your capital. As for me, I am now going to the great city of Vanji."

Covered with jewels, Manimekhalaï flew away on the paths of heaven.

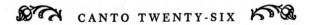 CANTO TWENTY-SIX

Manimekhalaï Arrives at Vanji

Manimekhalaï of the precious jewels left the isle of Manipallavam and, flying through space, soon landed near the city of Vanji. First of all, she wished to pay homage to Kannaki, the virtuous wife of her noble father Kovalan, and betook herself to the sanctuary dedicated to her where her statue stood. She stood there a long while shedding tears and praising the saint's striking merits, after which she questioned her.

"How is it that you did not follow the custom of chaste wives who, from faithfulness to their husband, accompany him onto the funeral pyre, or else adopt the widow's austere life? Why did you choose to employ the powers acquired by your virtues to set fire to the city of Madura and take revenge for the injustice done?"

The holy Kannaki, unrivaled model of the highest virtues, replied, "Unable to bear the grief caused by the tragic death of my husband, in my fury I destroyed the whole city of Madura by fire. The goddess Madurapati, the divine protectress of the town, then appeared to me and explained that everything that had come to pass was but the result of our faults in our former lives.

"In the fertile country of Kalinga (Orissa) with its marvelous gardens, two princes, cousins by birth, called Vasu and Kumâra, reigned over the twin kingdoms of Simhapura and Kapila. They hated each other and waged furious war the one against the other. Their battles had devastated the land for more than ten miles around, and people avoided passing through the territory separating the two capitals because of the violence of the combats.

"A merchant named Sangama, seeking to reach the town of Simhapura to expand his trade, strayed with his wife of the sparkling bracelets into the forbidden area. When he arrived at the town, where he was known to none, to sell jewels and other articles, the people, seeing this stranger come to do business, informed an officer of the royal guard called Bharata, a cruel man, who immediately seized the unfortunate Sangama. Having made King Vasu believe he was a spy of his enemy Kumâra, he had the innocent merchant put to death.

"Made desperate by such an ignominious end, his wife ended her days by throwing herself from a rocky height. But, before dying, she pronounced a curse. 'May those who have caused my misfortune in this life undergo the same suffering in their next existence.'

"This Bharata was my husband Kovalan in his former life and the curse which threatened him in due time produced its effect. Neither our good nor evil acts are ever washed away and we must inevitably suffer the consequences. Despite the explanations of the goddess protectress of the city, in my fury I was the instrument of the destruction of Madura by fire. I know that one day I must pay the price for this crime. In the meantime, as a reward for our accumulated merits, my husband and I have acquired the status of gods and live in the higher worlds where the heavenly beings dwell. When we have exhausted our credit, however, in the future we shall have to pay for our evil deed. Nothing can stay it from following us. Once we have exhausted our due of enjoyment in the heavenly worlds, we must return to earth and will continue to stray from one birth to another, tossed on the ocean of successive lives from which the other shore is not easily reached. We shall once again be caught up in the spiral of birth and death, until the day when, thanks to the Buddha, the One of boundless perfection, we may be released.

"The city of Kapila, renowned throughout the universe, shines like a precious jewel on the brow of the land of Magadha. Never have the rains failed in their proper season. There it was that the Sun called the Buddha appeared, the Illuminated One, who realized the perfection of the ten transcendent virtues, thanks to which living beings can attain the shore of the world and eternal release. He appeared on earth without causing any cataclysm and reached perfection seated in the shade of the tree of wisdom, the Bodhi, the sacred fig tree. Free from passions such as eroticism, anger, and the taste for error, he realized the four truths and broke the links of the chain that conditions existence. In his goodness, he spread the light of the *dharma* so that all might renounce the errors which are the source of their sufferings.

"Manimekhalaï! Already in your father's company have I been able to acquire the merit of venerating the seven monasteries (*vihâra*) built at Puhâr by Indra in the Buddha's honor. We have renounced the pleasures of this world and, when we have been sufficiently constant in following the teachings of the *dharma,* we shall no longer have to be reborn either on earth or in the nether worlds. We hope to break the interminable cycle of birth. Meanwhile, for a long time we must remain among the spirits who wait until their meritorious deeds bear fruit, and we shall continue to try and help the spiritual progress of all kinds of beings.

"Dear child, with your scented hair! The time has now come for you to go and visit the adepts of the various religions, those who use the most skillful arguments. You must try honestly to learn the portion of truth that each religion may include. If it then seems to you that none of them leads to transcendent truth, you may dedicate your life to following unswervingly the rules (*yama*) enounced by the Buddha (and transcribed in the *Pitaka*, the sacred texts of the Buddhists). This shall be your immediate task."

With these words, Kannaki, her (adoptive) mother, showed Manimekhalaï her duty.

Remembering that the goddess Manimekhalâ had explained that none of the learned preachers of the various religions would wish to expound the secrets of his faith to a young girl adorned with bracelets, Manime-khalaï, using one of the goddess's magic formulas, took the appearance, more in keeping with her student role, of a respectable monk. In this form, she landed outside the walls of the great city of Vanji, the capital of King Chera Senguttuvan of the unfailing scepter. First she visited the temple, the vast squares, the public buildings, the houses where the students of the various schools lived as well as the numerous ornamental lakes and gardens situated outside the town, where there dwelt a great number of ascetics who practiced their exercises in the hope of attaining salvation, as also the sages, masters of their passions, and the wise men, learned in the sacred texts which are the repositories of ancient wisdom.

When the Great King Chera Senguttuvan reigned over the city, he resolved to conquer the world, and set out on an adventurous expedition. His brow encircled with a crown of palm leaves, the emblem of his dynasty, he left the city at the head of a vast army formed of regiments of elephants, chariots, horsemen, and valorous warriors wearing ankle-rings.* Their marching produced an uproar like the sea made rough by a hurricane. Traversing the mountains, he reached the southern bank of the Ganges. There, on rafts called *vanga*, used by the people of Bengal, he crossed the river and encamped on the north bank. Having vanquished the Aryan kings, such as Kannaka, Vijaya, and others, he made them carry on their heads blocks of stone cut from the spurs of the Himalayas, which he wished to take back in order to have a statue of Kannaki sculpted, the most virtuous of wives. Shining with glory, he returned to Vanji, where he celebrated the festival of the "nets of victory," wearing a garland of red cassia flowers.

The time having come for her to turn to account the merits acquired in her former lives, Manimekhalaï entered Vanji, the magnificent city that bears the name of the palm tree. She devoted herself to good works, awaiting the day when by the ripening of events she

---

* The reward of their great deeds.

would be ready to receive the teaching of the four basic truths concerning suffering, its causes, its elimination, and the means of eliminating it.

CANTO TWENTY-SEVEN

Manimekhalaï Embarks on the Study of the Various Doctrines

Having reached Vanji, Manimekhalaï betook herself to the place where the representatives of the various sects with followers in Tamil country gather. One after the other, she met with the most learned of them, beseeching them to expound to her the tenets of their respective religions. She was thus able to approach the representatives of Vedism, Shivaism, Non-dualism, Vishnuism, Mîmâmsâ, Sâmkhya, Vaisheshika, and of the Materialists who believe in no reality apart from matter, as well as the wandering ascetics like the Ajivikas and Nirgranthas (Jains). She listened attentively to their theories and gradually acquainted herself with the doctrines of the various philosophic and religious schools.

Vedism and the Other Deist Traditions and the Philosophy of Mîmâmsâ (Rites and Theologies)

Before inquiring of the chief representative of the Vedic tradition, Manimekhalaï first contacted a logician (*pramânavâdi*) who belonged to this sect. He expounded to her the logical conceptions and "means of proof" (*pramâna*) envisaged by Mîmâmsâ, or theological reflection.

In explaining the means of knowledge, the logician referred to three teachers or sages: Veda Vyâsa, who divided the *Vedas* into four parts; Kritakoti (the Commentator); and the infallible logician Jaimini.*

* Veda-Vyâsa is the author of the *Pûrva Mîmâmsâ*, dealing with rites and sacrifices; Jaimini of the *Uttara Mîmâmsâ*, de-

126

These three thinkers have established that the instruments of knowledge through which the validity of any theory can be determined are, according to the school, either ten, eight, or six in number.

The Means of Proof

(Pramâna)

The means of proof are: *katchi* (*pratyaksha*), direct perception; *karuda* (*anumâna*), deduction; *upamâna*, analogy; *âgama* (or *shabda*), cultural heritage, the words of the ancients; *arthâpatti*, implication or presumption; *iyalbu* (*svabhâva*), common sense, the evidence inherent in the nature of things; *itheyam* (*aïthiya*), tradition or popular belief; *abhâva*, non-existence; *mitchi* or *olibu* (*parishesha*), elimination by inference or correlation; and finally, *undaneri* or *ulaneri* (*sambhava*), probability.

1. *Katchi* (*Pratyaksha*): Direct Perception.

Direct perception, free from doubt, is of five kinds (depending on which of the five senses is the intermediary): perception of color by the eyes; of sound by the ears; of odor by the nose; of taste by the tongue; of touch by the skin. It is through these perceptions that the sensations of pleasure and pain are felt.

Perception, in contact with the vital energies (*uyir*, *prâna*), reaches the mind (*manas*) through channels of internal communication (*vâyil*) called the sun, the moon, and fire (*ida*, *pingala*, *sushumna*). The mind (*manas*), which functions ceaselessly, receives the message. Thus is obtained an adequate knowledge of an object situated in a given place: its name, its nature, its activities, and not only knowledge of its appearance, without confusing it

---

fining the nature of the gods and heavenly hierarchies; Kritakoti, rarely mentioned outside the *Manimekhalaï* (except in a little-known text, the *Prapancha Hridaya*), is the name of a commentator on the whole of the two *Mîmâmsâs* by Bodhayana, generally mentioned only as the "author of the commentary" (*vrittikara*). This vast work is only known through the abridged editions of Upavarsha and Devavâmin.

with another object, but without leaving the least doubt as to its nature.

2. *Karuda* (*Anumâna*): Deduction.

Deduction or inference allows what is not perceived directly to be deduced according to what is perceived or seen. This kind of knowledge is of three types: simultaneous (*podul, sâmânya*); derived (*eccham, sheshavat*), proceeding from cause to effect; and ascendant (*mudal, purvavat*), returning from effect to cause.

Podul (*Sâmânya*): Simultaneous deduction.

Although two things are not necessarily connected to one another, the perception of one may lead to the deduction of the other, as in the case of the deduction of the presence of an elephant in the forest on hearing a trumpeting-like noise.

Eccham (*Sheshavat*): Deduction of the cause according to the effect.

On seeing rivulets pouring into a river, we may deduce that it has rained on the hilltops.

Mudal (*Purvavat*): Deduction of the effect from the cause.

On seeing black clouds gathering, we may deduce that it is going to rain.

Perception only exists in the present, whereas deduction is equally valid for both past and future.

3. *Upamâna:* Analogy.

The third instrument of knowledge is analogy, which consists of comparing what is not known with what is. For example, to somebody who has never seen one, a wild ox may be described in terms of a domestic bull.

4. *Âgama,* the sacred texts, or *Shabda,* the words of the wise: The cultural heritage.

This means of proof consists of having certain things admitted by quoting authors considered to be authorities. On this basis, heavenly or infernal worlds are admitted to exist where beings dwell in beatitude or suffering.

5. *Arthâpatti:* Presumption, implication.

An approximation is used to make an assertion understood. If, for example, we say that the cowherds live "on the Ganges," we mean "on the banks of the Ganges."

6. *Iyalbu* (*Svabhâva*): Common sense, evidence inherent in the nature of a thing.

The meaning of a word is determined by its context. When a man perched on an elephant's neck says, "Pass me the stick," he means the goad he uses to guide the animal, since he has no other stick.

7. *Itheyam* (*Aïthiya*): Tradition, popular belief.

One accepts the fact that a certain spirit dwells in a certain tree because this fact is generally accepted.

8. *Abhâva:* Non-existence.

The fact that an object is not to be found in a given place at a given moment means that it is not in that place, but not that it does not exist elsewhere.

9. *Mitchi* (*Parishesha*): Implication by correlation.

Saying that Râma was victor in his fight with Râvana implies that Râvana was the loser.

10. *Ulaneri* (*Sambhava*): Probability.

On seeing a piece of iron move, it can be concluded that a magnet is present, since otherwise the iron would be unable to move.

The Appearances of Proof

(*Prâmana-Âbhasa*)

Besides these ten means of examining the real, there are also eight appearances of proof that could lead us into error.

1. *Shuttunarvu:* Inexact perception.

Seeing something from afar, we cannot discern whether it is a man or a tree trunk: we merely know that something is there.

2. *Tiryak-kodal:* Deceptive appearance.

One thing can be mistaken for another, as, for example, mother-of-pearl for silver.

3. *Aïyam:* Indecision.
We are incapable of deciding whether a distant object is a man or a tree trunk.

4. *Teradu-teridal:* Arbitrary choice.
In the palace stable, there is a post for attaching horses as well as a stable boy standing nearby; we take the post for the stable boy without checking.

5. *Kandu-narâmaï:* Inattention, seeing without understanding.
Seeing something move, we do not realize it is a tiger and do not warn the person it is approaching.

6. *Valakku:* Mistaken association.
Believing in the reality of something that exists only in words: to speak of "hare's horns" is verbally comprehensible, but the thing described does not exist in reality.

7. *Unardandaï Unardal:* Truism, demonstration of what is evident.
For example, deciding after due reflection to sit near the fire to counteract the cold when one knows with certainty that heat is the opposite of cold.

8. *Niraïppu:* Indirect knowledge.
The fact of recognizing a couple as our parents can only be based on the affirmation of others.

The Means of Proof According to the Philosophical Schools

The six main philosophical schools differ in their acceptance of the means of proof, according to whether the latter were recognized or not by their founders. Thus, Lokâyata (atheism), founded by Brihaspati, only recognizes direct perception. Buddhist philosophy, inspired by

Jainism (founded by Rishabha), accepts perception and deduction. The Sâmkhya (cosmology) defined by Kapila accepts perception, deduction, and the authority of the texts (*âgama*). The School of Logicians (*nyâya*), whose founder was Akshapada, adds analogy (*upamâna*) to the list. The Scientist School (*vaisheshika*) of Kanada also accepts presumption (*arthâpatti*). As far as Mîmâmsâ is concerned, the deist school of Jaimini, all eight prime means of proof are accepted, including *abhâva*, non-existence.

Shivaism

After listening to the logician (*pramâna-vâdi*), who explained to her the logical means of discovering the truth, Manimekhalaï saw an adept of Shivaism (*Shaïva-vâdi*) approaching. She asked him what were the tenets of his religion. The man, for whom Shiva is the supreme god, explained as follows:

"The living being is formed of eight components, which are the five elements, plus the sun and moon (meaning the vital forces *ida* and *pingala*) and the ego, which acts. Shiva represents the indivisible principle (*nish-kalâ*), which exists outside the multiple world, who, for his own amusement, incarnates in the divisible world (*sa-kalâ*), the world of appearances, in order to create all things and beings. After this he destroys them, thus freeing them from suffering. There is no principle, no god, equal to or higher than he."

The Worshipers of Brahmâ

(*Brahmâ-vâdi*)

An adept of the Brahmâ cult explained to Manimekhalaï that the creator Brahmâ (whom he called Biraman) was the supreme god and that the universe was born from an egg laid by Brahmâ.

A Vishnuite, who had studied the Purâna of Vishnu, the god who is dark-blue like the sea, explained to her that this god is Narâyana, the refuge of men.

Vedism (the Religion of the Book)

The representative of Vedism (*Veda-vâdi*) explained to her that, for them, "no other divinity exists but the sacred text of the *Veda*." The *Veda*, which he called *ârana* (unfathomable), was the fount of knowledge, an eternal law, which is not the work of any one, and neither has it beginning nor end. The *Veda* corpus is divided into four parts, to which are added six addenda or "members" (*anga*), which are: ritual (*kalpa*), prosody (*chhanda*), calculation (*ganita*), the etymologies (*nirukta*), phonology (*shikshâ*), and grammar (*vyâkarana*).

Kalpa (Ritual) is a treatise which in the form of aphorisms explains the technique of sacrifices, the rites, and rules of behavior.

Chhanda (Prosody) explains the various meters and rules of versification.

En or *Ganita* (Calculation) comprises astronomy and astrology (essentials for determining ritual ceremonies).

Nirukta explains the etymologies and the meaning of difficult words in the *Veda*.

Shikshâ (Phonology) defines the rules of pronunciation (essential for the efficaciousness of ritual and magic formulas).

Vyâkarana (Grammar) expounds the rules of Sanskrit grammar, the language of the *Vedas*, as well as a general theory of language.

The god Veda is conceived as a body whose arms are the *kalpa*, feet the *chhanda*, eyes the *ganita*, ears the *nirukta* (through which the meaning of words is clarified), nose the *shikshâ,* and face the *vyâkarana.*

"The *Veda* is born of itself. It did not come forth from anything else. It has neither beginning nor end. Our rule of life consists of following the teachings of the *Veda.*"

Manimekhalaï, who had carefully followed the information given her by the representatives of the various philosophies, concluded that they did not correspond to the criteria of the written texts nor to those of the world in general as envisaged by those who possess true knowledge.

She thus addressed herself to the venerable master who taught the doctrines of the wandering monks, the Ajivikas, and asked him what text gave authority to his teaching and what, in his opinion, was the nature of the supreme being. He then explained to her as follows.

The Philosophy of the Ajivikas

"According to the teaching of our prophet Makkhâli*
whose power of knowledge is boundless and whose presence is immanent at all times and in all things, nothing excepted, everything that exists is formed of five constituents, which are the principle of life and those of four kinds of atoms. These atoms are mutually perceptive and group together to form various objects. The four kinds of atom are: solid, liquid, igneous, and gaseous. One group can bind itself to others without losing its own characteristics. The combinations of atoms form mountains, trees, bodies, after which they disperse once more. The atom of life is the one that centralizes, comprehends, perceives,

---

* Makkhâli Gosâla, who reformed the Ajivika sect in the sixth century before our era, was the first teacher of the Buddha as well as of Mahâvîra, the Jainist reformer. No written text attributed to him is known to exist. The work considered as an authority concerning his predication is, according to Nilakeshi Tiratta, called the *Navakadir,* translated into classical Tamil under the name *Ombadukadir.*

The Ajivikas are wandering monks who transmit the esoteric aspects of the most ancient civilization of India.

and governs each conglomeration of atoms. One group of atoms can mix with another without losing its identity, after which they again divide.

"Solid atoms are hard and stable, liquid atoms are flowing and cooling. They fall to earth with a slight sound, penetrating and being absorbed by it. Igneous atoms are burning, bright, and ascendent. Gaseous atoms move on a horizontal plane.

"The four kinds of atom, as well as the atom of life, are eternal, omnipresent, and were not created. Although endowed with the faculty of transforming themselves, in combining together and in separating, they are indestructible, and no new atom ever appears to mix with the others.

"A liquid atom never transforms itself into a solid atom, nor the contrary. Each atom is indivisible. It cannot be deformed like a grain of rice flattened in a mortar.

"Atoms move, rise, and descend. The mountains, which are a combination of solid atoms, can vanish, become dust, and mingle with other objects. The atoms belonging to a combination can separate from the others and regain their individuality. Atoms can unite with such density that they become hard as diamonds, or can take on the soft texture of bamboo. They can form seeds and germinate. When they spread over the earth like the light of the moon, they take the form of the various elements.

"The four perceptible elements—earth, air, fire, and water—are formed of these atoms which are found in every object in a definite proportion and without ever being equal in number. They combine together in the proportions of one, three-quarters, half, and a quarter, to form the various elements.

"To form the element 'earth,' a solid atom combines with three-quarters liquid, a half igneous and a quarter gaseous atoms.

"To form water, the proportion of liquid, igneous, gaseous, and solid atoms, is one, three-quarters, one half and one quarter.

"For the element 'air,' for one volume of gaseous atoms there are three-quarters of solid, half of liquid and a quarter of igneous atoms.

"The elements are called by the name of the atoms

present in greatest number. If these proportions are not observed, the earth will not be hard, water will not run, fire will not burn and the wind will not blow.

"Only those beings who possess transcendent vision can see atoms. Other living beings, even when the atoms unite to form the elements (*bhûta*), are not aware that these elements are made of atoms combined in certain proportions. They have only a general view of things that does not reveal the existence of the atoms forming an object just as, in the evening twilight, we cannot distinguish a single hair, but can clearly see a lock of hair.

"The combinations of atoms that form living beings appear under six different colors: black, dark-blue, green, red, golden, or white. Only those beings who attain the pure white level can reach the 'cessation of existence' (*vidu*) which is release. Those who wish to escape from this world of sorrows will seek to attain the whitest rebirth in order to free themselves from the cycle of reincarnation. Gradually reaching higher levels throughout several births in order to attain final release is known as the 'right path.' The 'wrong path' is its opposite. It leads to an endless cycle of births, deaths, and rebirths in a particular world, with its resultant suffering."

The Ajivika concluded, "According to the teaching of the sacred texts of Makkhâli, pleasure and pain attach themselves to our atom of life, through which our deeds in former lives will be the cause of our joys or sorrows in our future lives. As soon as life penetrates the fetus, it is that atom of life that determines for that particular body fortune or misfortune, loss of goods, difficulties encountered in life, establishment in a certain place, way of life, loss of friends, goods, servants, pleasure and pain, birth and death. Such is the teaching of Makkhâli."

The Jain Doctrine of Nirgrantha

Nikkanta-vati

Finding contradiction between the premises and the conclusions of the Ajivika's discourse, Manimekhalaï went next to a naked Jain ascetic, whose doctrine is called

135

Nirgrantha, and asked him, "What is the divinity you worship? What is the content of the teachings of your holy books? What is it that binds human beings to life and how can the bonds be broken to be free of this slavery?"

The Jain ascetic replied, "We worship Arhat Parameshti, the supreme prophet, before whom the ten sovereign gods, the Indras,* bow. Our doctrine is expounded in various works, such as the *Anga-âgama*, the *Pûrva-âgama*, and the *Bahushruti-âgama*.

"These texts deal with ten main subjects: *dharmâstikâya* (evolution); *adharmâstikâya* (immutability); *âkâya* (*âkâsha*, space); *kâla* (time); *paramanu* (the atoms); *karma* (action, that is, the bonds created by our good or evil deeds); and *nirvâna* (release).

"All these subjects are dealt with separately as well as in relation to everything that exists since, on reflection, everything is at the same time permanent and impermanent, subject to birth, a span of life, and death. A valid teaching takes into account the importance of good and evil deeds, the resulting bonds (*bandha*), and the means of attaining the cessation of existence (*vidu*).

"An object has its own nature, but can modify it according to what it is associated with which is why all objects are at the same time permanent and impermanent, allowing the coexistence of the three states of appearance, duration, and disappearance.

"The fact that a margosa seed germinates, grows, and becomes a tree, demonstrates the permanent nature of the margosa. Nevertheless, the seed does not subsist in the tree and is therefore impermanent. In the same way, when lentils are cooked and made into a dish, the nature of the lentils is not destroyed, although they cease to be lentils.

"The principle of evolution (*dharmâstikâya*) exists in all things and allows change. At the same time how-

---

* There are forty-two Bhuvana-Indras, Regents of the Heavenly worlds; thirty-two Viyantara-Indras, Regents of the Spheres; twenty-two Kalpa-Indras, Regents of the Cosmic Cycles; the Spirit of the Sun, and that of the Moon; Nara-Indra, the Regent of Men; Mrigendra, the Regent of Animals.

ever, the principle of immutability (*adharmâstikâya*) is immanent and allows things to exist without change.

"The principle of time (*kâlâstikâya*) measures duration, from the smallest unit (a wink) to the immense cycle of the *kalpas* (eons).

"The principle of space (*akâshâstikâya*) determines dimension, within which objects exist.

"When the principle of life (*jivâstikâya*) combines with matter to take the form of a living body, the capacity of perception and enjoyment through the five senses (taste, sight, touch, sound, and smell) appears.

"The non-living (*ajivâstikâya*), meaning inert matter, is formed of atoms (*paramanu*). The atom exists of itself, independently, but can also form part of a unit or body. It is the atom of life that becomes the center of a body. The other atoms collect around it. On combining with a body, the principle of life (*jîva*) becomes capable of good and evil deeds and remains chained to existence as a result of its actions.

"The elimination of causes (the fruit of actions) and of their resulting bonds allows release to be attained (*nirvâna*). Release takes place when the emotions of pleasure and pain are completely eliminated thus suppressing the effects of our actions, whether good or evil."

Sâmkhya

Once the representative of Nirgrantha had left, an adept of Sâmkhya came to explain the principles of his school to Manimekhalaï. According to him, the universe was not created and has no beginning. Basic nature (*prakriti*) is the matrix from which everything that exists issued forth. Although difficult to conceive of, basic nature is omnipresent, but without any activities of its own, and is formed of three trends (*guna*): centrifugal (*tamas*), centripetal (*sattva*), and orbital (*rajas*).

From this primordial state of being came forth the Great Principle (*mahat*), also called intelligence (*buddhi*). It is from *mahat* that ether or space (*âkâsha*) was born; from the latter, the gaseous state, or air; from the gaseous state, the igneous state (*agni*); from the latter, the liquid state (*appu, apah*); from the liquid state came forth the solid state (the earth element). From their combination, thought (*manas*) was born. From thought sprang the notion of identity, the ego (*ahamkara*). From ether or space was born vibration, the sound perceived by the ear. From air was born touch, perceived by the skin. From fire was born sight, perceived by the eye. From water, taste, perceived by the tongue. From the solid element, smell, perceived by the nose.

In the body, these perceptions correspond to the organs of action: the tongue for speech, the hand to touch, the feet for directional movement, which depends on sight, the anus for evacuation (the solid element), the sexual organ for generation (the element water).

It is by transformations of the elements (*bhûta*) that mountains, trees, and so forth take form. Then in the same way they develop by means of an evolutionary process, they return to their source by the contrary process. They thus return to an undifferentiated state, which fills the whole of space and exists for ever.

The other basic principle is consciousness, called *purusha* (the universal man), which is easier to understand. The three trends, or *guna*, of matter have nothing to do with the nature of *purusha*. Matter is unconscious, whereas *purusha* is the embodiment of consciousness, entirely independent of matter. *Purusha*, too, is not born of anything. Consciousness is omnipresent and eternal, and is not divided into various aspects as in the case of the senses. It is present in our mental structure as the instrument of knowledge, but remains distinct from the body.

The perceptible world is thus formed of twenty-five entities (*tattva*), which are the five elements, the five senses, the five organs of action, the mind (*manas*), intelligence (*buddhi*), the notion of self (*ahamkara*), consciousness (*chitta*) and life (*jîva*), also called the soul (*âtman*). These twenty-five principles were born of *prakriti* (basic nature). *Purusha* is the soul, the principle of life.

Manmekhalaï listened to this account with lively interest.

Vaisheshika (Scientism)

After listening to this important account, Manimekhalaï pursued her inquiry with a teacher of Vaisheshika (experimental philosophy) requesting him to expound its essential tenets.

"We envisage," he said, "six permanent basic principles, which are: substance, nature (qualities), action, common characters, special characters, and collective characters.

"Of these principles, qualities and action depend on substance while action is the cause of all progress.

"Substance, or matter, comprises nine components: earth, water, fire, air, ether, direction, time, consciousness or soul (*âtman*) and thought (*manas*). Of these elements, earth is perceived in five ways by sound, touch, color, smell, and taste. Each of the four following elements is perceived by one sense less: sound, touch, color and taste for water; sound, touch and color for fire; sound and touch for air; and sound alone for ether.

"The qualities of matter are: sound, touch, visibility, taste, smell, largeness, smallness, hardness, softness, heaviness, lightness, shape, the right side, the left side, superiority, inferiority, anteriority, and posteriority. These characteristics, which are essential for capacity of action, are common to all forms of matter.

"Existence is the common superior aspect, duration and death the common inferior aspects. The fundamental element is the atom. Atoms are numberless and autonomous. It is impossible to separate quality from the object to which it belongs.

"Everything that exists is formed only of conglomerates of material elements. The qualities of an object are derived from its substance."

Thus concluded the teacher of Vaisheshika.

Finally, Manimekhalaï addressed herself to a member of the Bhûta-vâdi (elementalist) sect, who said:

"When fig leaves are macerated with sugar and other substances fermentation takes place. This phenomenon is similar to consciousness and sensation which develop when certain elements are put together. Then, when these elements separate and return to their individual state, consciousness gradually vanishes, like the resonance of a drum that little by little fades and dies away.

"By combining together, the various categories of elements in which consciousness is present give birth to living beings, while inert elements, on combining together, produce the various forms of inanimate matter. These two categories work independently as regards their formation, duration, and disappearance. Each living being is animated by a consciousness to which its components give rise at the very moment of its coming into existence. Such is the natural course of things. The other aspects of our doctrine concerning the *tattvas*, the world's constituent parts, which I could expound, are identical to the concepts of the Lokâyatas, the pure materialists.

"Of the means of proof, only direct perception (*pratyaksha*) is acceptable. All other means of knowledge, including deduction (*anumâna*), must be rejected. There exists no reality other than the one we perceive in the present and the enjoyments we derive from it.

"It is absurd to believe in the existence of another life in which we would gather the fruits of our deeds in this one. Our existence as well as our joys and sorrows terminate with our life."

Knowing the events of her former life, Manimekhalaï smiled when the materialist affirmed that no one could remember a previous life, but, when she told him of her own experience, he replied that she was laboring under a delusion, like those who believe in the gods and take their dreams for realities. This was why her statements proved nothing.

She then asked him how he could know who his parents were, since he rejected deduction as a means of knowledge, inasmuch as many basic realities could only be known by deduction.

In such a way, in the great city of Vanji, Manime-khalaï, in her male disguise, was able to listen to the teachings of the five major traditions, which are: the deist tradition, including Nyâya, Vedism, Shivaism, Vishnuism, and the cult of Brahmâ; the Ajivika tradition, which includes Jainism and Buddhism; and the philosophical theories—Sâmkhya (cosmology), Vaisheshika (scientism) and Bhûta-vâdi (materialism), which also embraces Lokâyata (atheism)—making up the ten philosophical systems mentioned in this chapter.

Realizing that none of these systems could give a proper solution to a good rule of life, she deemed it useless to criticize them.

 CANTO TWENTY-EIGHT

Manimekhalaï Goes to Kanchi

Searching for Mâdhavi, Sutâmati, and Aravana Adigal in the great city of Vanji, Manimekhalaï crossed the suburbs spreading outside the walls that protected many princely dwellings. Groups of soldiers with their officers kept watch over the inner city as though the fierce warriors of some enemy king were threatening.

The inner city was surrounded by a moat, into which by means of underground pipes flowed the waste waters coming from the luxurious dwellings, but only the scented waste waters like those used to wash the ladies' tresses or impregnated with the sandal paste men and women spread on their bodies which dissolves when they bathe in baths mechanically filled and emptied as desired. Into it there also flowed the perfumed waters used to spray the crowd during the celebrations for the king's birthday; the waters used by heads of family, practicing the five virtues, to wash the sublime feet of ascetics; the waters discharged when pious persons cleansed the basins of the public fountains, impregnated with the smell of smoke from aloe wood and other aromatic woods used in the rites; and the waters mixed with various perfumes, sprinkled for freshness on the floors of rich dwellings.

Only such waters flowed into the moat, spreading delightful fragrances, so that the crocodiles and fish that disported themseleves there lost the usually nauseating smell of their bodies.

On the surface of the water floated large lotus flowers, red and white water liles, and blue iris. All these many-colored flowers made the moats look like the bow of the god Indra.*

Various sorts of imposing machines could be seen on the very high outer walls, serving for attack or for repulsing the assault of enemies. Between the outer and inner walls grew impenetrable brushwood entanglements. At the center of the fortifications was a high gate surmounted by a tower of several floors, on which many flags were flying. Painted white and covered with frescoes, from afar it looked like a mountain of marble. It was through this gate that Manimekhalaï entered the city.

In a playful mood, with lively interest, the bracelet-wearing girl disguised as a boy visited the city. She saw the wide avenues where many guards kept watch over the rich dwellings; the quarter of the fishermen, where they sold their fish; that of the white-salt merchants; of the sellers of toddy (palm-wine) and other food products; the street of the butchers; the street of the merchants of betel and the five kinds of spices and aromatics; then the road of the potters and of the brass-vessel workers; the street of the smelters who cast bronze receptacles; the street of the goldsmiths and those who process nuggets to extract the pure gold; the street of the carpenters; that of the artists who make plaster statues; the street of the painters to whom we owe the pictures of the gods who pour their blessings on men; that of the tanners who make leather bucklers; of the tailors; of the makers of garlands of flowers; the street of the learned astrologers; that of the

* The rainbow.

musicians (*pânâ*), expert in vocal music and in playing the various instruments, who know the major and minor modes, as well as elocution and poetic meters.

There was the street of the jewelers who make mother-of-pearl bracelets; the street of those who make necklaces of precious stones; the street of the dancers, expert in the two kinds of dances, classical dances for the palace and dancing suitable for the public at large.

In the alleys of the bazaar, eight varieties of grain were sold: rice, grass seeds (wheat), four kinds of millet, and two sorts of wild rice.

Further on was the street of the panegyrists, who composed eulogies of the king, which they declaimed standing or seated; that of the experts who calculate time and announce it every *nâtika* (24 minutes); the street of the common prostitutes who sell men the pleasure of their body; the street of the weavers who make cloth so fine that it is difficult to distinguish the cross threads and dye it in bright colors.

The street of the controllers who check gold content on touchstones and own houses of many floors; the street of the Brahmans, who perform the daily rites, careful not to make an error; the street where the ministers have their magnificent houses; and the street of the high officials, like the chief of staff.

In the center were the public buildings with waiting areas arranged in the shade of great trees and the squares at the crossings of three, four, or five avenues.

There was a quarter where the elephant drivers lived, who tamed recently captured animals and trained them with skill, and also a quarter for the horsemen who teach the golden-collared horses to amble.

Manimekhalaï admired the artificial hills from which cascades fell by mechanical means; the parks whose trees laden with flowers inspired all with an overwhelming desire to go and relax there; the pools with such limpid water that the inhabitants of heaven left their paradise to visit their banks; hospices to welcome travelers; vast palaces with golden domes and monasteries for ascetics, which in their splendor rivaled the seven temples built by Indra at Puhâr.

These monasteries were the permanent residences of monks who preached the holy doctrine taught by the Buddha. The ascetics who travel through the air sometimes stop there for a few moments of agreeable repose.

There, Manimekhalaï found Kovalan's father who after the death of his only son had renounced the world to dedicate himself to the ascetic life, taking the name of Mashâttuvan. She prostrated herself at his feet and informed him of all that had happened and of how she took care of the misfortunate with the aid of her magic bowl Cow of Abundance, which she held in her hand. She recounted how the sovereign of Java had attained the state of royalty due to the good works he had performed during his previous life with the aid of the bowl, distributing food to the poor and derelict, and how she had led him to Manipallavam where the divine pedestal had revealed to him the circumstances of his former life. She also told him how the divine protectress of the isle, Tivatilakaï, had freed the king from the anguish caused by the events of his past life and had revealed to them that Mâdhavi, Sutâmati, and Aravana Adigal were safely in Vanji, having escaped the destruction of Puhâr, devoured by the sea.

She explained that she had then sent the king of Java back home and had come to Vanji, where she had taken on the appearance of a boy in order to interrogate the competent representatives of the various creeds and study their doctrines. She added that she deemed it useless to mention these theories, which were not worth taking seriously. For this reason, she had come to seek Aravana Adigal, to learn from him the wise teaching of the Buddha's doctrine, far superior to all others.

"Holy woman! For me it is a great privilege to have had this chance of meeting you. When I learned that your father and his noble spouse were dead as a consequence of the errors committed during their previous lives, and that the prosperous city of Madura had been delivered to the flames, I realized that worldly life was illusory and that wealth, like the body, was transitory. I thus decided to adopt the life of a begging ascetic and to follow the illuminating law of the *dharma* that the Buddha taught us. I will explain why, having chosen the monastic life,

I came to this beautiful city that bears the name of the Vanji flower.

"One day, many years ago, Kuttako Cheralâtan, the great and noble Chera sovereign of Kuttanâtu (Kerala), who planted his emblem, the bow, on the Himalayas, had come to visit a garden together with his concubines, whose lips were red as coral and whose waists were slim as those of drums shaped like an hourglass. He merely wished for a pleasurable rest surrounded by his courtiers.

"Now, in this garden there was a stone terrace set aside for ascetics. Some *dharmacharanas*, messengers of the faith, who preach the Buddha's *dharma* and possess the power of traveling through the sky encumbered with black clouds, came down there to rest. They were returning from a pilgrimage consisting of encircling, from left to right, the holy mountain of Samanoli on the isle of Lanka.

"In his previous life the king had practiced severe austerities. He welcomed these ascetics with joy, greeted them, washed their lotus-like feet, and offered them the four kinds of food (what is eaten, what is drunk, what is licked, and what is bitten), in which can be found the six kinds of flavors (bitter, spicy, sour, salty, astringent, and sweet). He also offered them several gifts, brought by the royal officials who accompanied him, after which he worshiped them and spoke their praises.

"The ascetics then spoke to the king about the *dharma*, of the sufferings that birth brings us and the bliss of those that cease to be reborn. They reminded him of the four truths proclaimed by him who first taught the *dharma*, the Being of Light, the incarnation of all virtues, whose precious words, like ambrosia, fill hearts with joy. They said to him, 'Your father's ninth ancestor, who was also called Kovalan, was a great friend of the Chera king Kottako Cherulatan. As a reward for the merits he had accumulated through his good deeds, he had the privilege of listening to the *dharma*'s teachings. After this, he gave away to the poor and wretched all the riches he had acquired as well as those honestly piled up by his forefathers. He put on the ascetics' garb and has become a great saint. He it was who, in favor of the Highly-endowed

145

(*Sugata*), had a *chaitya* (sanctuary) built of plaster on the top of a mountain in the Chera country. Its whiteness is dazzling and its towers rise up to heaven. This sanctuary, which is open to all, delivers those that visit it from all evil inclinations.'

"I myself came as a pilgrim to visit this temple and when I learned from the ascetics of limitless knowledge who dwell here that Puhâr was going to be swallowed up by the sea, I forwent returning there and stayed here alone.

"Manimekhalaï! You have chosen the *dharma*'s virtuous path! You must know that your father, who was put to death when the evil deeds he had committed in his former life reached maturity, has now attained a new existence in the heavenly world as a result of his previous virtuous actions, after which he must once more endure the effects of his evil deeds.

"However, O young liana, when he has finally exhausted the fruits of all his actions, he will be reborn for the last time in the holy city of Kapilavastu, where he once benefited from the teaching of the Buddha who, in the shade of the pipal, in his goodness, showed men the way of the *dharma*. This is why he will finally attain *nirvâna*, together with Kannaki his wife. I managed to learn what I am telling you from the ascetics who have the power of knowing the past, present, and future, and who control the running of time.

"O daughter, beautiful as a peacock! You have been able to know your future thanks to the words of Tuvatikan, the genie who dwells in the statue on the pillar. I too have listened to the teachings of Aravana Adigal explaining the way of the *dharma*. It is to him that we owe all the good which happens to you and to the town of Kanchi. O flowering liana! The day on which Aravana Adigal left for Kanchi, your mother Mâdhavi and her companion Sutâmati departed with him.

"O charming girl with beautiful bracelets! Listen! Here you can meet monks who have emigrated from Kanchi, since, due to the lack of rain, the town of Kanchi with its golden parapets has lost its splendor. The whole surrounding countryside suffers from famine. Many have

146

died. The wealthy no longer have the means of offering ascetics even a symbolic offering of food.

"You possess the balm that assuages hunger and can save many precious lives. It is your duty to go to that town where, like a rain cloud in the proper season, you can give back life to the land which languishes and to its inhabitants."

Such was Mashâttuvan's discourse to Manimekhalaï.

Manimekhalaï of the splendid jewels prostrated herself before Mashâttuvan and took her leave. Then, holding the divine bowl Cow of Abundance in her hands, she rose in the air and flew westwards, over the ancient city with its flag-surmounted walls, and then turned to the north. Soon she saw the city of Kanchi and her heart was moved when she perceived that this town, formerly like Amaravati, the capital of the god Indra descended to earth, had lost its splendor due to the misery that follows after famine.

Circling the old town's surrounding walls where many standards waved, she descended in the midst of the city and went to pray in the sanctuary (*chaitya*) built by Ilamkilli, the younger brother of King Killi who wore ankle-bracelets as a sign of his noble deeds. In this place the image of the tree of knowledge, the Bodhi, was worshiped. The tree's trunk and main branches were of solid gold and its leaves were made of emeralds.

She then went south-west and reached a magnificent orchard filled with honey-scented trees.

The liveried guardian, seeing Manimekhalaï in the garden of flowers, betook himself to Ilamkilli, the sovereign protector of the land. Greeting him with hands joined, he said, "Manimekhalaï, the daughter of Kovalan, saint without equal in the whole jambu-rose-apple continent, has arrived in this land, holding in her hand the magic bowl Cow of Abundance, like a black rain-bringing cloud. She is now in the flower garden called Dharmada-Vanam."

The news of Manimekhalaï's arrival was greeted with joy by the king, happy to see the predictions of the statue of the pillar come true. Surrounded by his ministers and the dignitaries of the realm, he went to visit the girl, who had kept her male disguise, and said to her, "I am unable to understand why this land, once so flourishing, has now fallen into misery.

"Has my scepter failed to maintain justice? Have the ascetics failed in their disciplines, or have the women with their flower-adorned braids strayed from the path of duty? The fact is that the land suffers from lack of rain. Not knowing what could be the cause of this disaster, I was plunged into the deepest perplexity, when a goddess appeared before me.

"She said, 'Abandon your grief! As a reward of your former good deeds, a young woman will appear in this town, holding a divine bowl in her hands. All living beings nourished thanks to this inexhaustible bowl will come back to life and this great country will be saved from disaster. Thanks to her, at Indra's order, the rains will arrive abundantly and many other miracles will take place after her arrival.

" 'Never again shall the waters fail in your realm, even though the rains delay their arrival. Near to the city you shall command a pool and a park to be constructed with the greatest skill, exactly reproducing the isle of Manipallavam and the lake of the Bull's Muzzle (Gomukhi). It will be filled with an abundance of water, just as those of old did there.' Having spoken thus, the goddess disappeared.

"Following the goddess's order, we constructed the lake and planted the park."

The king conducted Manimekhalaï there, and she was filled with joy at the sight of the park which looked just like the isle of Manipallavam. She at once exerted herself in having a pedestal built, according to the very same measurements as the Buddha's pedestal on Manipallavam, which had revealed to her her previous existence. She also caused a temple to be built with statues of Tivatilakaï and the goddess Manimekhalâ and placed the divine bowl Cow of Abundance on the sacred pedestal. Then, in the Buddha's name, she invited all creatures to come and nourish themselves on the food that the divine bowl ceaselessly produced. The news of her coming at once spread through the various communities of the town, where eighteen languages were spoken.

Around Manimekhalaï, beautiful as a doll, her pubis resembling a cobra's hood, there soon gathered the blind, the deaf, the crippled, the orphans, the idiots, the ascetics who performed severe practices, all those that were hungry, the poor dressed in rags, and hundreds of thousands of other living beings, who crowded together to approach her.

To all she distributed such quantities of food that the hands of those who received it could hardly bear its weight.

The divine little bowl produced incredible quantities of food and thus a great number of precious lives were saved. Its effect was similar to that of water, earth, the season, and good tillage, which at sowing time, together with the ascetics' blessing, give forth an abundant harvest.

All those that survived thanks to the Cow of Abundance then came to thank Manimekhalaï and showered her with blessings for having saved them from the pangs of hunger. Because she had fed a very holy person in her former life, she now appeared as a dispenser of prosperity in her native land.

Once the seasonal rains had returned, the people began to come back to the ancient city, formerly so prosperous. Mâdhavi, Sutâmati, and Aravana Adigal, leaving their refuge, arrived at the travelers' hospice where they found Manimekhalaï who, rising quickly, came to receive the sage and bowed before his sacred feet which she washed with fresh water. She then caused him to sit on a raised seat and, at the appropriate hour, offered him and his companions the four kinds of food and the most exquisite beverages, representing the six different tastes. When they had taken refreshment, she offered them betel, areca nuts, and camphor, praying that what she had so long and so ardently desired should be accomplished.

Renouncing her male disguise and returning to her natural form, she came and prostrated herself at the feet of Aravana Adigal, the sage.

Manimekhalaï Receives from Aravana Adigal the Teaching of the *Dharma* and Adopts the Monastic Life

Aravana Adigal, who exerted himself in spreading the Buddhist *dharma*, blessed Manimekhalaï prostrated before him and explained to the young girl the reason for the destruction of Puhâr, devoured by the sea.

"Pilivalaï, the daughter of the king of the Nâgäs (the serpent race), on pilgrimage to the isle of Manipallavam, entrusted the child she had had by the Chola king Neduvel Killi of the high crown to Kambala Chetty, a merchant in woolen blankets, whose vessel was the only one to stop over at the island on the route to India, for him to take back to his father.

"Having taken the newborn child with all the respect due to his royal origin, Kambala Chetty set sail for his homeland, but in the darkness of the night, the vessel was shipwrecked not far from the shore. Chetty, the only survivor, sought the child in vain. He then had to inform the king of his loss and the king was overwhelmed with dismay. Wandering along the shore for many days, he sought in vain some trace of his son. Forgetful of his official duties, he neglected to celebrate the annual festival in Indra's honor, which provoked the god's fury. The sovereign of the gods then summoned Manimekhalâ, the sea goddess, to order the sea to swallow up Puhâr as had been predicted.

"One of the ancestors of your adored father, Kovalan, who bore his very name, well-known for his benevolence to all living creatures, was journeying a long time ago on a shark-infested ocean. His boat was shipwrecked and disappeared under the waves, like a needle lost in a woolen rug. For seven days, your ancestor managed to struggle among the waves of the bottomless ocean.

"This man had unfailingly practiced the five virtues

and recognized the four truths. So, when the moment approached for him to lose his life, a shudder ran through the carpet that bears Indra's throne. The god at once summoned the goddess of the ocean and said, 'This merchant, struggling for seven days in the sea, possesses the same virtues as the Bodhisattva, the master of us all who, in the shade of the pipal, practiced the ascetic life. This man is a person of rare importance amongst the living. He must be delivered from danger, so that the ten rules of conduct (*paramita*)* are observed in the world and the wheel of the *dharma* goes on turning smoothly.'

"The goddess Manimekhalâ thus helped your ancestor and guided him to shore. It was the Charanas, the omniscient sages who travel through the air, who recounted this tale to your father, and it was as a sign of gratitude to the goddess who had saved his forebear that he wanted you to bear her name. On the night of your birth, the goddess appeared in a dream, as clear as reality, to your mother and predicted your future renunciation.

"When, by the will of the goddess and the curse of Indra, the city of Puhâr was devoured by the sea, your mothers and I had fled and, for love of you, we retired to the city of Kanchi."

Such was the discourse of Aravana Adigal.

Having listened respectfully to the holy man, Manimekhalaï bowed before him and said, "Tivatilakaï, the guardian of the Buddha's pedestal, had already told me of all these events, and it is by her instructions that I adopted a disguise to come and learn the doctrines preached by the representatives of the various sects and study their Scriptures (*Nûl, Sûtra*). In truth, I was attracted to none of them, because they were unconvincing. Nevertheless, I listened with patience in the disguise I had adopted. I now wait for this most holy man to teach me the true *dharma*."

* The perfections (*paramita*) are generally considered as ten, sometimes reduced to eight, or even six. These ten rules are: *dâna* (charity), *shîla* (purity of conduct), *kshanti* (patience), *vîrya* (courage), *dhyâna* (meditation), *prajñâ* (intelligence), *upaya* (utilization of the proper means), *pranadhâna* (dedication), *bala* (energy), and *jñâna* (knowledge).

The first Master (on whose teachings Buddhist logic rests) is Jinendra (the great Jain prophet), according to whom the means of knowledge are limited to direct perception and deduction.

Shuttunarvu (pratyaksha)*: Perception.

Perception is the recognition of the existence of something through the organs of sense. Name (*nâma*), category (*jâti*), quality (*guna*), and action (*kriya*) are not included since they can be known equally by deduction or inference.

Karuda (anumâna): Deduction.

Deduction rests on a syllogism that comprises a given fact (*paksha*), an argument or reason (*hetu*), an example (*tittantam, drishtanta*) or illustration (*udahârana*), and the application (*upayana*) to a particular case. The conclusion (*nigama*), or general formulation, appears once the given fact is demonstrated and confirmed by the illustration.

Example:

Given fact (*paksha*): There is fire on the mountain.

Reason (*hetu*): Because smoke can be seen.

Example (*udahârana*): As in a kitchen.

Particular case (*upayana*): It is the mountain that is smoking.

Conclusion (*nigama*): There is no smoke without fire.

The argument uses a comparison with elements of the same nature (*sadharma*). These are then confirmed by comparing them with elements of a different nature (*vaidharmiya drishtanta*), such as: "Water does not smoke." Thus the general conclusion is reached: "There is no smoke without fire."

The case changes if the argument implies a notion

---

* For clarity's sake, the more generally known Sanskrit terms have been added and sometimes used instead of the Tamil or Pali terms found in the text. The glossary at the end of the book provides definitions of the terms as well as identifying them as either Sanskrit or Tamil.

affecting the "nature of the given fact" (*paksha-dharma-vachana*) or when the proposition goes without saying (*svabhâva*).

If, for example, we affirm "The 'Word' is not eternal because it is the result of an action." In speaking of action, we introduce a notion into the given fact (*paksha-dharma*) of which the implication by analogy (*sapaksha*) is that whatever is the result of an action, like a clay pot, cannot be eternal. On the other hand, by considering the opposite argument (*vipaksha*), we see that some things exist which are not the result of an action and are eternal, like space. We thus obtain a favorable argument (*sapaksha*) and a counter argument (*vipaksha*). We cannot therefore generalize the counter argument (*vipaksha vyâpi*) and affirm that the Word is eternal, in the absence of a concordance (*vijatireka*) of the arguments (*pramâna*).

Negative arguments (*pramâna*) are of two kinds. We can affirm that there is no clay pot in a given place because the person concerned does not see any. But if we speak of hare's horns, we do not see them because they do not exist.

If we pretend that the clay pot does not exist because it is not visible in a given place, we introduce too general a term into the given fact (*paksha-dharma-vachana*), thus extending a conclusion to the kind "whatever is not visible does not exist," like the hare's horns, to what is not visible at a given time and place, like the clay pot. If, in another connection, we envisage the inverse argument: "anything that exists in a given place is visible," this is not applicable to a myrobolam seed enclosed by your fist.

To demonstrate a proposition properly, both positive and negative arguments must therefore be used. The effect "smoke" proves the existence of the cause "fire." The cause can therefore be deduced from the effect, saying, "there is no smoke without fire." But the effect cannot be deduced with any certitude from the cause, saying, "there is no fire without smoke." The certitude of the connection between cause and effect is only possible in the sense effect-cause.

Anvayam (logical connection) implies a natural relation between an apparent effect and a cause. To deduce the cause from the effect can be misleading. Seeing smoke rising and spreading, we can deduce the presence of fire. But a dust cloud can also rise and spread out. A similarity of appearances can lead to an erroneous generalization.

Ananvayam anumâna (occasional connection) refers to a supposed relation between an effect and a presumed cause.

A person who, one day, in a given place, sees a prostitute beside an ass, and the next day sees the ass alone, risks deceiving himself if he thereby deduces the presence of the prostitute. Negatively, the absence of smoke tends to make us believe there is no fire—which is false.

Vijatireka anumâna (absence of logical connection) It being understood that an ass has neither a fox's nor a dog's tail above its posterior parts, when someone declares that his ass has not got a fox's tail, it cannot be deduced that it has a dog's tail.

In order to reach a certain conclusion (*nigama*), it is therefore essential that the example (*drishtanta*), the particular case (*upayana*), and the conclusion are implicit in the given fact (*paksha*).

Aravana Adigal then explained to Manimekhalaï that a generalized conclusion cannot be drawn on the basis of a particular case (*upayana*). According to him, the only elements for valid deduction are therefore the proposition (*pratijña*) or given fact (*paksha*), the argument or reason (*hetu*), and the example (*drishtanta*).

Having thus criticized the other opinions, Adigal then expounded his own point of view on inference.

The Buddhist Theory of Deduction as an Instrument of Knowledge

Certain ways of envisaging given fact, argument, and example (*paksha, hetu, drishtanta*) in a syllogism are correct, while others are wrong.

First of all it is important to determine clearly whether the given fact (*paksha*) to be demonstrated refers to a "concrete object possessing its own qualities" (*dharmi*), and whether the said qualities belong to it exclusively and are not common to other objects.

When, for example, the question is to know whether the "Word" (the primordial vibration of the ether that gave birth to the world) is eternal or impermanent (belonging to the created), the subject envisaged is the divine word (*shabda*), and the quality to be demonstrated (*sadhya-dharma*) is the fact of being eternal or impermanent.*

A clear definition of the nature of the given fact (*paksha-dharma-vachana*) is indispensable to a valid demonstration. It is therefore necessary to determine whether the characteristics of the given fact are met with in analogous cases (*sapaksha*) and are absent in others (*vipaksha*).

If, for example, we declare that the Word is impermanent (qualificative to be demonstrated) by comparing (*sâmânya*) it to a clay pot, we suggest that the Word is impermanent because it is created, the implication being that all non-created objects are eternal, like space (*âkâsha*), and all created objects are perishable, like the clay pot. Inherent qualities are found, however, only in objects of the same nature (*sapaksha*), and never in objects of different nature (*vipaksha*). Examples (*drishtanta*) are thus valid only if they refer to an object of the same nature (*sadharmya*) as the one envisaged in the given fact, whereas if a difference in nature is evident in the argument, the conclusion is uncertain.

A concrete given fact (*paksha*), a conclusive argument (*hetu*), and an evident example (*drishtanta*) are essential for the demonstration of a proposition beyond any shadow of doubt. A valid argument (*hetu*) requires three elements: it must be applicable to the given fact;

---

* According to Indian concepts, the basic element is ether (*âkâsha*), whose expansion gave birth to space. Sound (*nâda*) is the vibration of the ether from which all other elements sprang. The term "Word," used by the Gnostics for the primordial vibration (*In principium erat Verbum*) corresponds to the Indian term *nâda* (sound) in this context.

attributable to a similar subject; and not attributable to a different subject.

Non-valid Given Facts (Paksha)

In an argument, there are nine kinds of non-valid propositions.

1. *Pratyaksha viruddham* (Contrary to the evidence of the senses): such as, "Sound is not perceptible to the ear."

2. *Anumâna viruddham* (Contrary to deduction or experience): affirming that a clay pot is immortal.

3. *Suvachanam viruddham* (Contradiction of terms): saying, for example, "My mother is barren."

4. *Loka viruddham* (Contrary to general opinion): saying, for example, "The luminary of the night is not called the moon."

5. *Agama viruddham* (Contrary to authoritative texts). Since for Scientist Philosophy (Vaisheshika) the Word does not exist, to say it is immortal contradicts the text.

6. *Aprasiddha visheshana* (Non-existent qualificative). To speak of the immortality of the Word to a Buddhist, for whom the theory of the Word is a fiction, has no meaning, whereas it is admissible for an adept of Sâmkhya.

7. *Aprasiddha visheshyam* (Non-existent subject). To speak of the nature of the Word to a Buddhist, for whom the Word does not exist, is meaningless.

8. *Aprasiddha ubhayam* (Non-existent qualificative and subject). This is a case of a Buddhist saying, "eternal happiness is an experience of the soul" to a materialist (Vaisheshika), who believes neither in the soul nor in eternal happiness.

9. *Aprasiddha sambandham* (There being no question of relation). To try to demonstrate to a Buddhist that the Word is not eternal is pointless, since for him the

156

Word does not exist and there is therefore no question of its being eternal or not.

Non-valid Arguments

(*Hetu*)

Reasonings of which the fault lies in the argument are of three kinds: *asiddham* (unconvincing); *anaikantikam* (non-exclusive); *viruddham* (contradictory).

1. *Asiddham* (Unconvincing arguments) are of four kinds:

Ubhaya asiddham (Not valid from any point of view). To say, for example, "The Word is eternal because it is invisible," is not an argument for anyone.

Anyantara asiddham (Unacceptable for one of the parties). The assertion, "The Word cannot be eternal because it is the result of an action," is not acceptable for a Sâmkhya adept for whom the Word is an integral part of the prime cause and cannot therefore be a result.

Siddha asiddham (Non-determining argument). Without being certain whether what one sees is mist or smoke, the presence of fire cannot be affirmed.

Ashraya asiddham (Argument resting on an unproven fact). To say, "The Word exists because it is the vibration of the ether," is valueless for those who deny the existence of the ether.

2. *Anaikantikam* (Non-exclusive arguments) are of six kinds:

Sadhârana (General). To say, for example, "The Word is not eternal because it is intelligible," when the fact of being a knowable object belongs both to ephemeral things (the clay pot) and permanent things like space.

Asadhârana (Particular). Example: "The Word is eternal because sound is audible." But even if sound is audible other eternal things are not. The argument is not valid.

Sapaksha ekadesha vritti and *Vipaksha vyâpi* (Proposition valid in a single case, but also in contrary cases). If we say, "The Word is not eternal because it is not the result of an action," this is also the case of lightning which is transitory and is not the result of an action. But space, which is permanent, is not the result of an action and ephemeral things, like the clay pot, are the result of an action. An argument that applies to a similar thing, as well as to different things, cannot be used for demonstration.

Vipaksha ekadesha vritti, sapaksha vyâpi (Argument applying to a single different case and to all similar cases). If we say, "The Word is a result of an action because it is impermanent," we place it parallel with the clay pot, the result of an action, which is ephemeral. But lightning, which is not the result of an action, is also ephemeral. Moreover, the ether, which is not the result of an action, is eternal. The argument is therefore not valid.

Ubhaya ekadesha vritti anaikantikam (Argument applicable to another particular case, but also to various contrary cases). Example: "The Word is immortal because it is immaterial." There are similar things that are immortal, such as space or the atom, etc. However, although space is immaterial, the atom is material. The argument does not apply to all similar things. Among the different things that are transitory the clay pot, pleasure, etc. can be included. The pot has substance (material), while pleasure does not, even though it is also ephemeral. The argument applies to the pot, but not to pleasure. The argument thus applies both to similar and dissimilar things. Doubt remains as to whether an immaterial object can be immortal, like space, or ephemeral, like pleasure. The argument is not valid.

Vritti vyabhichari (Indetermination). In this case, the argument is not sufficient to demonstrate the proposition. The first says, "The Word is ephemeral because it is the result of an action." The second affirms, "It is immortal because it is perceived by the ear as a word (*shabdatva*)." The two arguments are equally inadequate.

3. *Viruddham* (Contradictory argument). This kind of non-conclusive argument is of four types: contrary to the qualificative attributed to the subject; contrary to a particular aspect of the qualificative attributed to the subject; contrary to the very nature of the subject; contrary to a characteristic of the nature of the subject.

Dharma svarûpa viparita sâdhana vritti (The characteristics of the argument are in contradiction to the qualificative attributed to the subject). If we say, "The Word is eternal because it is the result of an action," the argument does not prove the eternity of the world, but on the contrary, implies it is ephemeral.

Dharma vishesha viparita sâdhana vritti (The argument contradicts a particularity of the quality attributed to the subject). Consider the proposition, "The organs of the senses, which are the instruments for perceiving things, are utilized by the soul which is independent of them": the senses, which are several, are here taken in the aggregate, like the pieces forming a suite of furniture. But the components of a suite (bed, chairs, etc.) can be used by others apart from their owner. The organs of perception form a part of the body of their owner; but the body, here identified with the ego, is distinct from the soul. The soul, which is indivisible and organless, is presented as having organs. The argument contradicts this particularity of the soul.

Dharmi svarûpa viparita sâdhana vritti (Argument contradicting the very nature of the subject). In this case, it is the inherent qualities of the subject envisaged which are contradicted by the argument. Proposition: "Existence (*unmaï, bhava*) is a state and not an action and does not therefore possess any peculiar properties. Consequently, it is independent of the qualities of objects." But all existence implies an existing object, and an object inevitably possesses qualities and the possibility of action. The state of existence in general is thus envisaged as something different from the existence of objects. There is therefore no "unity of category" (*samânya*) and the general must be differentiated from the particular. There is, in fact, no general state of existence independent of the existence of objects, qualities, and actions.

Dharmi vishesha viparita sâdhana vritti (Argument contrary to a particular characteristic of the subject). This is the case of a proposition such as, "The state of existence (*bhava*) is not found in objects, their qualities or their actions," under the pretext that existence itself differs from the existence of objects, qualities, and actions. The argument is clearly inconsistent.

Wrong Examples

(*Drishtanta*)

Wrong examples may be based on misleading similarities (*sadharmya*) or incompatibilities (*vaidharmya*) and are therefore of two kinds:

1. *Sadharmya drishtanta abhâsa* (Examples based on the appearance of misleading analogies). These are of five kinds:

Sadhâna dharma vikalam (Example contradicting the argument). For the argument, "The Word is immortal because it is immaterial, since whatever is immaterial is immortal, like the atom (*paramanu*)," the example of the atom, which is suitable for the subject, is not suitable for the argument, inasmuch as the atom is material.

Sâdhya dharma vikalam (Example contrary to the desired conclusion). For the argument, "The Word is eternal because it is immaterial, since whatever is immaterial is eternal, like intelligence (*buddhi*)"; now, intelligence, which is immaterial, is not eternal. The example thus contradicts the conclusion.

Ubhaya dharma vikalam (Example contradicting the given fact and conclusion). These are of two kinds, according to whether existing (*sat*) or non-existing (*asat*) objects are involved.

For the argument, "The Word is eternal because it is immaterial, since whatever is immaterial is eternal, like a clay pot": inasmuch as the pot is material and perishable, the example is absurd.

For the argument, "The Word is ephemeral because it is material, since whatever is material is ephemeral, like the ether (*âkâsha*)": for someone for whom the ether does not exist, it is neither ephemeral nor material; for someone who believes in the existence of the ether, it is eternal and material. The example is inconsistent in both cases.

Ananvayam (Lack of logical connection). The connection between the given fact and the example may not be evident.

For the argument, "The Word is impermanent because it is the result of an action, like a clay pot": if the conclusion "whatever is the result of an action is impermanent" is not made explicit, the connection is not evident.

Viparita anvayam (Unestablished logical connection). This is the case when one tries to justify the given fact directly by means of the example, without taking account of the argument, as in the assertion, "The Word is ephemeral because it is the result of an action. Whatever is the result of an action is ephemeral."

Here, the subject (the Word) is the result of an action. The fact of being ephemeral is a resultant quality. To explain the contents from the container is fallacious. Thus, one can say, "Wherever there is smoke, there is fire," but not "wherever there is fire there is smoke," since fire can exist without smoke, but not smoke without fire.

2. *Vaidharmya drishtanta abhâsa* (Examples based on incompatible objects). These are of five kinds:

Sâdhya vyavritti (Example compatible with the given fact, but incompatible with the argument). This is the case of "The soul is immortal since it has no form, like the atom (*paramanu*)," because the atom is immortal, but has a form.

Sâdhana vyavritti (Example compatible with the argument, but incompatible with the given fact). This is the case of "The Word is eternal, since it has no form, like action (*karma*)," because action has no form, but is not eternal.

Ubhaya vyavritti (Example incompatible with both the given fact and the argument). There are two kinds of illustration, according to whether existing or non-existing objects are concerned:

For existing objects, the assertion "The Word is eternal because it has no form, like the ether (*âkâsha*)," implies that whatever is eternal has no form. For those who consider the ether a substance, it has no form and is not eternal. For those who deny its existence, the example has no meaning.

For non-existent objects, the assertion "The Word is ephemeral since it has a form, like the ether," implies that whatever is not ephemeral has no form. For those who do not consider that ether is a reality, the example concerns neither the given fact nor the argument.

Vyatirekam (Logical discontinuity). According to the assertion, "The Word is eternal because it is the result of an action, like a clay pot," it follows that whatever is eternal is necessarily created.

Viparita vyatirekam (Logical misconception). The argument, "The Word is eternal because it is material," implies that eternalness depends on materiality and that the absence of materiality involves an absence of eternalness.

We thus have nine non-valid propositions, fourteen non-valid arguments, and ten inadequate examples, totaling thirty-three kinds of erroneous reasoning.

Aravana Adigal then said to Manimekhalaï, "You can now see that there are thirty-three forms of mistaken deduction according to the laws of logic. By analyzing them, truth can be distinguished from error, and reality apprehended without confusion or doubt."

Manimekhalaï Is Freed from
the Cycle of Births

Now knowing all the events of her former life, Manime-khalaï resolved to follow the way of the Buddhist *dharma* and dedicate herself to works of charity. She took refuge in a monastery, thrice rendering homage, in spirit, word, and deed, to the triple jewel represented by the Buddha, the *dharma*, and the *sangha* (the community of the faithful). Aravana Adigal, whose teaching she had followed, explained to her the reason for the Buddha's incarnation.

"At a time when the population of the earth increased inordinately, so that knowledge and virtue declined, the heavenly beings who inhabit the *Tushita Loka,* the Paradise of Perfect Bliss, quitted it, leaving it almost empty, in order to go and bow before the 'Guardian of Light' (*Prabhâpâla*), who is the first Buddha, begging him to be incarnate on earth to teach men the path of wisdom. Leaving his paradise of light, the *Dutita Loka,* he was born in the terrestrial world. Having vanquished Mâra, the perfidious god of love, and having dominated all his passions, lust, anger, and the vagaries of human ideologies, he appeared as victor, seated at the foot of the tree of knowledge, taught the four truths, essential to the salvation of living beings, and undertook to exterminate the three kinds of error.

"After him, many have been his disciples who, for love of mankind, have taught the rules of the *dharma* which I will explain to you, since an understanding of the four truths is essential in order to break the chain of the *nidâna,* whose twelve rings form the fissureless obstacle to our freeing ourselves from the cycle of birth and reaching the other shore of the ocean of existence."

The Twelve Nidâna*

The Bonds That Determine Human Condition

The twelve *nidâna*, the bonds which fetter us, are the source of the misfortune of existing. They can be considered as determining the condition of existence. The strength of these bonds depends on our attachments. They lie at the root of our mistakes, our actions, and their consequences.

The *nidâna* are linked together like a chain of causes and effects, each following from the previous one. When a link breaks, the others are undone. When one reappears, the others inexorably emerge.

The chain of the *nidâna* can be divided into four parts, with three junction points. It is the chain that determines the three kinds of birth (among the gods, men, or in the infernal world) in the three forms of time (past, present, and future).

The desires, attachments, and ignorance resulting from our past actions determine our condition at birth, while the acts committed in our present life determine our future. Our misfortunes are the fruit of our errors.

Only by understanding the nature of the twelve *nidâna* which fetter us and realizing their importance, their interdependence, and the suffering they cause, can one escape them and attain the unchangingness that leads to *nirvâna* (or release). One can then understand the four realities: suffering, the causes of suffering, the cessation of suffering, and the means of freeing oneself from suffering.

By applying the six rules of critical reasoning (*anu-mâna*) to the five "branches of experience" (*skandha*), truth can be discerned and true knowledge attained.

* According to the Commentary: In the infinitude of creation, the individual being exists only within the limits that determine his nature. These limits are represented as the links of a chain forming a kind of magic circle from which the living being cannot normally escape. It is only by managing to break this chain that he dissolves into non-existence, which is known as release. The living being exists only within these limits, and the *nidâna*, the links of the chain imprisoning him, are the very cause of his existence.

The four kinds of relation, the four teachings, and the four types of reply to questions can be established on the basis of the *nidâna*.

Forming a continuous chain of interdependent elements, the *nidâna* are indestructible. They are incapable of independent action and must be put into motion by someone. Their existence can only be perceived through their effect on those who put them into motion.

The *nidâna* belong neither to the past nor to the future. They are neither born nor do they die. Nothing can cause their end. They themselves are both the cause and the result of actions. They are the cause of existence and of the cessation of existence, the origin of all life.

Every being born into the world exists only by means of the twelve *nidâna*, which are: ignorance; action; consciousness; name and form; the organs of sense; perception; sensation; desire; attachment; development; birth; decline and death. These twelve elements form the links of the chain that separate the individual from transcendent reality and immortality. Those that manage to escape return to eternal bliss. The others remain imprisoned in the world of appearances or fall into hells from which there is no escape.

1. Ignorance (*pedamai, avidyâ*).

Ignorance consists of not understanding what is explained to you or being inclined to choose false ideas, believing hearsay without checking whether it is true or not, believing in the hare's horns because someone spoke of them.

2. Action (*sheykai, karma*).

The beings that people the three worlds are innumerable. They belong to the six categories that include humans, gods, Brahmâs, the inhabitants of the nether regions, animals and birds, and demons or evil genies.

According to his acts, good and evil, a being is installed in a human or other embryo. The effect of past actions is thus already present in the embryo. The ripening of those actions will be the cause of the living being's anguish, joys, and pleasures during its whole life.

Maiden of the beautiful bracelets! Evil actions may

be physical, verbal or mental. Physical evil deeds include murder, stealing, lechery. Verbal evil deeds include lying, slander, cruel words, and useless verbiage. Mental evil deeds include covetousness, anger, false ideologies. Those that seek to avoid these errors during their life improve their fate. Those that give themselves over to evil deeds are reborn as animals, demons, or denizens of hell. Their spirit will be obtuse, their body will suffer, and they will live in anguish.

Only those that observe the *shîla*,* the rules of "good conduct," and practice charity (*dâna*) will know happiness and will be reborn among the higher beings that include gods, men, and the Brahmâs.

3. Consciousness (*unarvu, vijñâna*).

Consciousness is the basic faculty of perceiving things. Such impressions do not lead to action nor to enjoyment, as in the case of a dream when one is asleep.

4. Name and form (*aru-uru, nâma-rûpa*).

Of itself life has no form, but the body that it animates, which shelters consciousness, has a form and a name.

5. The organs of sense (*vâyil, indriya*).

These, with the addition of the mental, form the six instruments (*shadayatana*) that transmit perception to consciousness (*ullam, vijñâna*).

6. Perception or touch (*uru, sparsha*).

Perception, which is the source of suffering, establishes the contact (*veru-pulangal*) between the senses and the mind with the objects.

7. Sensation (*nuharvu, vedanâ*).

Pleasure and pain are the result of the contact between the senses and objects, informing the consciousness (*vijñâna*) which enjoys or suffers accordingly.

* The *shîla* (rules of conduct) of the Buddhists are ten in number, five of which are important and binding: do not kill; do not lie; do not steal; practice sexual abstinence; do not accept gifts. Five are secondary (facultative), mostly concerning monks: do not use raised seats or beds; do not use ointments or rich clothes; touch neither silver nor gold; do not practice either music or dancing; eat before sunrise.

8. Desire or thirst (*vetkai, trishnâ*).

Desire is the insatiable demand of the organs of sense for objects whose contact give pleasure to the sentient being.

9. Attachment (*parru, upadâna*).

This consists of not desiring to leave objects in which the senses take pleasure and for which we have an insatiable desire.

10. Development (*pavam, bhava*).

This is the accumulation of our past actions through our successive lives, determining what we are as well as our experience of pleasure and suffering.

11. Birth or rank in the hierarchy of beings (*tonral, jâti*).

This is the result of our past actions, obliging the sentient being to be born in one or the other of the six categories of living beings. According to an ineluctable law, we carry with us in the various bodies we inhabit over numerous lives, the heritage of joys and sorrows we have accumulated.

12. Birth, old age, and death (*vinaippayam, janmamaranam*).

Sickness (*pini*) is due to changes in our balance as a result of our actions, but can also come from external causes. Old age (*mûppu*) is part of the normal development of one approaching the end. Death (*shakkadu*) is the disappearance of the body which vanishes like the setting sun. The transmigrating principle of life, which is formless but permanent, separates itself from the matter of the body, which has form and is ephemeral.

The Interdependence of the *Nidâna*

Action is born of ignorance, consciousness from action, name and form from consciousness, the organs of sense from form, perception from the organs of sense, sensation from perception, desire from sensation. Of desire is born attachment which results in the mass of our actions.

The accumulation of our actions causes rebirth; each birth brings with it sickness, old age, and death as well as the anguish that comes from the impossibility of freeing oneself from endless suffering.

In this endless cycle of experience, if ignorance disappears, action ceases, and with action consciousness vanishes. Without consciousness, name and form cease to exist, and in turn the organs of sense and the mind. Without the organs of sense, there is no perception, and without perception there can be no sensation. When sensation ceases, desire also disappears. Without desire there is no longer any attachment.

No attachment means no longer any accumulation of actions, and without the latter there can be no development. Without development, there is no more birth, sickness, old age, and death, and therefore no more anguish nor despair. That is how the suffering of existence disappears.

The Grouping of the *Nidâna*

Of the *nidâna*, ignorance and action (*avidyâ* and *karma*) are the basis of the others and thus form a group apart.

Tied to the body, consciousness, name and form, the organs of sense, perception, and sensation, form the next group.

The third group includes desire, attachment, development, and the accumulation of actions, which represent the bad utilization of the previous group. It is the madness of desire and attachments which result in becoming (*bhava*).

The fourth group comprises birth, as well as sickness, old age, and death, which are the consequences of birth.

The Junction Points of the *Nidâna*

The first is the action-consciousness junction which is the basis of life. The second is the junction of sensation and desire, which is the source of behavior. The third is the point at which the accumulation of actions causes birth.

Nidâna and Birth into a Family (Jâti)

Birth into one of the main categories or families of beings, as man, god, or animal, is the result of the state of consciousness in the previous life and depends on the mental structures born of ignorance.

Birth in a particular family is not the beginning of existence, nor the cessation of another kind of existence, but rather a transfer in which the continuity of existence appears. Consciousness cannot be manifest without taking a form or body in which to dwell. From birth, consciousness and form coexist in a body, whether it be a man, animal, or spirit.

The Nidâna and Time

The ignorance and the actions that determine the orientation of a life issue from the past.

Consciousness, the body animated by life, the senses and the mind, perception, sensation, the experience of pleasure and pain, desire, attachment, the accumulation of actions causing future rebirths, and social status from birth, belong to the present.

All that occurs after birth, sickness, decrepitude, and death, distress, tears, anxiety, and despair, belong to the future.

The Way of Release

In order to progress toward release, one must be conscious that desire, attachment, and ignorance are the result of our past actions and the cause of our future rebirths; that action (i.e., our present behavior), is the cause of our destiny; that birth (the category of beings to which one belongs), decline, sickness, and death are the effects of our errors and deeds; that the body, the result of our errors and deeds, is impermanent and the instrument of our sufferings, and that neither human beings (nor any other sort of being) possess a soul that is their own.

The Four Truths

The four truths are: suffering; the causes of suffering; freeing oneself from suffering; and the means of freeing oneself.

1. Suffering concerns consciousness, the body animated by life, the senses and the mind, perception, pleasure, birth, sickness, growing old, death, distress, tears, anxiety, despair.

2. The causes of suffering are ignorance, wrong action, desire, attachment, and the accumulation of past errors which gives rise to rebirth.

3. To free oneself from suffering, it must be realized that it is attachment that binds us and causes rebirth and its resultant sufferings.

4. The means of freeing oneself from suffering is detachment, which is the source of happiness and salvation.

The Five *Kântam* (*Skândha*) or Branches of Experience

Life's experience consists of five factors or "branches": instruments, objects, forms, relations, and goals.

The instruments of experience are: the body (which constitutes the basis); sensation (pleasure/pain which directs choice); perception (the mind and the five senses that characterize the state of life); action (*karma*, i.e., the good or evil use of the facts given by experience); intelligence (which allows us to utilize the other branches of experience).

The objects of experience are: ensembles (or conglomerates); continuity; evolution; entities circumscribed by a name. Ensembles (or conglomerates) are, for example, a body, water, a country. The body is the assemblage of blood, bones, flesh, nerves, etc. Water is an assemblage of water drops. A country is an assemblage of villages and towns. Continuity is a series of causes and effects such as: seed, shoot, stalk, seed, and so on, indefinitely. Evolution concerns birth, growing old, and disappearance. Things delimited by a name: A name is not only a group of letters. It implies a content. A month, for example, is a length of time containing a certain number of days.

The forms of experience are six in number: true experience of a real object; false experience of an unreal object (e.g., the hare's horns); true relation between real things (for example, pleasure and pain are tied to perception); false relation between real things (for example, consciousness which is eternal cannot be compared to lightning which is ephemeral); false relation to a true object, like the deduction of an invisible object from a visible effect (fire and smoke); deduction of a false object from another false object, such as the affirmation that hares do not exist because they do not have horns.

The four types of relation are based on unity, diversity, the unknowable, and the evident. Unity means that the object considered as cause and the object considered as effect are of the same nature. Diversity implies that cause and effect are of different natures. The unknowable implies a relation that is incomprehensible to us, such as that existing between eternal principles and ephemeral objects. The evident is the result of experience, such as the prediction that the rice shoot will come from the grain.

From this, we can deduce four teachings: There is nothing that is at the same time cause and effect. We must not become attached to things. We must not confuse the act with the person who commits it. Continuity must not be confused with the transitory reality of the moment: The seed, shoot, and stalk of the rice plant form a continuity of cause and effect, but the seed is not the shoot, and the shoot is not the stalk.

There are four kinds of answers to questions.

Definite answer: To the question: "Must what is

born die?," the answer is "Everything that is born has to die."

Deferred answer: To the question: "Will this dead man be reborn?," the reply is first of all a question: "Was he attached to the things of this world?" If he was not, he will not be reborn.

Dilatory answer: To the question: "Which comes first, the seed or the palm tree?," the answer is, "To which seed and which palm tree do you refer?"

Silence: To the question: "Are the flowers that fall from heaven fresh or faded?" the best answer is silence.

The choice between the slavery of transmigration and release is the final goal of the *skândha,* of life's experience. It is by realizing that everything is impermanent, painful, soulless, and unclean, that desire is done away with.

It is by love towards all beings, by pity towards those who suffer, by a feeling of joy at the success and happiness of others, that one acquires inner peace and rids oneself of anger.

One extricates oneself from mistaken ideologies by studying the sacred texts (*shruti*), meditation (*chintana*), comparison with the real (*bhâvana*) and methodological reasoning (*darshana*).

It was through these four stages that Aravana Adigal led Manimekhalaï towards the truth, by his exposition of the *dharma,* free from all inconsistency, and lit for her the bright light of knowledge.

Manimekhalaï, as beautiful as a doll, having put on the monastic habit, henceforth led the life of austerity that is indispensable for attaining wisdom and being free of the burden of faults that bind us to the interminable cycle of birth.

❧ GLOSSARY ❧

[Asterisks indicate Sanskrit terms.]

Abhâva*: non-existence.

Accâ (or Sâl): *shorea robusta.*

Adharmâstikâya*: immutability.

Âgama*: traditional text. The Âgamas or holy books of the Jains are the *Anga-âgama, Purva-âgama,* and *Bahushruti-âgama.* Also, generally, a term for cultural heritage.

Âgama viruddham*: contrary to authoritative texts.

Agastya*: mythical sage who spread the Vedic religion in the south of India. He lived on Mount Podiyil.

Agni*: the god of fire. His wife is Svaha (the Offering). Also a term for the igneous state.

Ahamkara*: the ego or the notion of the self.

Airavata*: the white elephant, mount of the god Indra.

Aïthiya: tradition or popular belief.

Aiyai-Kumarî: Kâlî, the goddess of death.

Aïyam: indecision.

Ajivika: the main sect of pre-Aryan origin of wandering monks who transmit the esoteric aspects of knowledge.

Ajivâstikâya*: inert matter.

Akam: love.

Âkâsha*: space or ether.

Âkâshâstikaya*: the principle of space.

Âkâya: space.

Akshapada: considered to be the founder of Nyaya, the school of logical philosophy.

Amaravati: the capital of the god Indra.

Amrita-Surabhi*:   Cow of Abundance, the name of the magic bowl belonging to Aputra and Manimekhalaï.

Anaikantikam*:   non-exclusive argument.

Ananvayam*:   lack of logical connection.

Anga*:   members of a larger corpus.

Anga: a region of Bengal, located to the north of Maghada.

Antalaï: vulture.

Anumâna*:   deduction or critical reasoning.

Anumâna viruddham*:   contrary to deduction or experience.

Anvayam*:   logical connection.

Anvayam anumâna*:   occasional connection.

Anyantara asiddham*:   unacceptable argument to one of the parties.

Apah*:   liquid state.

Appu: liquid state.

Aprasiddha sambandham*:   no question of relation.

Aprasiddha ubhayam*:   non-existent qualificative and subject.

Aprasiddha visheshana*:   non-existent qualificative.

Aprasiddha visheshyam*:   non-existent subject.

Aravana Adigal, the perfect master of the *dharma:* the propagator of *Mahâyana* Buddhism in southern India. He can probably be identified with Nâgarjuna.

Arhat-Parameshti: the supreme Jain prophet.

Arthâpatti*:   implication or presumption.

Arûpa-brahmâs*:   the four groups of world planners.

Aru-uru: name and form.

Asadhârana*:   of a particular nature.

Asat*:   non-existent.

Ashoka*:   red-flowered tree (*jonesia ashoka roxbi*), the sacred tree of Jain and Buddhist hermit magicians. Its flower is one of the seven arrows of the god Eros.

Ashotaram: a city of the north.

Ashraya asiddham*:   argument resting on unproven fact.

Asiddham°: unconvincing arguments.

Asura°: anti-gods or genies; one of the main celestial co-horts.

Âtman°: consciousness or soul.

Atti: *bauhinia tormentosa* or *recemosa:* the mountain ebony tree, symbol of the Chola dynasty.

Avanti: a city of the north.

Avidyâ°: ignorance.

Ayiraī: nowadays the river Ponnani.

Bala°: energy.

Bali: the king of Genii.

Bâna: the prince of demons, son of Bali.

Bandha°: bonds.

Bhârata°: the Indian continent.

Bhava°: development.

Bhâvana°: what is real.

Bhûta°: genies or cruel spirits. Also, elements.

Bhûta-vâdi°: elementalists, absolute materialists. One of the philosophical schools, whose best-known theorist was Chârvâka.

Black-heads: monastic order, see Kâlâmukha.

Bodhâyana: author of a commentary on the two *Mîmânsâ*.

Brahmâ°: the third god (after Shiva and Vishnu) of the Hindu trinity; the creator or craftsman of the world.

Brahmâs°: the planners and regents of the world. There are four groups of planners (Arûpa-Brahmâs) who are without form and sixteen regents of the visible world (Rûpa-Brahmâs) who are endowed with a body.

Brahmâ-vâdi°: worshiper of Brahmâ.

Brihaspati: founder of the atheist school (Lokâyata) of philosophy.

Buddhi°: intelligence.

Chakravâla°: the heavenly spheres.

Chakravâla-kottam°: the heavenly city, the place where the gods are gathered together.

Chaitya°: Buddhist sanctuary.

Champa: kingdom beyond the seas. (Possibly Cambodia.)

Champa: city of the north, located in the region of Bhagalpur in Bengal, where the Karalars live.

Champaka: a kind of jasmine (*orchna squartiosa*).

Champâpati: the name of the city of Puhâr.

Champapuri: Kacchayam, the capital of King Durjaya in the Anga country (Bengal).

Champu: Pârvatî, wife of the god Shiva, and divine protectress of the Rose-wood continent, Nâvalan Têvu, which includes India and the neighboring countries.

Charana°: wandering Jain or Buddhist monks, who travel through the air.

Chedi: the Vidyâdharas' capital, situated near Mount Kailasa in Tibet.

Chera: the dynasty reigning over the west of southern India, whose capital was Vanji.

Chetty: a noble title conferred on merchants.

Chhanda°: prosody.

Chintâ: the goddess of knowledge, another name of Sarasvatî.

Chintana°: meditation.

Chit°: consciousness.

Chitrasena: celestial genie, companion of Tuvatikan.

Chola: the dynasty of the sun, reigning over the east of southern India, whose capital was Puhâr.

Cohorts of the celestial spirits: these are eighteen in number: Apsaras, Nâga, Siddha, Gandharva, Vidyâdhara, Pishâcha, Taraka, Bhogobhumiya, Kimpurusha, Sena, Asura, Bhûta, Muni, Deva, Garuda, Rakshasa, Yaksha, Charana. The cohorts of the gods are four in number, comprising thirty-three gods, called: Vasu, Rudra, Aditya, and Ashvini. The Ganas, Shiva's companions, are eighteen.

Dâna*: charity.

Darshana*: methodological reasoning.

Devasvâmin: commentator on the *Mîmânsâ.*

Dharma*: the *dharma* or "natural law" is taken by the Buddhists to mean the body of rules of life prescribed by the Buddha.

Dharmacharanas: messengers of the Buddhist faith.

Dharmâstikâya*: evolution.

Dharma-shrayaka: an ascetic, preacher of Buddhism in Java.

Dharma, svarûpa viparita sâdhana vritti*: the characteristics of the argument are in contradiction to the qualificative attributed to the subject.

Dharma vishesha viparita sâdhana vritti*: the argument contradicts a particularity of the quality attributed to the subject.

Dharmi*: concrete object possessing its own qualities.

Dharmi svarûpa viparita sâdhana vritti*: argument contradicting the very nature of the subject.

Dharmi vishesha viparita sâdhana vritti*: argument contrary to a particular characteristic of the subject.

Dhavala-malaï: the white mountain, a tall mountain on the island of Java.

Dhyâna*: meditation.

Drishtanta*: example.

Drishtivisham*: serpent so venomous its sight alone is fatal.

Durgâ*: the terrible form of the goddess Kali.

Dutita Loka*: the paradise of light, the ninth of the thirty-three celestial spheres.

Dvârakâ: the native city of the god-hero Krishna.

Dvîpa-tilaka*: Tivatilakaï, literally, the adornment of the isle.

Eccham: derived deduction.

Eratti: the jujube tree.

Etthy or Etthy shalayam: a noble title conferred on merchants.

Gândhâra: a country of the east, whose capital was Idavayam (Rishavayam).

Gandharva*: celestial musicians.

Gandharvas (rite of)*: one of the eight forms of marriage, marriage by elopement or mutual consent.

Ganita*: calculation.

Gautama: mythical sage, founder of Nyâya (logic).

Gridhra-Kuta*: "Hill of the Vulture," near Rajagriha, where the Buddha preached.

Gomukhi: "The Bull's Muzzle," the sacred lake on the isle of Manipallavam.

Guna*: trend.

Hetu*: reason.

Hinâyana: "The Little Vehicle," the original monastic form of Buddhism.

Ida*: the sun. One of the arteries of the body.

Idavayam: Rishavayam, capital of East Gândhâra.

Ilam Killi: Chola king.

Ilandaï: jujube tree.

Ilangô Adigal: brother of a Chola king, author of *The Ankle Bracelet* (*Shilappadikaram*).

Indra: the king of heaven, an important deity of the Aryans, Dravidians, and Buddhists. It is on him that the rains (source of all prosperity) depend.

Indriya*: the organs of sense.

Itheyam: tradition or popular belief.

Iyalbu: common sense or the evidence inherent in things.

Jaimini: founder of the Mîmâmsâ, the school of deist philosophy.

Jaïna: an ancient moralistic and atheist religion. The wandering Jain monks carry a beggar's bowl (*katjnai*), a mesh bag (*uri*), and peacocks' feathers. They practice non-violence, the strictest vegetarianism, and nudity.

Jambu-dvîpa*:   the rose-wood (rose-apple) continent, including India and neighboring countries.

Janma-maranam*:   birth, old age, and death.

Jâti*:   birth, or rank in the hierarchy of beings.

Jayanta: son of the god Indra.

Jivâstikâya*:   the principle of life.

Jñâna*:   knowledge.

Kacchayam: Champapuri, the capital of King Durjaya in the Anga country (Bengal).

Kâdam: a measurement of approximately ten miles.

Kadamba: an empire beyond the seas, conquered by Shenguttuvan: probably Champa (modern-day Cambodia).

Kadamba: sea-side oak, symbol of the god Murugan.

Kakanda: ancient sovereign of the Chola country.

Kâla*:   time.

Kâlâmukha*:   "Black heads," one of the sects of wandering monks who, according to the rule of their order, have to feign madness.

Kâlâstikâya*:   the principle of time.

Kalinga: modern Orissa.

Kalli: euphorbia

Kalpa*:   ritual; also, eon.

Kalpataru*:   the tree of abundance.

Kâma*:   Eros, the god of love.

Kâma-Sûtra*:   treatise on eroticism.

Kambala Chetty: merchant in woolen blankets.

Kampul: species of heron.

Kanada: founder of the scientist philosophy (Vaisheshika).

Kanchanapuram: "the golden city," capital of the Vidyâdharas in Tibet.

Kanchi: the capital of the Chola kings, modern Conjeevaram, near Madras.

Kandu-narâmaï: inattention; seeing without understanding.

Kannaka: Aryan king vanquished by the Chola king Senguttuvan.

Kannaki: wife of Kovalan, heroine of *The Ankle Bracelet*.

Kannan: Krishna.

Kantan: Skanda, ancient king of the Chola dynasty.

Kântam: The branches of experience.

Kanyâ-Kumari°: "Cape of the Virgin," Cape Comorin in the extreme south of India.

Kâpâlika°: "Wearers of skulls," a sect of wandering monks.

Kapila: a city of Maghada, the native town of the Buddha.

Kapila: a city of Kalinga (Orissa).

Kapila: founder of Sâmkyhyâ (cosmology).

Kârâlar: a people of the north, living in the city of Champa in Bengal, Sutâmati's native town.

Karikâl Valavan: Chola king, conqueror of the northern kingdoms.

Kariyura: a river in the south of India.

Karma°: action, i.e., the bonds created by our good or evil deeds.

Kârtika°: the constellation of the Pleiades.

Karuda: deduction.

Katchi: direct perception.

Katjnaï: the beggar's bowl of the Jain monks.

Kausambi: a city of the north of India.

Kaveri: an important river in the south of India.

Kaveripumpattinam: another name for the city of Puhâr, the Kaveris Emporium of Ptolemy.

Kavir: coral tree.

Kayankaraï: a river of the north.

Konku: tree with yellow and white flowers.

Konrai: laburnum.

Korkai: the ancient capital of the Pandya kingdom, the Kolkhoi of Ptolemy. The modern name of the city is Quondam.

Kovalan: merchant prince, lover of Mâdhavi and father of Manimekhalaï, hero of *The Ankle Bracelet*.

Kovvai: *coccinia indica*.

Krauchna*:   heron.

Kritakoti: commentary on the *Mîmânsâ* by Bodhâyana.

Kshanti*:   patience.

Kumil: gardenia, *gruelina parviflora*.

Kurinji: *strobilanthes*.

Kurava: amaranth.

Kuruntu (or Kurunda):   wild lemon tree, *atalantia*.

Kusha*:   a sacred herb, *poa-cynosuroides*.

Kutasham: *milingtonia*.

Kuttako Cheralâtan: mythical sovereign of Kerala.

Kutta-nâtu: Kerala.

Lakshmi*:   the goddess of Fortune.

Lakulisha: an Ajivika who reestablished Shivaism just prior to the beginning of the Christian era.

Loka virudham*:   contrary to general opinion.

Lokâyata: the atheist and materialist school founded by Brihaspati.

Maduraï: the capital of the Pandya kingdom.

Mahâ-Brahmâ*:   the creator of the gods.

Mahat*:   the great principle.

Mahâvira: the reformer of Jainism, a contemporary of the Buddha.

Mahâyana: "Great Vehicle" of Buddhism: reformed or popular form of Buddhism.

Makara-yâl: crocodile harp.

Makkhâli Gosâla: prophet of the Ajivikas, the teacher of the Buddha and Mahâvira.

Manas*:   the mental or the mind.

Manimekhalâ: goddess of the ocean.

Manipallavam: isle to the east of southern India.

Mantras: magic formulas.

Mâra: "The Slayer," a version of the god Eros.

Marutavega: "Fast as the wind": the name of a Vidyâdhara, lover of Sutâmati.

Mayä: the heavenly carpenter. He is the architect of the Asuras or genies, here called the architects of the gods.

Meru: the golden mountain, the axis of the world, located in Tibet.

Mesgrits: a kind of flower.

Mîmâmsâ°: spiritual or theological reflection. The deist philosophy (rites and theology) founded by Jaimini.

Mîmânsâ: Two of the orthodox philosophical texts of Hinduism, collectively known as *Vedanta,* though this name is usually reserved for the later, or *Uttara, Mîmânsâ.* The earlier, or *Purva, Mîmânsâ* is a system of rationalism applied to the study of the *Vedas.* The *Uttara Mîmânsâ* is more metaphysical, teaching that God is the sole reality.

Mitchi: elimination by inference or correlation.

Mudal: ascendant deduction.

Mudra°: the language of gesture.

Mullai: jasmine. Also a mode of music played at twilight.

Muni: sage.

Mûppu: old age.

Murava: marine oak.

Murugan: the ancient Dravidian god of youth and war, identified with Skanda, son of the god Shiva. He is also the god of beauty.

Nâda°: sound.

Nadi: the sixtieth part of twenty-four hours.

Nâga: race of naked savages.

Nâgä: a serpent-people living in a subterranean world, the splendor of which, according to the Jains, surpasses Paradise. Their king is Valaivanam.

Nâga-nadu: the land of the Nâgas.

Nâga-puram: the capital of the isle of Java.

Nakam: white basil.

Nalal: orange-cup, *brasiletto-climber wagaty.*

Nâma-rûpa*: name and form.

Nappimaï: Râdhâ, lover of the god Krishna.

Narantan: orange tree.

Nâtika: twenty-four minutes.

Nâvala: rose-apple tree or rose-wood.

Nâvalan Têvu: the Rose-apple or Rose-wood tree continent, which includes India and the neighboring countries. Its center is Mount Meru in Tibet.

Neytal: the funeral chant.

Nidâna*: the twelve rings of a chain whose links constitute the state of existence.

Nigama*: conclusion.

Nilam*: blue lotus.

Niraïppu: indirect knowledge.

Nirgrantha*: the philosophical theory of the Jains.

Nirukta*: etymologies.

Nirvâna: the Buddhist paradise of non-return.

Nish-kalâ*: the indivisible principle which exists outside the multiple, divisible world, but incarnates in it for his own amusement.

Nuharvu: sensation.

Nyâya*: logic. The founders of the Indian school of logic are Akshapada and Gautama.

Olibu: elimination by inference or correlation.

Pada-pankaja-malaï: "Mount of the Lotus Feet." Name given to the Hill of the Vulture, near Rajagriha, where the Buddha preached.

Paksha*: given fact.

Paksha-dharma-vachana*: nature of the given fact.

Palai: the plagal mode in music, corresponding to the Murchhana of the Sanskrit treatises.

Pânâ: musicians.

Pandya: the dynasty reigning over the extreme south of India, identified with the Pandavas of the *Mahabharata*.

Paramita*:   the ten perfections of the Buddhists.

Paramanu*:   atoms.

Parashurâma: "Rama with the axe," an incarnation of the god Vishnu who destroyed the princely order.

Parishesha*:   elimination by inference or correlation.

Parru: attachment.

Pavai: dance.

Pavam: development.

Pedamai: ignorance.

Pêdi: male transvestites and prostitutes.

Pingala*:   the moon. One of the arteries of the body.

Pini: sickness.

Pitaka: the sacred texts of the Buddhists.

Pitavan: ipeca.

Podiyil: a mountain in the south of India, source of the river Tamrapani. Mount Podiyil is the legendary abode of the sage Agastya. It was called Bettigo by Ptolemy and is known today as Malaya or Chandanâchala.

Podul: simultaneous deduction.

Polikal: a plant called "hare's ear."

Potikaï: the snowy mountain (see Podiyil).

Prabhâpâla: "Guardian of the Light," the first Buddha.

Pradyumna: assumed name of Kama, son of the god-hero Krishna.

Prajñâ*:   intelligence.

Prakriti*:   basic nature.

Pramâna*:   means of proof in logic.

Pramâna-vâdi*:   logician.

Prâna*:   vital energies.

Pranadhâna: dedication.

Prapancha Hridaya: commentary of the *Mîmânsâ*.

Pratijña*: proposition.

Pratyaksha*: direct perception.

Pratyaksha virrudham*: contrary to the evidence of the senses.

Puhâr: "City of the estuary," situated at the mouth of the river Kaveri. Also called Kaveripumpatinam or Champâpati, this city is the Kaberis Emporium of Ptolemy. It was destroyed by the sea at the epoch of the *Manimekhalaï*.

Punga: *pongamia glabra.*

Punnaï: Alexandrian laurel, *canophyllum-inophyllum.*

Punya Râja: king of Java, reincarnation of Aputra.

Puram: glory.

Purâna: a work containing traditional knowledge.

Purusha*: concept of the universal man.

Pûrva-desha: Gandhara, a renowned country to the east of Pûhar.

Purvavat*: ascendant deduction.

Rajas*: orbital trend of motion.

Rakshasa: Shiva's faithful demonic genies.

Râma: an avatar of the god Vishnu.

Ratna-dvîpa: "Isle of Jewels" situated to the east of India (probably Burma).

Rishabha: "The Bull," the name of the founder of Jain philosophy.

Rishi: sage or seer.

Rudraksha*: "eye of Shiva." Yarcum seed used to make Shivaite rosaries.

Rûpa-Brahmâ*: The sixteen regents of the visible world.

Sadhâna dharma vikalam*: example contrary to the argument.

Sâdhana vyavritti*: example compatible with the argument but incompatible with the given fact.

Sadhârana*: of a general nature.

Sadharma*:   elements of the same nature.

Sadharmya drishtanta abhâsa*:   examples based on the appearance of misleading analogies.

Sadhya-darma*:   the quality to be demonstrated.

Sâdhya dharma vikalam*:   example contrary to the desired conclusion.

Sadhya vyavritti*:   example compatible with the given fact, but incompatible with the argument.

Sa-kalâ*:   the divisible world.

Sâmânya: simultaneous deduction.

Sambhava*:   probability.

Sâmkhya: cosmology, the philosophical theory defined by Kapila.

Sampati: mythical vulture.

Sangha: the community of faithful Buddhists.

Sapaksha*:   analogy.

Sapaksha ekadesha vritti*:   proposition valid in a single case, but also in contrary cases.

Sapaksha vyâpi*:   argument applying to a single case and to all similar cases.

Sat: existence.

Sattva*:   centripetal trend of motion.

Shabda*:   cultural heritage; also, divine word.

Shabdatva*:   pertaining to the word.

Shaïva-vâda*:   Shivaite philosophy.

Shakkadu: death.

Shavakam: the isle of Java.

Sherunti: gold-flowered pear tree.

Sheshavat*:   derived deduction.

Shetti: noble title granted to merchants.

Sheykai: action.

Shikshâ: phonology.

Shîla*:   the five rules of conduct of the Buddhists. Also, generally, purity of conduct.

Shilappadikaram: *The Ankle Bracelet* by Prince Ilangô Adigal, of which the *Manimekhalaï* is the sequel.

Shiva: the first of the gods. He bears a third eye on his forehead. As the principle of expansion and destruction, he is one of the members of the Hindu trinity.

Shivaism: the main theistic religion of pre-Aryan origin.

Shruti°: sacred texts.

Shudukâttu-kottam: "City of the Dead," the name of the cemetery of Puhar.

Shurai: jujube tree.

Shuttunarvu: direct perception.

Siddha asiddham°: non-determining argument.

Simhapura: a city of Kalinga (present-day Orissa).

Skandha°: the five branches of knowledge.

Sugata°: "The most endowed," epithet of the Buddha.

Sushumna°: fire. One of the arteries of the body.

Suvachanam viruddham°: contradiction of terms.

Svabhâva°: common sense or the evidence inherent in things.

Tâla: musical rhythm.

Talai: pandanaus, tamarisk (screw pine).

Talavam: golden jasmine.

Tamas°: centrifugal trend of motion.

Tamrapani: river of southern India.

Tanri: myrobolam.

Tapas°: mortifications.

Teradu-teridal: arbitrary choice.

Tilakam: coral tree.

Tirukkural: celebrated work of the Tamil poet Tiravallur.

Tiryak-kodal: deceptive appearance.

Tittantam: example.

Tittivitam: serpent whose poison works from a distance.

Tivatilakaï: *dvîpa-tilaka,* "adornment of the isle," the name of the fairy protectress of Manipallivam.

Toddy: palm wine.

Tonral: birth or rank in the hierarchy of beings.

Tondaï: Indian caper.

Trishnâ*: desire or thirst.

Tukku: mimicry, the art of posture.

Tushita Loka*: the paradise of the perfect, one of the thirty-one heavenly spheres.

Ubhaya assidham*: argument not valid from any point of view.

Ubhaya dharma vikalam*: example contradicting the given fact and conclusion.

Ubhaya ekadesha vritti anaikantikam*: argument applicable to another particular case, but also to various contrary cases.

Ubhaya vyavritti*: example incompatible with both the given fact and the argument.

Udahârana*: example.

Udayakumâra: crown prince of the Chola kingdom.

Ujjaina: a city of the north of India.

Ulaneri: probability.

Unardandaï unardal: truism.

Unarvu: consciousness.

Undaneri: probability.

Unlicil: albizzia.

Upadâna*: attachment.

Unmai: existence.

Upamâna*: analogy.

Upavanam: garden.

Upavarsha: commentator on the Mîmânsâ.

Upaya*: utilization of proper means.

Upayana*: particular case.

Urandai: capital of the Chola kings. Puhar was only the second capital.

Uri: mesh bag crarried by wandering Jain monks.

Uru: perception or touch.

Uyir: vital energies.

Vahai: cassia tree.

Vaidharmiya*: contradictory example.

Vaidharmiya drishtanta*: elements of a different nature.

Vaidharmya drishtanta abhâsa*: example based on incompatible objects.

Vaigaï: river running through Madura.

Vaishakha: month running from April 15 to May 15.

Vaisheshika*: scientific materialism, the scientific school founded by Kanada.

Vajra*: lightning, Indra's weapon.

Vakula: species of cassia tree.

Valakku: mistaken association.

Valiyon: Bâladeva, brother of Krishna.

Vanga: raft.

Vanji: palm tree; the palm is the symbol of the Chera kings.

Vanji: capital of the Chera kings (Malabar coast).

Vanni: mesgrits.

Varanam: ancient name of the city of Uraiyur.

Vatuku: the country to the north, or Telugu country on the east coast.

Vâyil: channels of internal communication; also, the organs of sense.

Vedanâ*: sensation.

Veda-vadi: follower of vedism.

Vedas: the sacred writings of the Hindus.

Veda Vyâsa: author of the *Purva Mîmânsâ* dealing with rites and sacrifices.

Vellil: camellia.

Venkai (or Vengaï): Kino, *pterocarpus marsupinum.*

Venvêlân: Skanda, Shiva's son.

Vetchi: scarlet ixora.

Vetiram: bamboo.

Vetkai: desire or thirst.

Vidu: cessation of existence; release.

Vidyâdhara*: "genies of knowledge," demi-gods and servants of Shiva. They form one of the eighteen heavenly cohorts. Their city is Chedi, situated not far from Kailasa, the sacred mountain of Shiva in Tibet.

Vihâra: a monastery of Buddhist monks.

Vijatireka*: a concordance.

Vijatireka anumâna*: absence of logical connection.

Vijaya: the hero Arjuna.

Vijñâna*: consciousness.

Vila: pine tree.

Vinaippayam: birth, old age, and death.

Vipaksha*: opposite or counter argument.

Vipaksha ekadesha vritti*: argument applying to a single case and to all similar cases.

Vipaksha vyâpi*: a proposition valid in a single case, but also in contrary cases.

Viparita anvayam*: unestablished logical connection.

Viparita vyatirekam*: logical misconception.

Virrudham*: contradictory argument.

Virya*: courage.

Vishnu: the second member of the Hindu trinity and the principle of conservation.

Vishvamitra: a sage of princely origin.

Vrittikara*: "author of the commentary."

Vritti vyabhichari*: indetermination.

Vyâkarana*: grammar.

Vyatirekam*: logical discontinuity.

Yak of the Kaveri: a long-haired grey animal, now extinct.

Yâl: Indian harp, unkown today, whose number of strings

varied from seven to one hundred. The *makara-yál* or crocodile harp had seventeen strings.

Yama*:   the rules of conduct.

Yavana*:   Greek.

Yojana*:   league, about three miles.

New Directions Paperbooks—A Partial Listing

For a complete listing request a free catalog from New Directions, 80 Eighth Avenue, New York, NY 10011; or visit our website, www.ndpublishing.com

†Bilingual

Five Plays. NDP506.
In Search of Duende.† NDP858.
Selected Poems.† NDP1010.
Nathaniel Mackey, Splay Anthem. NDP1032.
Xavier de Maistre,Voyage Around My Room. NDP791.
Stéphane Mallarmé, Mallarmé in Prose. NDP904.
Selected Poetry and Prose.† NDP529.
A Tomb for Anatole. NDP1014.
Oscar Mandel, The Book of Elaborations. NDP643.
Abby Mann, Judgment at Nuremberg. NDP950.
Javier Marías, All Souls. NDP905.
A Heart So White. NDP937.
Tomorrow in the Battle Think On Me. NDP923.
Your Face Tomorrow. NDP1081.
Written Lives. NDP1068.
Carole Maso, The Art Lover. NDP1040.
Enrique Vila-Matas, Bartleby & Co. NDP1063.
Montano's Malady. NDP1064.
Bernadette Mayer, A Bernadette Mayer Reader. NDP739.
Michael McClure, Rain Mirror. NDP887.
Carson McCullers, The Member of the Wedding. NDP1038.
Thomas Merton, Bread in the Wilderness. NDP840.
Gandhi on Non-Violence. NDP1090.
New Seeds of Contemplation. NDP1091
Thoughts on the East. NDP802.
Henri Michaux, Ideograms in China. NDP929.
Selected Writings.† NDP263.
Dunya Mikhail, The War Works Hard. NDP1006.
Henry Miller, The Air-Conditioned Nightmare. NDP587.
The Henry Miller Reader. NDP269.
Into the Heart of Life. NDP728.
Yukio Mishima, Confessions of a Mask. NDP253.
Death in Midsummer. NDP215.
Frédéric Mistral, The Memoirs. NDP632.
Teru Miyamoto, Kinshu: Autumn Brocade. NDP1055.
Eugenio Montale, Selected Poems.† NDP193.
Paul Morand, Fancy Goods (tr. by Ezra Pound). NDP567.
Vladimir Nabokov, Laughter in the Dark. NDP1045.
The Real Life of Sebastian Knight. NDP432.
Pablo Neruda, The Captain's Verses.† NDP991.
Love Poems. NDP1094.
Residence on Earth.† NDP992.
Spain in Our Hearts. NDP1025.
New Directions Anthol. Classical Chinese Poetry. NDP1001.
Robert Nichols, Arrival. NDP437.
Griselda Ohannessian, Once: As It Was. NDP1054.
Charles Olson, Selected Writings. NDP231.
Toby Olson, Human Nature. NDP897.
George Oppen, Selected Poems. NDP970.
Wilfred Owen, Collected Poems. NDP210.
José Pacheco, Battles in the Desert. NDP637.
Michael Palmer, The Company of Moths. NDP1003.
The Promises of Glass. NDP922.
Nicanor Parra, Antipoems: New and Selected. NDP603.
Boris Pasternak, Safe Conduct. NDP77.
Kenneth Patchen, Collected Poems. NDP284.
Memoirs of a Shy Pornographer. NDP879.
Octavio Paz, The Collected Poems.† NDP719.
Sunstone.† NDP735.
A Tale of Two Gardens: Poems from India. NDP841.
Victor Pelevin, Omon Ra. NDP851.
A Werewolf Problem in Central Russia. NDP959.
Saint-John Perse, Selected Poems.† NDP547.
Po Chü-i, The Selected Poems. NDP880.
Ezra Pound, ABC of Reading. NDP89.
The Cantos. NDP824.
Confucius to Cummings. NDP126.
A Draft of XXX Cantos. NDP690.
Personae. NDP697.
The Pisan Cantos. NDP977.
The Spirit of Romance. NDP1028.
Caradog Prichard, One Moonlit Night. NDP835.
Qian Zhongshu, Fortress Besieged. NDP966.
Raymond Queneau, The Blue Flowers. NDP595.
Exercises in Style. NDP513.
Gregory Rabassa, If This Be Treason. NDP1044.
Mary de Rachewiltz, Ezra Pound, Father and Teacher.
NDP1029.
Margaret Randall, Part of the Solution. NDP350.
Raja Rao, Kanthapura. NDP224.
Herbert Read, The Green Child. NDP208.
Kenneth Rexroth, 100 Poems from the Chinese. NDP192.
Selected Poems. NDP581.
Rainer Maria Rilke, Poems from the Book of Hours.† NDP408.
Possibility of Being. NDP436.
Where Silence Reigns. NDP464.
Arthur Rimbaud, Illuminations.† NDP56.

A Season in Hell & The Drunken Boat.† NDP97.
Edouard Roditi, The Delights of Turkey. NDP487.
Jerome Rothenberg, Pre-faces & Other Writings. NDP511.
Triptych. NDP1077.
Ralf Rothmann, Knife Edge. NDP744.
Nayantara Sahgal, Mistaken Identity. NDP742.
Ihara Saikaku, The Life of an Amorous Woman. NDP270.
St. John of the Cross, The Poems of St. John ... † NDP341.
William Saroyan, The Daring Young Man ... NDP852.
Jean-Paul Sartre, Baudelaire. NDP233.
Nausea. NDP1073.
The Wall (Intimacy). NDP272.
Delmore Schwartz, In Dreams Begin Responsibilities. NDP454.
Screeno: Stories and Poems. NDP985.
Peter Dale Scott, Coming to Jakarta. NDP672.
W.G. Sebald, The Emigrants. NDP853.
The Rings of Saturn. NDP881.
Vertigo. NDP925.
Aharon Shabtai, J'Accuse. NDP957.
Hasan Shah, The Dancing Girl. NDP777.
Merchant-Prince Shattan, Manimekhalai. NDP674.
Kazuko Shiraishi, Let Those Who Appear. NDP940.
C.H. Sisson, Selected Poems. NDP826.
Stevie Smith, Collected Poems. NDP562.
Novel on Yellow Paper. NDP778.
Gary Snyder. Look Out. NDP949.
The Real Work: Interviews & Talks. NDP499.
Turtle Island. NDP306.
Gustaf Sobin, Breaths' Burials. NDP781.
Voyaging Portraits. NFP651.
Muriel Spark, All the Stories of Muriel Spark. NDP933.
The Ghost Stories of Muriel Spark. NDP963.
Loitering With Intent. NDP918.
Symposium. NDP1053.
Enid Starkie, Arthur Rimbaud. NDP254.
Stendhal, Three Italian Chronicles. NDP704.
Richard Swartz, A House in Istria. NDP1078.
Antonio Tabucchi, It's Getting Later All the Time. NDP1042.
Pereira Declares. NDP848.
Requiem: a Hallucination. NDP944.
Nathaniel Tarn, Lyrics for the Bride of God. NDP391.
Yoko Tawada, Facing the Bridge. NDP1079.
Where Europe Begins. NDP1079.
Emma Tennant, Strangers: A Family Romance. NDP960.
Terrestrial Intelligence: International Fiction Now . NDP1034.
Dylan Thomas, A Child's Christmas in Wales. NDP1096
Selected Poems 1934-1952. NDP958.
Tian Wen: A Chinese Book of Origins.† NDP624.
Uwe Timm, The Invention of Curried Sausage. NDP854.
Morenga. NDP1016.
Charles Tomlinson, Selected Poems. NDP855.
Federico Tozzi, Love in Vain. NDP921.
Tomas Tranströmer, The Great Enigma. NDP1050.
Yuko Tsushima, The Shooting Gallery. NDP846.
Leonid Tsypkin, Summer in Baden-Baden. NDP962.
Tu Fu, The Selected Poems. NDP675.
Niccolò Tucci, The Rain Came Last. NDP688.
Frederic Tuten, Adventures of Mao on Long March. NDP1022.
Dubravka Ugrešić, The Museum of Unconditional Surrender.
NDP932.
Paul Valéry, Selected Writings.† NDP184.
Luis F. Veríssimo, Borges & the Eternal Orangutans. NDP1012.
Elio Vittorini, Conversations in Sicily. NDP907.
Rosmarie Waldrop, Blindsight. NDP971.
Curves to the Apple. NDP1046.
Robert Walser, The Assistant. NDP1071.
Robert Penn Warren, At Heaven's Gate. NDP588.
Wang Wei, The Selected Poems. NDP1041.
Eliot Weinberger, An Elemental Thing. NDP1072.
What Happened Here. NDP1020.
Nathanael West, Miss Lonelyhearts. NDP125.
Paul West, A Fifth of November. NDP1002.
Tennessee Williams, The Glass Menagerie. NDP874.
Memoirs. NDP1048.
Mister Paradise and Other One Act Plays. NDP1007.
Selected Letters: Volumes I & II. NDP951 & NDP1083.
A Streetcar Named Desire. NDP998.
William Carlos Williams, Asphodel ... NDP794.
Collected Poems: Volumes I & II. NDP730 & NDP731.
In the American Grain. NDP53.
Paterson: Revised Edition. NDP806.
Wisdom Books:
The Wisdom of St. Francis. NDP477.
The Wisdom of the Taoists. NDP509.
The Wisdom of the Zen Masters. NDP415.
World Beat: International Poetry Now From New Directions.
NDP1033.

For a complete listing request a free catalog from New Directions, 80 Eighth Avenue
New York, NY 10011; or visit our website, www.ndpublishing.com

†Bilingual